W9-BUY-381

ROOMS

Also by

LAUREN OLIVER

Before I Fall
Delirium
Pandemonium
Requiem
Panic
Delirium Stories
The Spindlers
Liesl & Po

ROOMS

LAUREN OLIVER

ecco

AN IMPRINT OF HARPERCOLLINS PUBLISHERS

This book is a work of fiction. The characters, incidents, and dialogue are drawn from the author's imagination and are not to be construed as real. Any resemblance to actual events or persons, living or dead, is entirely coincidental.

 For information address HarperCollins Publishers, 195 Broadway, New York, New York 10007.

HarperCollins books may be purchased for educational, business, or sales promotional use. For information please e-mail the Special Markets Department at SPsales@harpercollins.com.

FIRST EDITION

Designed by Suet Yee Chong

Library of Congress Cataloging-in-Publication Data has been applied for.

ISBN 978-0-06-222319-7 (hardcover)
ISBN 978-0-06-234447-2 (international edition)

14 15 16 17 18 OV/RRD 10 9 8 7 6 5 4 3 2 1

To the brilliant Lexa Hillyer,
for her support, friendship, and many glasses of wine

Rooms

Rooms I (I will not say
worked in) once heard in. Words
my mouth heard
then—be
with me. Rooms,
you open onto one
another: still house
this life, be in me
when I leave

—FRANZ WRIGHT

ACKNOWLEDGMENTS

I'd like to thank, first, my wonderful agent, Stephen Barbara, who has for the past four years encouraged me, pushed me, and tolerated my insanity. Enormous thanks to Lee Boudreaux, whose energy and enthusiasm for this book initially made me believe that I could pull it off, and whose perceptiveness and guidance ultimately ensured that I did. I owe a huge debt of gratitude to the whole team at Ecco, including Ryan Willard; Sara Wood and Allison Saltzman; and Michael McKenzie and Ashley Garland, who (respectively) took care of the details, made sure the book looked absolutely beautiful, and worked tirelessly to get it into the hands of readers. Thank you, too, to Jeremy and Marie, whose wonderful house, Gunthorpe, served as the original inspiration for this book.

Last, thank you to my parents, for all of the books and beautiful rooms.

The fire begins in the basement.

Does it hurt?

Yes and no. This is, after all, what I wanted.

And I'm beyond hurting now.

But the fear is almost like pain. It is driving, immense. This body, our last body, our final chance, will be burned to dust.

What will happen to me then?

From the kitchen, to the pantry, to the dining room and the hall; up the stairs, a choking smoke, darkness, soot, and stifling heat.

From the attic to the roof, from the roof to the basement.

We burn.

Sandra wants to place a bet on whether or not Richard Walker will die at home. I don't know when Sandra became so crazy about gambling. She wasn't a gambler when she was alive. I can say with authority that it was one of the only vices she didn't have. Nowadays it's *bet you this, bet you that.*

"He'll croak right here, you'll see," Sandra says. And then, "Stop crowding me."

"I'm not crowding you."

"You are. You're breathing on my neck."

"Impossible."

"I'm telling you what it *feels* like."

Richard Walker moans. Is it possible that now, after all these years, he can understand us?

Doubtful. Still, an interesting idea.

How do we speak? In creaks and whispers, in groans and shudders. But you know. You've heard us. You simply don't understand.

The day nurse is in the bathroom, preparing Richard's pills, although she must know—we all do—that they can't help him now. The bedroom smells like cough syrup, sweat, and the sharp, animal scent of urine, like an old barn. The sheets have not been changed in three days.

"So what do you think?" Sandra presses. "Home? Or in the hospital?"

I like making bets with Sandra. It breaks up the space—the long, watery hours, the soupiness of time. Day is no longer day to us, and night no longer night. Hours are different shades of hot and warm, damp and dry. We no longer pay attention to the clocks. Why should we? Noon is the taste of sawdust, and the feel of a splinter under a nail. Morning is mud and crumbling caulk. Evening is the smell of cooked tomatoes and mildew. And night is shivering, and the feel of mice sniffing around our skin.

Divisions: that's what we need. Space and lines. Your side, my side. Otherwise, we begin to converge. That's the greatest fear, the danger of being dead. It's a constant struggle to stay yourself.

It's funny, isn't it? Alive, it's so often the reverse. I remember feeling desperate for someone to *understand*. I remember how fiercely I longed to talk to Ed about this or that—I don't remember what, now, some dream or opinion, something playing at the pictures.

Now it's only the secrets that truly belong to me. And I've given up too many to Sandra already.

"Hospital," I say at last.

"I'll bet you he croaks right in that bed," Sandra says, gleeful.

Sandra is wrong. Richard Walker does not die at home. Thank God. I've shared the house with him for long enough.

For a time, the house falls into quiet. It is ours again, mine and Sandra's. Its corners are elbows, its stairways our skeleton pieces, splinters of bone and spine.

In the quietness, we drift. We reclaim the spaces that Richard colonized. We must regrow into ourselves—clumsily, the way that a body, after a long illness, still moves in fits and shivers.

We expand into all five bedrooms. We hover in the light coming through the windows, with the dust; we spin, dizzy in the silence. We slide across empty dining room chairs, skate across the well-polished table, rub ourselves against the oriental carpets, curl up in the impressions of old footprints.

It is both a relief and a loss to have our body returned to us, intact. We have, once again, successfully expelled the Other.

We are free. We are alone.

We place bets on when the young Walkers will return.

PART I

THE KITCHEN

A L I C E

Minna comes through the kitchen, flinging open the door as though expecting several dozen guests to jump out and yell, "Surprise!"

"Jesus Christ" is the first thing she says.

"It isn't," Sandra says. "It can't be."

But it obviously is: there is no mistaking Minna, even after so many years. Sandra claims it has been exactly a decade; I think it has been a little longer than that.

Minna is changed, but she is still Minna: the tangle of long hair, now lightened; the haughty curves of her cheekbones; the eyes, vivid, ocean colored. She is just as beautiful as ever—maybe even more so. There's something hard and terrifying about her now, like a blade that has been sharpened to a deadly point.

"Jesus Christ," she says again. She is standing in the open doorway, and for a moment the smell of Outside reaches me: clover, mud, and mulch; honeysuckle that must still be growing wild all over the yard.

For a brief moment, I am alive again, and kneeling in the garden: new spring sunshine; cool wind; a glistening earthworm, turned out of the earth, surprised.

A girl, probably six, barrels past Minna and into the house.

"Is this Grandpa's house?" she asks, and reaches out toward

the kitchen table, where a coffee mug—one of the nurse's mugs, half full, which has begun to stink of sour milk—has been left.

Minna grabs the girl's arm, pulls her back. "Don't touch anything, Amy," she says. "This whole place is crawling with germs." The girl, Amy, hangs back obediently, while Minna takes several tentative steps into the kitchen, keeping one hand in front of her, as though she's walking in the dark. When she is within reach of the kitchen table, she makes a sudden grab for it, letting out a noise somewhere between a gasp and a laugh.

"*This* thing," she says. "It's even uglier than I remembered. Christ, he couldn't get rid of *anything*."

"Well, that settles that," Sandra says gleefully. "Minna's grown into a hopeless bitch. I always knew she would."

"Be quiet, Sandra." In the many, many years I have been here, in this house, in the new body, my faith in the Christian conception of the afterlife has been considerably taxed. But there is no doubt about one thing: having Sandra with me is hell.

"Any girl that pretty . . ."

"I said be quiet." Poor Minna. I can't say she was my favorite. But I felt sorry for her all the same.

Amy starts to come out of the doorway, but Minna puts up a hand to stop her. "Honey, stay there, okay? Just hang on a second." Then she calls out, a little louder, "Trenton! You've got to come see this."

I no longer have a heart, so to say my heart speeds up is inaccurate. But there is a quickening, a drawing together of whatever pieces of me remain. For years, I've longed to see Trenton. He was the most beautiful child, with feather-blond hair and eyes the electric blue of a summer sky. Even at four or five he had a slightly tragic look, as though he had come into the world expecting beauty and elegance and had suffered such tremendous initial disappointment that he had never recovered.

But it's not Trenton who comes into the house, practically doubled under the weight of two duffel bags, and lugging an additional rolling suitcase behind him. It is an absurdly tall, skinny adolescent, with a sullen look and dingy-dark hair, wearing a black sweatshirt and long jeans with filthy cuffs.

"What did you *pack*?" he mutters, as he steps into the kitchen, straightens up, and unslings both duffel bags, piling them on the kitchen floor. He bumps the suitcase through the doorway. "Did you put rocks in here or something?"

Sandra begins to laugh.

"It isn't him. It can't be," I say, unconsciously parroting her remark about Minna.

"It's him," she says. "Look at his eyes."

She's right: under that jutting, unattractive forehead, covered with a smattering of pimples, his eyes are still the same startling electric blue and fringed with a girlish quantity of lashes.

"God, what a piece of shit," Minna says. She leans over and places both hands on the kitchen table, as though to verify that it's real. "We used to call it the Spider. Do you remember?"

Trenton says nothing.

The table is white and plastic—*Lucite,* Sandra informed me, when it was first delivered—and has jointed, twisted legs that do, in fact, make it look like a spider crouching in the corner. It cost $15,000, as Richard Walker was always fond of telling his guests. I used to find it hideously ugly. Sandra informs me that that is just because I have no modern sensibility.

"Modernity is ugly," she always says. On at least that one point, we agree.

Over the years, the table has grown on me. I guess you could say, actually, it has grown *into* me, the way objects do. The table is my memories of the table, and my memories of the table are: Minna hiding, brown knees drawn to her chest, sucking on a scab; Trenton trimming paper for a Valentine's Day card, holding blunt-edged plastic scissors, his fingers sticky with glue; Richard Walker sitting in his usual place at the head of the table the day after Caroline had left him for good, newspaper folded neatly in front of him, a mug of coffee cooling, cooling, as the light grew and swelled and then began to narrow over the course of the afternoon, until at last it was no more than a golden finger, cutting across the room on a diagonal, dividing him from shoulder to hip.

Other memories—from different times and places, from my old life—have weaseled their way in alongside these. It's transfiguration, the slippery nature of thought. Wine turns to blood and wafer to body, and table legs to church spires white and stark against the summer sky—and the spiderwebs in the old blueberry bushes behind my childhood home in Newport, draped across the branches like fine gray lace—the spare pleasure of a boiled egg and bread, eaten alone for dinner. All of that is the table, too.

"It smells," Trenton says.

Minna takes the coffee cup from the table and moves it to the sink. She turns on the faucet, letting the flow of water break up the surface of mold and run it down the drain. She moves in electric bursts, like miniature explosions. When she was little, it was the same way. She was on the floor. Then, suddenly, she was kneeling on the countertop; then she was striking her palm—bang!—against the window.

Now she leans over and strikes the window, hard, with her palm, just the way she used to. The catch releases; the window shoots upward. The smell of Outside comes sweeping into the room. It is like a shiver, or the touch of someone's hand.

"Did you see that?" she asks Trenton. "The trick still works."

Trenton shrugs and puts his hands in the pocket of his sweatshirt. I can't believe that this awkward, gummy, sullen thing is beautiful, tragic Trenton, who liked to lie in the sunshine on the wooden floor of the dining room, like a cat—curled against me, cheek to cheek, the closest I have come to an embrace since I was alive.

I used to imagine, sometimes, that he could feel me hugging him back.

"Mommy." Amy has been straining onto her tiptoes, exploring the countertop with her fingers. Now she tugs on the hem of Minna's shirt. "Is Grandpa here?"

Minna kneels so she is eye level with her daughter. "We talked about that, sweetpea. Remember?"

Amy shakes her head. "I want to say hi to Grandpa."

"Grandpa's gone, Amy," Trenton says. Minna shoots him a murderous look. She places her hands on Amy's shoulders.

She speaks in a lullaby voice. "Remember the chapter in *The Raven Heliotrope,* where Princess Penelope gives up her life to save the Order of the Innocents?"

"Oh, God." Trenton rolls his eyes. "You're reading her that crap?"

"Did you hear that, Alice?" Sandra says to me. "*Crap*. No wonder it was never published."

"I never tried to get it published," I say, and then regret it. She's only trying to goad me into an argument.

"Shut up, Trenton," Minna snaps at him. Then she continues, in a soft voice: "And remember Penelope has to go away to the Garden of Forever?"

Amy nods. "To live in a flower."

Minna kisses her forehead. "Grandpa's in the Garden of Forever."

Trenton snorts. Minna ignores him, stands up, and switches off the faucet. It's a relief. We're very sensitive to sound now. The noise of the water is thunderous. Water running through the pipes is an uncomfortable feeling, and it still fills me with anxiety, the way I used to feel when I had to go to the bathroom and was made to laugh: a fear of leaking.

"But will he come back?" Amy asks.

"What?" Minna turns around. For a moment I see that underneath the impeccable makeup, she is just as tired as anybody else.

"In Part Two, Penelope comes back," Amy says. "Penelope wakes up. And then Prince Thomas joins forces with Sven and saves everybody."

Minna stares at her blankly for a second. It's Trenton who answers.

"Grandpa's not coming back, Amybear," Trenton says. "He's going to stay in the garden."

"As long as the old grout stays away from here," Sandra says.

Of course she isn't really worried that he'll return. It's just the two of us. It will no doubt always be the two of us, and the spiny staircases, and the ticking furnace, like a mechanical heart, and the mice, nibbling at our corners.

Unless I can find a way to light the fire.

M I N N A

Minna hadn't been back to Coral River in a decade. She hadn't stepped inside the old house in even longer than that, since she'd spent the last six months of high school living with her mom and Trenton in a two-bedroom condo in Lackawanna, although in reality she'd spent most of that time staying with her first boyfriend, Toadie.

She hadn't wanted to come back at all. She didn't give a shit about the old place other than what it might sell for, had no use for memory lane and digging up a past that she'd deliberately left behind. But her shrink had encouraged it—recommended it, even.

"You can't keep running, Minna," she'd said. "You have to face your demons at some point."

Minna liked her therapist, and trusted her, but she felt superior to her, too. Dr. Upshaw had a wide, comfortable sprawl of a body, like a human sofa. Minna sometimes imagined Dr. Upshaw having sex with her husband, lying there almost motionless, fat sticky thighs sagging on the bed, saying, "I think you're onto something, David," in her low, encouraging voice.

"Why?" Minna had answered, trying to make a joke.

"Because you're not happy," Dr. Upshaw had answered, and

then Minna had remembered that Dr. Upshaw had no sense of humor.

She was right, though; Minna wasn't happy and hadn't been in as long as she could remember. The last guy she'd dated—she counted it as dating, since they'd gone to dinner a few times before screwing back at his place, her skirt hitched up, underwear pulled down to her knees, both of them pretending it was spontaneity rather than laziness—had turned to her once and said, "Do you *ever* laugh?" That was their last date. Minna had been less offended than she was irritated; she hadn't known she was so transparent.

She couldn't remember the last time she'd truly laughed. She couldn't even come anymore. She could get close, and did, as often as possible—pushing against the deep darkness inside her, stretching toward that warmth, the break in the wall—but it never happened; she couldn't get through.

Trenton went upstairs with the duffel bags. She could hear him thumping around up there—the floor groaned awfully, even worse than she remembered, like it was actually feeling physical pain.

The kitchen was disgusting. Used plates everywhere, even the stub of old cigarettes floating in a saucer—had one of the nurses smoked? was that even legal?—and Trenton was right. It smelled. Minna started piling dishes in the sink, sweeping old crumbs from the counter into her palm, straightening and reordering. She'd been here five minutes and already needed an Ativan.

Trenton reentered the kitchen. "Where's Mom?" he asked, nudging a chair out from the table and sitting down. He was moving well, barely limping anymore. "What's taking her so long?"

"Probably getting drunk somewhere," Minna said. "No, Amy." This as Amy reached for a wooden spoon lying on the Spider. Trenton caught Amy and pinned her between his legs and she squealed and writhed away.

Sometimes Minna found for the briefest spark of a second that she was jealous of Amy—for being young and dumb, the way all kids were dumb, and not knowing better than to be so happy. Then she hated herself. What kind of fucking person was jealous of a six-year-old? Her own *child,* for Christ's sake?

"Are you going to be nice?" Trenton asked.

"Are *you*?" Minna fired back. She felt a headache coming on and squeezed her temples. Maybe a Valium, instead of an Ativan. She didn't want to fight with Trenton, and had been told by her mother that he'd been extremely moody since the accident and should not be upset in any way. Like dragging him up to Coral River to clean out the house of the father he'd barely ever seen wasn't going to upset him. "Did you remember to take your pills?"

"Uh-huh." Trenton was now hunched over his phone.

"What for, Mom?" Amy said, tugging on Minna's shirt.

"Remember when Uncle Trenton was in the hospital?" Minna said, scooping Amy up. She was so heavy now. Soon Minna wouldn't be able to carry her at all. "And we went to visit him?" Amy nodded. "Well, now he has to take medicine so he stays healthy and strong."

"Like your medicine?" Amy said, and Trenton smirked.

Minna kissed Amy on the cheek. Her skin smelled like Dove soap and a little bit like the grape gum she'd been chewing in the car, proud that she could keep it in her mouth without swallowing it, as she had several times in the past.

"Exactly," Minna said, staring at Trenton, daring him to say something. But he just kept smiling his half smile, like someone chewing on a secret. She wished she didn't feel like smacking him half the time. It hadn't always been that way. They'd been close when they were younger, even though Minna was twelve when he was born. She'd watched over him, protected him, watched him transform—like one of those miniature sponges you put in a glass to grow into a complex shape—from a small pink blob with a permanent expression of wide-eyed alarm, to a toddler trotting after her, grabbing always at her jeans, her shirt, whatever he could reach, to a skinny kid with a feathered mop of hair and a slow, shy grin.

She could still remember the time she'd dared him to sled down the driveway and he'd split his lip on the side of the garage, and blood had poured down his chin, so red and bright she couldn't believe, at first, that it was real. She remembered that in that moment before he began to cry, as he mouthed silently to her, his fingers covered in blood, how everything else went still and static and there was only the rush of her heartbeat in her ears and a soundless scream going through her, sharper than fear.

It was the same way she'd felt three months ago, when her mother had called out of the blue on a normal Tuesday evening.

"Trenton's in the hospital," Caroline had said. "St. Luke's. They don't know if he'll make it. It would be nice if you came by."

That was it. *It would be nice if you came by.* Like someone inviting you to Sunday fucking brunch. And Minna had stood, frozen, in the middle of the crosswalk, opening and closing her mouth like Trenton had all those years ago, until the sudden blast of horns brought her back to reality, realizing the lights had changed.

He was her little brother. She loved him. But in the past few years she couldn't help but be annoyed and sometimes disgusted by him. He pinched his pimples when he thought no one was looking. He chewed his fingernails to raw bloody stubs, insisted on being a vegetarian to be difficult, and grew his hair long so that he could practically chew on his bangs—partially, she suspected, so he wouldn't have to make eye contact with her when they saw each other.

On the other hand, she couldn't blame him. She'd been a shitty sister. Sometimes she wished she could sit him down and explain, tell him that it wasn't his fault, confess her deepest, truest secret:

there was something rotten growing inside of her. She had hoped, in an inarticulate way, that having Amy would change things—would change her.

Amy was an Innocent.

Minna, too, had read *The Raven Heliotrope,* and although she was far too old for fairy tales, she had clung to one of its major tenets for a long time: the Innocents could save. They could redeem.

"It's weird being here," Trenton said. His head was still bent, his voice raw. "It doesn't feel the same." Then: "Why wouldn't he let us see him?"

"You know Dad," Minna said.

"Not really," Trenton said.

Minna nudged a chair out from the table—the Spider—with her toe and sat down. The chair creaked underneath her and she felt suddenly weird, like this had never been her house, like everything had been set up to test her. Like a stage set for an actress, to see if she could figure out her role. She wouldn't put it past her father. Maybe he'd planned all of this.

Minna put an arm around Amy, to keep her from wandering and touching things. Trenton still hadn't looked up, and he was swiping at his phone, but she realized this must be hard for him. He had been young when their father and mother had divorced, and since then had seen their father only sporadically, when Richard would appear suddenly in Long Island like Father Christmas, toting gifts and a wide, jolly grin and a big laugh that made you temporarily forget that it would all be over by tomorrow.

"He was sick," she said. "He didn't want us to remember him that way." That, at least, was true. It wasn't for their sake, but for his. Richard Walker had been in control until the end.

"It's fucked," Trenton said. Amy put her hands over her ears.

"Christ, Trenton," Minna said.

"Trenton said a bad word," Amy said in a singsong. Then,

keeping her hands pressed tightly to her ears, she spun away from Minna, twirling around the kitchen, humming to herself, her cotton blue skirt fanning around her knees.

"Home sweet home," Minna said.

A large part of her wanted to leave already: to get back into the small white BMW she'd leased exactly two weeks before being fired from her latest job; to sink down into the upholstery that smelled like Amy's shampoo and old juice bottles; to drive as far and as fast as she could from Coral River, and the Minna who had been stuck there.

But there was another part of her that suspected—that *remembered*—that she had once been happy here. For years she had carried the image of a different Minna with her, a faint, heartbeat-shadow of a girl who had existed before the rot took hold.

So she was here. To face the demons.

To put them to rest for good.

A L I C E

Caroline Walker, like Minna, walks into the kitchen as though expecting a party and seems bewildered to instead encounter an empty room filled with old belongings, stacked newspapers, and crusted dishes in the sink—as though everyone else must have mistaken the date.

"She got fat!" Sandra crows. "Didn't I tell you she would?"

I do *not* remember that Sandra ever said this. Although, to be fair, I spend the majority of my time trying to ignore Sandra, so it's possible that I missed it.

Caroline removes her sunglasses and, without going any farther into the house, calls: "Minna? Trenton? Amy? Where *is* everyone?"

I can tell you where they are. Trenton is in the upstairs bathroom, next to the Blue Room, which was always his; he has a magazine unfolded on his lap, and his pants around his ankles. Amy is sitting on the floor of the Yellow Room, where Minna has installed her. Minna is lying on the bed, staring up at the ceiling, talking on the phone.

"I just don't see why he couldn't do us a favor and die somewhere decent," she is saying. "I told Trenton in the car—as far as I'm concerned, we can just *burn* the damn place . . . "

Amy is braiding the tassels on the worn yellow rug, humming to herself.

"Well, *of course* there's nowhere to eat around here," Minna is saying. "It's a miracle I even have cell-phone reception."

In the kitchen, Caroline removes her coat—an enormous fur coat, despite the fact that it is unseasonably warm. She did get fat; it's true. Her beauty is still there, but with age it has softened, blurred, and become faintly ridiculous, like the kind of amateur watercolor you might see in an office building.

"*And* she's drunk." Sandra gets still, and very alert. "Drunk as a whore on Sunday. Do you smell it?"

"No." I smell perfume, and mildew, and Trenton's bathroom, which I am trying hard *not* to smell.

"Vodka," Sandra says, the way a music lover might say *Bach*. "I'd swear to it. Absolut. No, no. Stoli, with just a splash of tonic . . . "

When Sandra was alive, she would drink anything she could get her hands on. Wine or beer when there were guests—she would top off her glass with bottles stashed behind curtains, or in the shower, so no one would know she was drinking more than double their amount—and vodka when she was alone. But she wasn't picky. Whiskey, gin, and even—after a brief period of sobriety, when she had cleaned her entire house of liquor—rubbing alcohol.

It's only now that she has developed a palate.

"And lime," she says. "Definitely lime."

If only it could have been *anyone* else but Sandra . . . that nice, quiet girl from down the road, whom Maggie used to be so fond of. Or Sammy, the butcher—he always had interesting things to say, and he was polite, even to the black customers. Even Anne Collins, who was constantly going on about her husband's finances and bragging about the new coats she would buy, would have been preferable.

Trenton flushes. Water runs; pipes shudder; the system pulses. Rhythm and flow; ingestion, excretion. Input, output. These are laws of the universe.

He pounds down the central staircase—(the feeling of a doctor knocking on a kneecap, testing for reflexes; painless and unsettling)—and slouches against the kitchen door frame.

"Trenton!" Caroline says, extending her arms to him, although he makes no move to go toward her and she stays where she is. "How was your drive?"

"What happened to you?" he responds.

"What do you mean?" Caroline's voice is the same as it always was—high, shot through with nervous laughter, as though someone has just told a joke whose punch line she hasn't completely understood.

"I mean you left just after us." Trenton goes to the Spider and slumps into a chair, tilting his head back to lean against the dark stone walls of the fireplace. He seems exhausted by the energy required to cross the room.

"Traffic," Caroline replies shortly. "Terrible traffic."

"Bullshit," Sandra says.

"Sandra, please." I've never been able to abide her mouth; she's worse than Ed was.

"It's bullshit. She was in a bar having a tall one. Ten to one. I'll bet you."

"It was smooth sailing for us," Trenton says neutrally. He watches his mother through half-narrowed eyes. She moves around the kitchen, picking things up and replacing them: an empty vase, whose glass is crusted with a thin film of brown; a balled-up napkin; a bottle of vitamins, cap removed. Even though she's heavy now, she still manages to give the impression of a moth: fluttering and fragile.

"How strange," she says. "There must have been an accident. It was a parking lot on I-80."

"You made it," Minna says. She, too, has come downstairs. Her bra and the contours of her spine are visible through her T-shirt.

Caroline looks from Minna to Trenton. Her voice turns shriller. "Well, of course I made it. For God's sake. Anyone would think I had . . . " She turns to Minna. "And *you* were probably speeding the whole way."

"Did you see it?" Trenton asks.

"Did I see *what*?" Caroline snaps.

"The accident," he says. The more agitated his mom gets, the further he sinks into stillness. Only his eyes are moving. "Did you see it?"

"No, I didn't . . . " She breaks off, setting down a coaster with a bang. "What are you saying?"

He lifts a shoulder. "I don't know. Thought there might have been a fire. A head lying in the road or something."

Minna snorts.

"Trenton. How can you—?" Caroline shakes her head. "I really don't know what's wrong with you. How could you even say that?"

"It's a normal question," Minna says. She peels herself away from the wall and is across the room in a flash. She sits in a chair across from Trenton and draws her knees to her chest. For a second, she looks just like the old Minna.

"Normal," Caroline repeats. "It's morbid, that's what it is. It's horrible. I didn't come here to be attacked." She's opening and shutting each cabinet now. Each time she slams a door, it sends a tiny shiver through me.

"The liquor's in the dining room now," Minna says.

Sandra says, "I told you she was drunk."

Caroline shoots Minna a dirty look and stalks out of the kitchen. The lights are off in the hall. For a moment Caroline stands, disoriented, and I feel almost bad for her: this new hulk of a woman, changed and old, in a space she no longer recognizes.

Trenton and Minna sit for a moment in silence.

Minna says, "You shouldn't tease her. You're the one who told me to be nice."

"I wasn't teasing," Trenton replies.

"It *is* morbid, you know. I don't know why you're so fixated on accidents all of a sudden. What's that game on your iPhone?"

Trenton sighs deeply. "I don't know what you're talking about."

"You do so. *Crash,* or whatever. Where you're always sending characters over cliffs or into fireballs. There's no goal to it, is there? Except to kill them, I mean."

In the dining room, Caroline has located the liquor cabinet. She removes a tumbler and pours a half glass of vodka, straight. She downs it in one go, then pours another and does the same.

"Points," Trenton says. His eyelids flutter.

Minna stares at him. "What?"

"Points," Trenton repeats. "You get points for killing them. That's the goal."

In the dining room, Caroline wipes out the glass with a tissue and then replaces it. She takes a wineglass next and selects a bottle of red wine. She is much calmer now.

"Well, I think it's idiotic," Minna says. I'm reminded of the way she used to stand in the dining room, telling Trenton where to place the candlesticks when they were playing Roll-Your-Ball. *There,* she would say, in a tone of exasperation, pointing. *No,* there. *That's slanted. Don't be stupid, Trenton. It will make the ball go crooked.*

Trenton mutters something. What he says is: *Like the* Heliotrope*'s any better.* When I was alive, I doubt I would have understood him. But now we are dispersed among the sound. We are the waves; we carry the crests of his voice to her mouth, and her voice back to him, and so on. We are the endless swells.

"I can't understand you when you mumble," Minna says.

"*The Raven Heliotrope*'s full of murder," Trenton says, a little louder. "A whole forest of nymphs gets wiped out. And half of the Order gets beheaded. Sven gets trampled by a Tricorn."

"*The Raven Heliotrope* is a book about morals, Trenton." Minna swings her legs to the floor and stands up. Caroline comes back into the room, holding two wineglasses and the bottle. She is cheerful again, vague and smiling. She roots around for the wine opener, becoming briefly agitated when she doesn't find it. Then it is located and her body relaxes again. She uncorks the bottle and ostentatiously pours herself a very small glass.

"A pinot," Sandra says. "From Oregon, I think."

"You're making that up," I say, finally losing patience.

"I'm not," Sandra says.

"You can see the label."

"I'm not looking."

"That's impossible," I say. Another hellish thing: we can't choose *not* to look, or smell, or feel. We just are, always.

"Would you like a glass, Minna?" Caroline says.

"I'm fine," Minna says.

"Have a glass," Caroline says. "You look like you need it."

"I'll have a glass," Trenton says.

Caroline turns her large, watery blue eyes toward him. "Don't be silly, Trenton. Go and get my bags from the car, will you? They're in the trunk."

"Why do *I* have to do it?" he says, but he's already standing and moving toward the door. His motions are erratic, like a scarecrow that has just come to life and has to compensate for a spine full of stuffing. He plunges headlong several steps, then overcompensates by slumping backward; then lopes, then shuffles.

Trenton. My beautiful, graceful, perfect Trenton.

As soon as Trenton is gone, Minna stands, approaches the kitchen island, and pours herself a glass of wine. She's at least four inches taller than her mother, and much thinner, but the fact that Minna has lightened her hair increases the resemblance between them. Minna is the angular, modern version of Caroline's watercolor.

"Where's Amy?" Caroline says.

"Upstairs," Minna says. She pauses, then adds, "She wanted to know why Grandpa isn't here."

"That's normal." Caroline drinks again, this time forgetting to be so careful. Her glass is now more than half empty, and she sets it on the counter. "My glass must have sprung a leak," she says, with a high, nervous trill, before refilling.

For a second, there's silence. Then Minna says: "It's strange being back here. It looks so . . ."

"Different?"

Minna shakes her head. "No. The same. That's what's weird about it." She reaches for a small porcelain pig saltshaker, one of a dozen saltshakers Richard Walker accumulated. "Why did he *keep* all this junk?"

"Oh, you know." Caroline takes another sip of wine. "Your father was never very good at parting with things." The words sound unexpectedly bitter.

Richard Walker was a collector. He brought back hand-painted ashtrays from Mexico and beads from Guatemala as well as Buddha statues from India and cheap posters from Paris, which he hung, without shame or irony, next to original Warhols in his study. He collected foreign coins and clocks, cheap Venetian masks and original Eskimo art, mugs and key chains and magnets.

Minna walks a small circle around the kitchen, like a caged animal. "Junk, junk, junk, junk," she says. "Junk everywhere. It'll take forever to sort. I say we just trash it all."

"It's not all junk, sweetpea," Caroline says, and then sighs. "Some of it must be worth something. And money is money, after all."

"Did you schedule the auction?" Minna asks.

The kitchen door bangs. Both Minna and Caroline jump; neither had noticed Trenton push his way back into the kitchen, dragging his mother's luggage. The suitcases remind me of Ed's shoes, after they'd been worn for too long and polished often and painstakingly. The luggage has no visible spots or imperfections, just a kind of sad, sagging look.

"What are you talking about?" Trenton says. "What auction?"

Minna and Caroline go momentarily still. Caroline is the first to unfreeze. "An auction to sell off your father's things," she says brightly. "Whatever we don't want, of course."

"When?" Trenton stands with his back pressed against the door, as far away from his mother and sister as possible.

"At the end of the month," Caroline says, reordering the saltshaker Minna displaced.

Trenton looks from his mother to his sister. Minna avoids his eyes. "Sick," Trenton says. "Truly sick. We've been here less than an hour—"

"It isn't like he can *hear* us," Minna says, rolling her eyes.

He stares at her. "And *I'm* morbid." Then he jerks forward and bursts out of the kitchen. His feet are hard on the stairs. Each time he stomps, deliberately loud, I feel a distant explosion of pain and sensation—like the bursts of color I used to see behind my closed eyes after accidentally staring at the sun.

"I don't understand that boy," Caroline says.

"He's sensitive." Minna waves a hand. "Besides, he hardly remembers Dad. He can't be expected to know what an asshole he was."

"Don't talk about your father that way," Caroline says mildly.

"He *was* an asshole," Minna insists.

"I'm hungry," Caroline says. "Are you hungry?"

"Not really," Minna says.

"Amy must be hungry." Caroline begins opening cabinets: these, too, are overflowing, although Richard Walker hardly ever cooked. There are boxes of pancake mix and half-eaten bags of chips; a half-dozen cereals, cans of beans and tuna, two jars of honey, cemented to the shelf by a sticky, golden ring of overspill; sardines and pasta and bags of rice in which mites have started to nest.

"What are you doing?" Minna asks.

"I'm looking for something to have for dinner," Caroline says. "What does it *look* like I'm doing?"

Minna leans over the kitchen island and slams the cupboard shut. "We can't eat his *food*," she says, as though Caroline has just suggested she eat an insect.

Caroline tries to open the cupboard again; Minna keeps her hand on it firmly. "Minna, please. You're as bad as Trenton. He won't miss it, will he?"

"No, I mean—" For a second, Minna looks ashamed. "I mean it's disgusting. I mean, it's been sitting here just—just absorbing his germs."

Caroline widens her pale blue eyes. "For heaven's sake, Minna. The last time I checked, death isn't contagious. It isn't an infection, you know."

Minna wrenches her hand away from the cupboard. "I won't eat it. And I won't let Amy eat it, either."

"Oh, Minna." Caroline sighs dramatically, but she removes her hand from the cupboard and instead picks up her wineglass and drains it.

SANDRA

I'm not afraid to say that what you've heard so far is a big honking load of bullshit. And no, I won't mind my language. Jesus Christ, it's practically the only thing I have left.

I bet she didn't even tell you this: my death was no accident.

I'm not saying Alice lies, per se. Her problem is she's a prude, straight out of the *wash-your-mouth-out-with-soap* generation, and secretive as anything.

Take Minna. Alice is always going on about how beautiful she is. Yeah, if you like that look—a great big pair of fake tits screwed on like a lid, and eyes that always look like they're trying to see through your pants to how much money you've got in your wallet.

No thank you.

I know Minna had a rough start. All those years in that crusty basement practicing piano until her fingers ached and God knows what else. But listen, we all get served a deck with some cards missing. Get up and get on with it, is what I say. I've done my reading about all of it: neuroses, psychoses, anxieties, and compulsions, blah, blah. I used to work for *the* Dr. Howard Rivers, of the Rivers Center for Psychiatric Development, for God's sake. And I've seen my fair share of churches and twelve steps.

It all boils down to the same thing: are you going to play the cards you got, or are you going to fold?

For example: I didn't exactly have it easy growing up. We were in Silverlake, Georgia: land of shotgun houses and trailer parks, an all-white county park, peach trees with fruit like drooping tits, and summers that slapped you in the face like a dog's tongue. Dad had a mouth like a closed-up zipper, and when he looked at me at all, it was usually to ask how come I couldn't play nice like the other girls and stop getting into brawls on the playground and *why can't you ever learn to listen.*

I don't think I ever once saw him kiss my mother or even hold her hand. He spent all his time with his friends at the Rotary Club, especially his friend Alan Briggs, and my mom used to go into hysterics on the phone with her sister, wondering where he was and whether he was cheating on her and what she would do if he left her for some young tramp. And then one day when I was seven, she came home early from her once-a-month steak-and-lobster buffet dinner with the girls in Dixie Union and found my dad and Alan in bed, buck naked. At least, that's the way my mom told it to me later.

My dad and mom divorced, and Mom and I had to move to a small one-bedroom in what was still called the colored part of town. It was 1960 in the South, which was like 1940 anywhere else in the world, and at school whispers went around that my dad was a queer and I was a nigger lover besides. Those aren't my words. Silverlake, Georgia, was a pretty place, full of ugly people. I remember houses set up in a row like dominoes, yellow in the morning sun, explosions of bright red trumpet creeper, and picket fences dusty with pollen; and I remember "Whites Only," and fields crawling with chiggers, and cockroaches the size of a child's palm wriggling out of the drain.

Colored, black, white, yellow, queer, straight—from the beginning, it never mattered to me, maybe because even though my dad hardly ever said a word to me, and liked to diddle his male friends behind my mother's back, and wore the same bowling shirt every Saturday and Sunday, I still loved him. Who knows why or how. Maybe only because he brought me candy buttons, or let me sit on his lap while he cruised down Main Street in his sky-blue El Dorado, big as a boat, shark finned and smooth.

Parents teach us our very first lesson about love: that you sure as hell don't get to choose it.

My point is, I didn't sit around sobbing about my problems and expecting everyone to feel sorry for me. I wanted out of Georgia, and so I got out of Georgia, and I didn't wait for some man to saddle me with a ring and a lifetime of laundry to do it.

By then it was 1970, anyway, and things were changing. The farther north I got, the more they changed, until finally, in New York City, I discovered it had been the future all along.

Funny, isn't it, how quickly the future becomes the past? I bet Trenton doesn't even know who Jimi Hendrix was. Joplin, Neil Young, Jerry Garcia—forget it.

What can I say about Trenton? A sad sprout of a human being, halfway between a boy and a broccoli. Then there's Caroline, a big sodden biscuit, soaked morning through night. I'm not one to talk—I liked getting knockered sometimes, who doesn't?—but at least I had the decency to do my drinking alone.

Richard was probably the worst of all of them. Couldn't keep his prick in his pants and made everybody's lives miserable with his whims and his moods and demands, especially at the end. *No chicken soup, I want tomato. Turn the heat up. Now turn it down. Now up again.* We used to catch his poor nurses crying in the dining room, hidden in the dark, hunched between dusty furniture—grown women, blubbering silently into their palms. The biggest favor Richard Walker ever did for anyone else was die.

Do you think I'm being harsh? I've never been one to sugarcoat the truth, and at least I've still got a sense of humor, even if I'm all splinters and dust everywhere else. That's another thing that drives me crazy about Alice: no sense of humor at all. I can feel her, wound up tight, like a soda about to explode, like clenched butt cheeks.

So I ask you: What's she holding in?

TRENTON

The truth: that's all Trenton wanted. For someone in his family to tell the truth.

It was seven o'clock and he was lying in his old bedroom, which looked almost exactly the same as he remembered it except for the piles of junk everywhere, listening to the murmur of his sister's and his mother's voices. They were arguing about what to do for dinner. And it occurred to him that since the last time he'd been to Coral River, he probably hadn't heard a single word from either one of them that wasn't some kind of lie.

He didn't know why it still mattered to him. Maybe it was because he'd been hoping for *integrity*. He liked that word, *integrity,* had picked it up in Brit Lit II, which among the guys at Andover was known as Boner Lit. The teacher, Ms. Patterson, was hot. Most of the teachers at Andover were really old, past forty, and strapped into their clothes like psychos into straitjackets, as though their fat might attempt an escape.

But Ms. Patterson wasn't. She was twenty-eight—she'd told them so—which wasn't *that* old. And she looked even younger. She wore her hair loose. It was soft and brown and kind of fuzzy, and all the girls made fun of her because they said it was frizzy and she didn't know how to blow-dry it right. They made fun of her clothes, too, because she wore sneakers sometimes with her skirts and dark old-lady tights; and other times, loose black pants and a shapeless fleece on top.

But Trenton liked that. He found he couldn't even jerk off thinking about the girls at Andover, even the girls younger than him. They were all out of his reach. Their jeans were suctioned to their butts and their hair was slick as an oily river, and their mouths were always curled up and laughing at a joke he was never a part of, and on weekends they took planes and cars down to New York and came back, triumphant and smirking, with a new story: they'd gone down on so-and-so in a cab. They'd done ecstasy and taken over the DJ booth at Butter.

Plus they were smart. He, Trenton, slouchy and barely hanging on to his grades, had nothing to offer them.

Integrity. Integrity was showing up with your hair fuzzy, in a fleece. Integrity was doing your best in school because you liked it, even if people called you a fag and elbowed you into the walls, when they weren't busy pretending you didn't exist.

Everyone in his family lacked integrity. They were *corrupt* (antonym). His mom, Caroline, was the worst. She had lied to everyone for so long, Trenton wasn't even sure she knew the difference anymore. He thought probably she'd always been fake, and he had only noticed recently. Now he knew he couldn't trust anything she said, especially things about his father. *"He loved you, Trenton, very much . . ."*

Bullshit.

He had believed for a long time that Minna had integrity, but he'd been wrong. He could hardly look at her, ever, without noticing her *additions,* which seemed to point at the world like an accusation. And he knew, from his mom, there had been other stuff:

tugs and pulls, needles and pills, all things she didn't need. He might have been prepared to forgive her if it hadn't been for what had happened during Family Weekend in the spring.

And Minna hadn't even apologized. She avoided the subject neatly, the way she avoided everything, because she *lacked integrity,* because she was *corrupt,* because she was *full of shit.*

Amy was all right. But Amy didn't count because she was six and didn't know better. She would probably grow up to be as full of shit as the rest of them.

He'd hardly seen his dad since his parents divorced, and Trenton had never been back to Coral River. Instead, Richard came to New York. He took Trenton to shows he didn't care about seeing and dragged him to restaurants where everything on the menu had some disgusting ingredient, when Trenton would have preferred to get a burger. But in a weird way, Trenton had been closest to his father. Trenton knew his dad was impossible—particular, obsessive, pompous (another word from Ms. Patterson), a complete egomaniac and kind of a dick.

But he'd also been honest. Brutally, totally honest. Trenton still remembered the time they'd been at Boulud, and Trenton had been trying to conceal the fact that he had a hard-on (why the fuck did he have a hard-on? The waitress, who wasn't even that hot, touched his shoulder with her breasts for one second, as she leaned down to take away his wineglass), and his dad had suddenly said to him: "Look, you'll hear a lot of bullshit from your mother. And I was a shit husband. I was. But the woman is batshit crazy and I did my best. Remember that, Trenton. It's not your fault. *It's not your fault.*" And later, after half a glass of wine, Trenton had found himself in the back of a taxi, blinking away tears and feeling grateful.

"Dinner, Trenton!" His sister's voice came through the floorboards, and he thought he heard a slight sigh.

Integrity. That word was still there, like a small staircase in his mind, leading up to the inevitable.

Trenton wanted to die with integrity. There was one reason—and one reason only—that he had agreed to come back to this place that was no longer a home: to die.

As he passed into the dark hallway, and felt his way to the stairs and the light down below, he turned that idea over inside of him, and it brought him comfort.

And he ignored the wisp of a whisper that seemed to say, from very far away, "I wish they'd let the whole place burn."

A L I C E

Dinner is delivery from Mick's Coffee Shop and Restaurant. I recognize the name from the dinners the night nurse would pick up for Richard, when he was still eating solid foods. Macaroni salad and roast beef sandwiches were his favorite.

I've never been to Mick's. In my day, Coral River had only a general store, a Woolworths, a post office, a bar, and a movie theater that showed one film a month. Sandra informs me that when she was alive, Coral River added an Italian restaurant and a McDonald's, a new bar, two more gas stations, a hardware store, a bookstore, and a clothing boutique called Corduroy. The town can only have grown since then.

Minna, Caroline, Amy, and Trenton eat their dinners straight from the deli containers, not even bothering to throw out the plastic bag, which they leave balled on the center of the table. Trenton eats a cheese sandwich, plain, on white bread. He chews moodily, noisily, occasionally letting a bit of cheese drop onto the wax paper the sandwich came in, now unfurled on the table like a stiff white flower.

Caroline eats cold macaroni salad—an unconscious echo of her ex-husband's preferences—and hot chicken soup, and becomes increasingly withdrawn as the vodka in her water glass takes effect.

Minna picks at a chef's salad and complains that the produce is disgusting. Amy eats a tray of baked ziti and winds up covered with tomato sauce, a ring of red around her lips like a second mouth.

Sandra misses drinking. I miss food. It's funny—I never had much of an appetite when I was alive. Even when I was pregnant with Maggie, I was hardly ever hungry, and what little I did eat came up just as quickly. My doctor said I was the skinniest pregnant woman he'd ever seen. I made it through all nine months on tinned green beans, tuna fish, and a little bit of beer. That was all I could keep down, and of course we weren't so concerned in those days about drinking when we were carrying a baby.

Now food is practically all I can think about: pork roast and gravy; buttered potatoes and my mother's spiced Christmas loaf; fried eggs, yolks high and proud and orange as a setting sun; toast dipped in bacon fat and the first summer peach; pools of cream; and fluffy biscuits.

I remember the first time Ed and I ate a TV dinner in front of our twelve-inch black-and-white, how happy we were balancing the small plastic tray on our knees and eating the mass of mushed peas, the disintegrating roast. And I remember the first time I took an airplane to visit Maggie, when I was already in my fifties: the shiny look of the pleather seats, and the way the stewardesses smiled; compartmentalized mashed potatoes, a flat gray disk of turkey, and Jell-O, each thing separated by small plastic dividers. That's modernity, if you ask me: endless division.

Yogurt and blueberries; margarine and brussels sprouts.

I remember:

A copper pot: a wedding gift from my mother, presented to me covertly, so my father wouldn't see. ("God help you," she said, her last words to me.)

A large saucepan, of blackened cast iron: a welt swelling on my thumb, shiny red and taut, like the head of a newborn.

The window: open above the stove; the smell of chicken fat and oil. Blue columbine clung to the windowsill; the shadows outside were long and lavender.

One shadow was longer than the rest and grew more quickly: this was Ed coming home.

This is how it always was, how it would be for almost every day in the thirty-four years of our marriage, except for the years when Ed was away in the war. The shadows grew on the hill; the kitchen was hot and smelled, when money was good, like cooked meat, and when it was not, like old bacon fat and potatoes. One shadow grew longer than the others, like a slowly spreading stain, until it seeped into the doorway and became a man.

"What's for dinner?" Ed would say, if he was in a good mood, as he shrugged off his coat and sat down to unlace his shoes before wiping them carefully with the stiff-bristled brush he kept by the kitchen door.

If he wasn't in a good mood, if he'd been drinking, he would say: "What the hell have you been brewing in here?"

But in the beginning it was always good. We had our own house, and the freedom to do what we wanted. After Ed's first day at the Woolworths in Coral River (we furnished half our house with things from there—half on discount, the rest on credit—smells of wool and furniture polish; so many objects crammed together in memory, jostling for space), I gathered handfuls of Jacob's ladder and leaves from the yard—burnt-edged and brittle, like ancient lace—and arranged them in the old stone hearth, which by then had been cold for twenty years.

"What's for dinner?" Ed asked, as he shrugged off his jacket. Ed Lundell was the most handsome man I had ever seen, and every time I looked at him, I could think only of my plainness and how lucky I was that he had chosen me. He had ink-black hair, a strong jaw, and walnut-colored eyes.

"Chicken," I answered. It was a joy to say the word. This was life, and being an adult: to respond this way to one's husband about dinner. I was twenty and believed we would always be happy.

We ate. We must have. I remember that Ed talked very little about the store, and a lot about the railroad. That was a favorite topic of his in those days. There were rumors that a train line would soon be laid between Boston and Buffalo, cutting within a mile of Coral River. It had been Ed's big reason for buying the house, which was, at the time, remote: it was a two-mile walk to and from the bus that carried him the remaining two miles into Coral River, and at least a mile jaunt to its nearest neighbor.

Once the train line came, Ed assured me, there would be houses cropping up and down the hills like mushrooms after a rainstorm, a forest of bleached white skeleton-houses, shingled siding, modern plumbing. We'd be the pioneers. He wouldn't be surprised if the rail company offered to buy us out for three times what we'd paid or more—he'd heard of such things happening.

In the end, the line never came; and the house remained as remote as ever—even more remote when Mr. Donovan, our closest neighbor, died in the war and his widow had to move in with a sister in Boston. That was when Ed began to lose his interest in progress, stopped saving up for the newest vacuum cleaner models, stopped exclaiming over the advertisements for electric kettles and televisions.

That was also when there weren't so many good days anymore.

But that was all down the road. We had years to get through first—a war, winters of cold and hunger, Maggie's birth, long, bitter seasons of silence. We couldn't have known that the railroad wouldn't come. We were kids and didn't know anything.

I overcooked the chicken. I remember that. The skin was rubbery but Ed was too hungry to notice, and he finished his plate and asked for seconds, and I was so glad. I kissed him on his beautiful forehead when I got up to make him another plate.

At the end of the meal he noticed the leaves and the Jacob's ladder in the hearth. He pushed away from the table.

"What is that trash?" he asked, standing up abruptly.

"Leaves and flowers from the yard," I said. "I thought they would look pretty."

He frowned. "Clean it up," he said, belched loudly, and left the room.

It was the first time in our married life that I felt like crying. But I didn't. I thought of my parents, and how pleased they would be to know I was unhappy—*we warned her,* they would say—and instead I went straight to the stone fireplace and began picking out the leaves, one by one. The hearth was coated with a fine layer of ancient ash, like a soft, gray snow, and by the time I was finished, it streaked my skin to the elbow. I couldn't bring myself to throw the flowers and the leaves in the garbage; instead, I gathered them in my arms and took them out into the yard, released them to the wind, and let them scatter over the hills, where the purple shadows had dimmed to uniform darkness. I had a sudden, desperate urge to run; but instead I stood still, frozen, while the wind picked up and the bats began to race across the moon, until Ed called out to me to come inside.

I went inside.

I remember:

The metal bed frame, knocking, knocking, knocking against the wall; the sound of a coyote screaming in the night.

You see? Even now, I can follow the memory thread down. The past stirs under the ashes and pokes its petals from the dust.

Once everyone is asleep—Minna in the Yellow Room, with one arm looped around Amy's waist, their hair intermingling on the pillows; Trenton in the Blue Room, lying on his back, arms flat at his sides, as though he has been felled by a blow; and Caroline in the Daisy Room, because at the last minute she expressed a horror of sleeping in the master suite, which looks identical to the way it did during the years of her marriage; and even Sandra, although awake, of course, has gone silent and still, so that her presence is nearly imperceptible—I can't stop thinking about what Caroline said to Minna about death.

It isn't an infection, she said. She might be right. Then again, we've nested in the walls like bacteria. We've taken over the house, its insulation and its plumbing—we've made it our own.

Or maybe it's life that is the infection: a feverish dream, a hallucination of feelings. Death is purification, a cleansing, a cure.

In the morning, Minna gets up early to pick up large boxes from the hardware store downtown. By the time the others are waking, she has assembled a dozen of them and lined them up neatly like a series of cardboard coffins, ready to enfold the remains of Richard Walker's earthly existence.

And so the cleansing begins.

PART II

THE STUDY

SANDRA

"Monstrous," Minna says. "Absolutely monstrous. It looks like a vulva."

I'll say this about Minna: she may be as deep as a puddle but she *is* funny. And she's right. The lamp on Richard Walker's desk is meant to look like a rose—all droops and loops of pink and white fabric, with tiny electric lights budding in between—but the effect is more like a fat lady peeling back her skirt.

"Minna." Caroline presses her fingers against her temples. It's 9:30 A.M. and she's on her first drink. She won't be over the hump until her second or third.

"A drooping vulva," Minna adds. She shakes her head and returns to wrapping up Richard's collection of clocks. "Who would buy something like that?"

"Your father."

"What did he think he would do with all of it?" Minna says, making a face. "It's like a trash heap in here. Like one of those hoarder shows."

"Your father wasn't a hoarder," Caroline says. "He was a collector. Be careful, Minna. Some of those clocks are valuable."

"Junk," Minna says, as she nestles a paperweight on top of a folded afghan, in yet another box. The boxes are slowly sprouting all over the house. "And more junk."

"I've talked to Dani Sutherland," Caroline says, keeping one hand on her temples and taking a sip from a plastic cup with the other. Screwdriver. Two parts vodka, one part orange juice.

Minna gives her mother a blank look.

"You don't remember Dani Sutherland? Her son, Hank, used to babysit? Oh, well. Dani does realty now. She's worried about the market. Says it might take two or three years to really get the price we want. We might get lucky, though, with a buyer from the city. I guess we'll have to see."

Minna rips off a bit of packing tape with her teeth. "Maybe we shouldn't sell," she says. "At least not right away."

"Of course we're going to sell." When Caroline frowns, her face looks like a collapsed pudding.

"It's not only your decision," Minna says.

"Yes, it is," Caroline says. "It's my house now. I call the shots."

Minna stares at her. "Trenton was right," she says. "You really don't care—about Dad and the house and all of it."

"Please, Minna. Don't be so childish. Of course I care. But I'm also broke. And you need the money just as much as I do." Caroline takes a sip that nearly empties her cup. Now it makes sense: the ugly luggage, all that expensive clothing showing its age, cashmere spotted with holes.

Minna starts assembling another box, wielding the tape aggressively, as if trussing a live animal. "You should have married that guy—what was his name?—the one from the cosmetics family. Henry something."

"Harry Fairfield," Caroline says.

"Then you would have been set."

"He had sweaty palms." Caroline sighs. "Besides, you can't fall in love with someone just because he has buckets of money."

Minna snorts. "Isn't that why you fell in love with Dad?"

"Minna. No. Of course not." Caroline's either shocked or doing a good job of pretending to be.

"He was ten years older," Minna says.

"He was sophisticated." Caroline's voice gets quiet, and for the first time she releases her death grip on her forehead. "I loved your father. I did. He was just . . . "

"An asshole?"

That's the understatement of the century.

"*Difficult,*" Caroline says, scowling down at her drink. It's nearly empty: pulp clings to the sides of the cup.

Minna opens the top drawer and makes a noise of disapproval. "Papers. Envelopes. Postcards. No order. No *system.*" She slams the drawer shut and moves on to the next one, then inhales sharply. "I didn't know Dad kept a gun."

"A gun?" Caroline repeats.

Minna lifts up a pistol slowly, holding it with two fingers, as if it's a dirty sock.

"Don't point that thing at me, Minna."

"I'm not pointing it."

"Put it away, please, before you hurt yourself."

Minna rolls her eyes and replaces the gun in the drawer. "It'll take weeks to go through all this stuff."

Caroline stares at her cup for a minute. Then she looks up. "Do you have *any* happy memories here?"

"No." Then, a pause: "Some. I remember you used to let me bowl in the hallway upstairs. Remember that? You set up pins and everything. And when it rained, we watched movies in your bed."

"*The Wizard of Oz* was your favorite," Caroline says. "You were always praying for a tornado."

"And I remember Trenton learning how to walk. Then he wouldn't stop following me. Jesus, it drove me crazy."

Alice stirs; I hope she won't start sniveling. You should have seen her when Caroline brought Trenton back from the hospital: a patchy red blob with a single tuft of hair growing from the center of his forehead, one of the ugliest babies I've ever seen. And the smells! Diapers, spittle, puke. Horrible.

But Alice just went to pieces. I'd catch her when she thought I was distracted, drawn close around his crib, singing nonsense songs and whispering to him as though he could hear.

"Do you remember the Christmas parties we used to have? Your father would sing. And you and Trenton always argued about who got to hang the angel. I remember you played the piano so beautifully . . . "

"I *hated* the piano," Minna says loudly—so loudly Caroline blinks.

"Did you?" she says. "But you were so good. Everyone said you would go to Juilliard." She tries to shake the last remaining drops of liquid onto her tongue.

Minna glares at her. "Are you serious? You really have *no* fucking idea, do you? About anything."

Caroline widens her eyes. "I don't know why you're being so hostile, Minna," she says. "We're just having a conversation."

Minna stares. "Have another drink, Ma," she says finally, then slams down a plate so hard it cracks in two, and storms out of the room.

TRENTON

Trenton was disappointed by the gun Minna had found. He'd been expecting something sleek and black. He'd pictured tucking it into his waistband, swaggering around with it for a bit, getting the feel. He'd pictured the kind of gun that would make you think twice about messing with someone—guns evened the score, turned losers into big shots.

This gun was old, first of all, and it was heavy. He couldn't even fit it into his waistband, and if he did, he thought he'd probably blow his balls off accidentally. It looked more like something you would see at a museum than at the scene of a crime. Plus he didn't know if it was loaded, and he wasn't sure how to check.

He'd seen a gun only once before, at the disastrous party last winter that had earned him his nickname. It had been, without doubt, the worst night of his life. Most people probably thought the accident had been the worst night of his life, but for Trenton, that had been a kind of liberation.

Everything afterward—the pain and the pills and the metal rods holding his shins together and the wire in his jaw and the shitty power shakes that tasted like sand sipped through a straw—had been awful. But in the moment of the accident, the sheer blazing terror of it and the certainty, just then, that he would die, he'd found a kind of peace he'd never known, or at least hadn't felt in years.

This is it, he had thought, just before the scream of metal on metal and the sparks and then the darkness. And he was, purely and simply, relieved. No more failing, no more fucking up, no more loneliness like a constant pressure on his bladder that he couldn't piss or sleep or drink away.

And then he'd woken up. He had never thought about suicide before. But lying in the hospital, it had occurred to him that suicide was the only possible solution. Clean. Elegant. Brave, even.

Suicide, he decided, had integrity.

He supposed he could just shove the barrel of the gun in his mouth and fire, but Russian roulette lacked integrity. If you were going to kill yourself, you had to know, in advance, that it was going to work. Chance was for idiots.

That's what Derrick Richards had suggested at the party: that they all play Russian roulette. Trenton had kept his mouth shut, like he did at every party, hoping that if he stayed quiet, no one would notice that he didn't belong. Derrick was dumb enough to do it and his friends were dumb enough to follow along. Fortunately Derrick was so drunk he'd stumbled backward and sent a bullet straight through the window, and after that someone had taken the gun away and everyone had moved on to strip poker, even though it was December and flakes of snow were swirling in through the shattered window.

From upstairs, Trenton thought he heard laughter, faintly, and shoved the gun quickly into his dad's desk drawer, where he had found it, where Minna had casually mentioned it would be—almost like she knew what he was planning and was encouraging it. Well. Why wouldn't she? Nothing was worse than being a disgusting pock-faced freak with a sister who looked like Minna. He was sure she suspected him of being a virgin.

If only she knew the truth: that he'd never even been kissed. At least not in a way that counted.

The laughter stopped. Maybe he was hallucinating. Last night, before falling asleep, he thought he'd heard whispers, voices in the creaking of the floorboards, the sighing of a woman. He would have blamed it on the painkillers, but he'd stopped taking them. He was saving them up, just in case.

He opened the drawer and removed the gun once again. It was heavy. What the hell had his dad used it for? What had his dad used *any* of this stuff for? Pencil sharpeners in weird shapes, antique toys, old radios. Craziness.

He was suddenly aware that the whole house had gone silent. His mom had left, he knew, probably to go buy more booze. Minna had gone to the kitchen to make Amy lunch.

He could do it. Right here. Right now. Could bite down on the metal, taste iron on his tongue, say boom, and head toward that place of calm again, where he wasn't such a nothing. Where he *was* nothing.

But he couldn't bring himself to lift the gun to his mouth. He kept thinking of stupid Derrick Richards and his salmon-colored pants pooled at his ankles, comfortable as anything, his pale chest exposed, already curling with a man's worth of hair, his fleshy thighs splayed like two fat white fish, losing hand after hand in strip poker and not caring. And Trenton, who wasn't even playing, sitting stiff as an arrow, mortified, desperate that no one move or even breathe in his direction, because Angie Salazar was sitting on his right (he'd never even thought she was hot) and down to her bra and underwear, and every time she moved to take a card the fat swell of her boobs moved with her, and he could see where her butt was compressed by the chair, and imagine the heat of her thighs pressed together, and he had such a raging boner he thought he might die or, worse, explode right there in front of everyone. *Bang.*

When he finally couldn't take it any longer, when it was too much, he'd gotten up stiffly, bowlegged as a sailor, holding his cup in front of his crotch, and hurtled into the bathroom. He'd slammed the door shut and locked it—at least, he thought he had, but in his desperation to get his pants down and release the explosion that had been building inside of him like some awful time bomb ticking away to social humiliation—well, he hadn't double-checked. And so when Lanie Buck had stumbled into the bathroom less than a minute later because she had to puke, the whole party had caught Trenton mid flagrante delicto, if you could be in flagrante delicto by yourself—head back, pants around his ankles, cock in his hand, eyes closed, and practically crying with the sheer, tremendous relief of it.

Splooge. Derrick had led the chant, and everybody had picked up on it. Splooge. Splooge. Splooge.

He hadn't even buckled his belt before fleeing. As he walked back to campus, the snow stinging his cheeks like new tears, he'd known that he was finished at Andover.

Sometimes he fantasized about killing Derrick, instead of himself. But he knew he'd never have the guts for it.

There was a footstep outside, in the hall. Before Trenton had time to put away the gun, Minna pushed open the door, carrying yet another box.

"Oh," she said. "Did you decide to help after all?"

Trenton had successfully avoided helping for most of the morning, claiming that his leg was acting up. He was pretty sure Minna knew he was faking, but she wouldn't say anything; besides, she had no right, after what she had done.

That was life, Trenton thought: people knew your secrets, but if you had shit on them, too, they couldn't rat you out. So everything evened out, piled under one huge shit sandwich.

Minna dropped the box, which was empty, and nudged it with a foot to turn it right side up. "You found Dad's dirty little secret, I see. One of them, anyway."

Now that she had acknowledged the gun, he felt he could safely return it to the drawer. He was relieved when it was out of his hands, and he opened a few drawers casually, so Minna might think he'd just been rooting around in the study, idly curious, when he'd happened on the gun. "I was just looking at it," he said.

"You weren't planning on shooting anyone?" she said.

"Not today," Trenton said. He wasn't sure if he was making a joke or not.

"I might shoot Mom," Minna said matter-of-factly. Some of her hair had fallen out of her ponytail and she brushed it back with a wrist. "We haven't even made a dent in this room, have we?"

In one of the lower desk drawers, Trenton found a half-dozen cards, stuffed haphazardly on top of some ink cartridges. He opened one and jerked back in his chair. "Ew."

"Ew what?"

"Hair." He held up a small brown curl, held together by a faded blue elastic. There was no signature on the card. No message, either. Just the words that had been printed: *Thinking of you.*

Minna stood up quickly, snatched the card and the lock of hair from him, and tossed it back in the drawer. "Don't touch Dad's stuff," she said.

"I thought I was supposed to be helping," he said.

"Well, you're not." She slammed the drawer closed with a shin. She stood for a minute, massaging her temples, and Trenton thought viciously that she would probably look just like his mom in a few years.

"I'm getting old," she said, as if she knew what he'd been thinking. Then Trenton felt guilty.

"You're twenty-seven."

"Twenty-eight next month." She moved another box—this one full of books—from the chair opposite the desk onto the floor and sat down with a small groan and closed her eyes. She said, "Someone died in here, you know."

Trenton felt the tiniest flicker of interest. "What do you mean?"

"Someone was shot. In here. Years ago, before Dad bought the house. There were brains splattered all over the wall." She opened her eyes. "I remember Mom and Dad talking about it when we first moved in."

It was the first interesting thing Trenton had ever heard about the house. "How come you didn't tell me before?"

Minna shrugged. "You were so little. And then I must have forgot."

Trenton turned this piece of information over in his mind and found that it gave him a little bit of pleasure. "Like . . . a murder?" That word, too, was pleasurable: a distraction, a temporary lifting away from the everyday. Like being just a little drunk.

"I don't know the whole story," Minna said. She seemed to lose interest in the conversation. She started picking out dirt from underneath her nails.

In the quiet, Trenton heard it again. A voice. Not quite a voice, though. More like a shape: a solidity and pattern to the normal creakings and stirrings of the house. It was the way he'd felt as a kid listening to the wind through the trees, thinking he could make sense out of it. But this wasn't just his imagination.

There were words there, he was sure of it.

"Do you . . . do you hear that?" he ventured to Minna.

"Hear what?" Minna looked up. "Did Amy shout?"

Trenton shook his head.

Minna tilted her head, listening. She shrugged again. "Nada."

Trenton swallowed. His throat felt dry. Maybe something had gone haywire in his head after the accident. Like a popped fuse or something. Because directly after Minna had spoken, he heard the word, uttered clearly in the silence.

The word was: *Idiot.*

A L I C E

How do ghosts see?

We didn't always; it had to be relearned.

Dying is a matter of being reborn. In the beginning there was darkness and confusion. We learned gropingly. We felt our way into this new body, the way that infants do. Images began to emerge. The light began to creep in.

Now I see better than I did when I was alive. I never liked to wear my glasses, and by the time I was thirty, I couldn't see from one side of the parlor to the other without squinting.

Now everything is perfectly clear. We do more than see. We detect the smallest vibrations, minuscule shifts in the currents, minor disturbances, molecules shifting. We are invisible fingers: we play endlessly over the surface of things.

Only memory remains slippery and elusive. Memories won't keep faith with you. They'll go sliding away into the ravenous void of nonbeing.

Memories must be staked to the back of something, swaddled in objects, wrapped around table legs.

Trenton is so motionless in the armchair, if it weren't for the way he occasionally reaches up to finger a pimple on his face, he might be dead. Amy sits at his feet with an enormous, leather-bound book on her lap. I recognize it as *The Raven Heliotrope.*

Minna was the one who found it, discovering the typewritten pages loosely stacked and stashed in an old crawlspace. She read it so many times she could recite whole passages from memory. When she was ten, she went crazy trying to figure out the writer's identity—the manuscript was anonymous—and Richard Walker, in one of his spells of good humor, had it bound, and even called in literary experts and a Harvard professor, who judged from the language and imagery that the book might date from the mid-nineteenth century.

This was endlessly amusing to me. I know for a fact that *The Raven Heliotrope* was completed between 1944 and 1947. I wrote it.

"Mommy!" Amy cries out suddenly, excitedly. "I'm at the part with the bamboo forest. Do you want me to read it to you?"

Amy's mention of the bamboo forest sends a small thrill through me. That was one of the passages I was proudest of: Penelope and the Innocents get attacked by a vicious band of Nihilis and are only saved by the sudden appearance of magical bamboo, which grows up around them, impaling the Nihilis army.

"Sure, honey." Minna dabs her forehead with the inside of her forearm.

Amy moves her finger across the picture of Penelope riding a horse. "Then Penelope went riding away . . . and there were Nihilis and they were ugly and they liked blood."

"You're a terrible writer," Sandra says neutrally. Believe it or not, I had actually managed to forget her existence for an hour, the way you do a shadow's.

"She's not reading," I snap. "She's making it up."

"Bamboo," Sandra says. "Bamboo! You might have at least used rosebushes. Thorns that punctured the eyes, and all that."

I don't bother responding. It was Thomas who told me about

bamboo—that it grows so quickly, and with such strength, it can go straight through a human body. We talked about how terrible the natural world could be.

Of course the bamboo is only doing what it must. Everything obeys its own inner laws. Everything is greedy, and moving toward a version of light.

"Penelope made a wish and then a forest grew up . . . " Amy says, after putting her finger, arbitrarily, in the center of the page. She trails off. She's butchering it. The forest doesn't grow because Penelope wished it. The forest grows out of the blood of the Innocents.

Minna scoots past the desk and pulls apart the curtains. She must be looking out at the driveway. I no longer know what the driveway looks like. Sandra told me it was paved. But I can still picture the hills—at this time of year, the poplars and the cottonwoods should be blossoming, and the daffodils will be pushing up, and the air will smell sweet as the sap begins to run: a painful smell, which brings back memories of other springs and other cycles, a continuity that exists beyond and apart from us.

"Who is it?" Amy pushes the book off her lap. "Is it Nana? Is she back?"

"It's not Nana," Minna says, frowning. "I don't know who it is." She sighs. "Stay here with Uncle Trenton, okay, sweetie? Trenton, can you watch her? Don't touch anything, Amybear."

Minna goes out into the front hall: a dim place that always smells like old shoes. No one uses the front entrance except for delivery people and the various groups that go door-to-door, petitioning for a clean water act or advocating for Mr. So-and-So for governor.

The man on the front porch is wearing a too-big suit and holding a briefcase that looks like a theatrical prop. He seems vaguely familiar. After he introduces himself as Dennis Carey, Richard Walker's lawyer, I realize I must have seen him before.

"Well, I guess you better come in," Minna says, and opens the door wider to admit him.

For a moment I'm swept away by a wedge of light that cuts into us, penetrates the layers of air and dust that have accumulated in the hall. Then Minna closes the door.

"You could have told us you were coming," she says, sticking her hands in her back pockets so he can't avoid looking at her breasts.

"Here comes trouble," Sandra says, obviously pleased. She loves a good spectator sport.

His eyes tick down and careen back up to her face. "I called," Dennis says, shifting his briefcase to his left hand. "I spoke to Caroline . . . ?"

Minna laughs. "No wonder I wasn't expecting you," she says. "Caroline isn't here."

"Not here?" Dennis tugs at his collar. He's probably in his forties and not completely unattractive, although he has too much stomach and too little hair.

I feel a brief flash of fear. Minna is like a spider, huge and hungry.

"My mom tends to be forgetful," Minna says, and pushes past Dennis, shouldering too close, so her body brushes against his. "You want something to drink?"

Dennis transforms his nervous cough into a laugh. "Better not," he says. He's uncomfortable, as he should be, without knowing why. "I'm still on the clock. I made the appointment with Caroline . . . "

Minna waves a hand. "Appointments have never stopped my mother from drinking. What do you say? Whiskey? Wine? Vodka? We're absolutely drowning in vodka . . . "

"I shouldn't," Dennis says, but I can feel him beginning to relent.

"You might as well relax." Minna takes another step toward

him. “Who knows how long we’ll be waiting for the others . . . ” She steps forward again, so they are standing less than a foot apart.

All the threads are pulled tight in that instant. Even I am swept along. The air vibrates like a plucked violin string.

Then Amy bursts out of the study.

“Nana’s back, Mommy!” She barrels down the hall, half sliding on bunched-up socks.

Just like that, the threads are cut. Dennis and Minna instinctively step away from each other.

“Honey, be careful!” Minna reaches out and catches Amy by the shoulders, forcing her to slow down.

“Who are *you*?” Amy says, looking up at Dennis.

“Don’t be rude, Amy,” Minna says.

Dennis laughs. “I’m Dennis,” he says, leaning down and offering his hand, solemnly, for Amy to shake. Instead she ducks around Minna’s leg, peeking at him from between Minna’s thighs.

“Oh, for heaven’s sake,” Minna says. “Say hi to Mr. Carey, Amy.”

“Hi,” Amy whispers.

Dennis straightens up again. “Is she yours?”

Minna nods. She won’t meet his eyes. I wonder whether she’s embarrassed about the fact that their moment was interrupted, or about the fact that it happened at all.

“She’s very pretty,” Dennis says.

“Say thank you, Amy,” Minna says sharply.

Amy says nothing.

The kitchen door opens.

“In here, Mom,” Minna says, before Caroline can ask.

Caroline comes into the hall a moment later. In her large gray cashmere jumpsuit, she looks like an overgrown dust mite. And yet there—underneath it, underneath *her*—I can’t help but see another Caroline: thin and beautiful, with the same wide, lost eyes, drifting from room to room. Even then, she was like dust—blown from place to place.

"The service here—" she starts to say, and then, seeing Dennis, stops. "Oh God. You must be Mr. Carey. I'd completely forgotten—"

"It's no problem," Dennis says, starting forward. He goes to shake her hand; she extends her hand limply and allows it to be engulfed. "I wasn't waiting long."

"You don't *look* like a lawyer," Caroline says, and she laughs as though she has made a joke. "Surely you're too young."

"A lawyer?" Trenton has skulked into the hall, too, and stands with his shoulders hunched practically to his ears.

Minna says offhandedly, "I never could stand lawyers."

Dennis clearly doesn't know who to address. He again adjusts the collar of his shirt. His neck is thin, and his Adam's apple prominent, as though he has swallowed a peach pit at some point in his life and it has been lodged there ever since. "I was lucky enough to work with Mr. Walker in the later years of his life," he says.

Caroline claps her hands. Her eyes are very bright. "I suppose we might as well get started," she says. "No point in delaying the inevitable."

"Get started on what?" Trenton asks.

Caroline looks from Trenton to Minna in her old, bewildered way, as though both of them have just materialized from nowhere. "Mr. Carey is here to read your father's will," she says. She turns a smile back to Dennis. "Let's go into the study, shall we? It's so much cozier in there. I'll just nip into the kitchen for a glass of wine. I have a feeling I'm going to need it."

S A N D R A

In my day, the study was the den. It wasn't as big then as Richard Walker made it during the Great Renovation of 1994, when we got cracked open like an egg, scrambled and remade, puffed up into a soufflé of useless rooms and spiral staircases and "breakfast nooks" and window seats.

My favorite place: in the armchair, feet up, cigarette burning in the ashtray and a drink in my hand, the deep purple walls pulsing in the light from the TV, like being at the center of a heart. Bay windows belly out over the back lawn, and in the distance stands a shaggy dark line of trees, thick as a group of sheepdogs.

Minna looks as if she needs a cigarette. Caroline, too. They're gaping at each other like two trout on ice at the grocery store. Even Trenton has straightened up.

Minna is the one to speak first. "*Trenton?* Why the hell would he leave the house to *Trenton*?"

"Probably because I'm the only one of us who didn't hate him," Trenton says. He shakes a bit of hair from his eyes. When he's not slouching and sulking and playing with his zits, he's not so bad looking. He's got a little of his father in him—straight nose, nice chin.

"Don't be Victorian, Trenton," Minna says. "I didn't hate him."

I'm feeling especially nice about Minna today. I can't help it if I'm a little aglow, a little warm and fuzzy, as though all the lights are on at once. She knows about me! She remembers. I'd bet my last dollar that means other people remember me, too. Everyone likes to be recognized and appreciated. Those were *my* brains on the study wall, *thankyouverymuch.*

I'm glad that Martin at least had the decency to kill me in the study.

"He can't possibly leave the house to Trenton," Caroline cuts in shrilly. "For God's sake—Trenton's only fifteen."

"Sixteen," Trenton corrects her.

"Exactly," Caroline says. "He's a minor."

"The property will be held in trust until Trenton turns eighteen," Dennis says. Over the course of the hour his skin has gone a mottled pink color, like he's just washed up in too-hard, too-hot water.

"In trust?" Caroline parrots. "In trust to who?"

Dennis jerks his head to the left, some kind of nervous tic. With his scrawny neck, and his paunch, he reminds me a little of one of those mechanical birds we used to perch at the edge of a bowl: dipping, dipping. "Mr. Walker appointed several trustees," he says, "myself included."

Caroline throws up her hands and settles back in her chair. "I see. So it's a scam."

"Mom," Minna says.

"It's one of those—what do you call them—pyramid schemes."

"My mother isn't a finance person," Minna says to Dennis.

"Don't speak about me as though I'm not here, Minna."

Trenton has lost interest already and slumps backward. "Forget it," he says. "I don't want it, anyway."

Caroline looks at Dennis as though to say, *See?*

"I'm afraid that isn't how these things work," Dennis says.

Up until now, the will has been as boring as laundry. Everything exactly as expected and all aboveboard. Richard is a whole lot nicer dead than he was alive, I'll tell you that. A whopping half a million for both children and another to Amy, and the contents of the house to Caroline, to sell if she wants. That should bring in a nice little bundle.

"I'm telling you, I don't care what you do with it," Trenton insists. "Sell it. Turn it into a hotel. Burn the whole thing down, like Minna said."

Alice makes a strangled sound. She's been wound up tighter than a nun's asshole since the Walkers came home.

She's afraid. She knows the truth will come out now. *Everything* will come up, like after the floods of '79 when whole sheets of mud slid up to the porch, battered the windows, uprooted trees, turned up rotten hats and stinking shoes and even a forty-year-old turtle with the face of an old man. Brought Maggie, Alice's daughter, to my door, too.

Remember that: remember that about Alice, when you're tempted to believe everything she tells you; when she says that I'm full of shit, that I'm paranoid, that I've rewritten the past. Her own child—her *only* child—didn't know her at all. She told me so herself.

"Minna!" Caroline pretends to look shocked.

Minna waves a hand. "I wasn't serious."

Dennis clears his throat. He's obviously in way over his head. He probably spends most of his time rezoning decks and settling divorces. He's getting plowed by the Walkers. "I'm afraid that's not quite how it works," he repeats again. "And you won't actually have the power to decide on a course of action—"

"Until I'm eighteen, I know," Trenton cuts him off.

"Look, are we done yet?" Minna asks, starting to stand. "I should check on Amy."

"Not quite," Dennis says, and he jerks his head to the left again as he fingers his collar. "Mr. Walker made several other provisions—"

"Of course he did," Caroline says. "He lived to be a pain. I don't know why I thought it would be different once he was dead."

Dennis presses on: "He requested, first, that his ashes be buried, not scattered. And he would like to be interred somewhere on the property."

"We knew that," Minna says. "He always said he wanted to stay here. Wouldn't be dragged out come death, hell, or high water."

"There's another thing," Dennis starts, and then stops. "A fairly large bequest . . . " He shuffles the papers in his hands and clears his throat. His skin is just getting pinker. It looks like he's sprouting a rash. For a moment he stands sputtering, opening and closing his mouth. Then he turns to Caroline. "Maybe it would be better if we discussed it alone?"

Caroline stares. "I don't care," she says. "What did he do? Leave half his money to a dog pound or something?"

"He hated dogs," Trenton says.

Dennis places the papers next to him on the desk and rearranges them so their corners match up. Minna has sat down again. He deliberately avoids her stare. For a moment, the room is still.

This is going to be good.

"Mr. Walker has left a sum of money to an Adrienne Cadiou," he says.

Minna and Caroline exchange a momentary glance, no more than a flicker of their eyes.

Minna says, "Trenton, can you go check on Amy?" Her voice is high.

"Who's Adrienne?" he asks.

"Please, Trenton." She looks at him, eyes dark, the same way she always did. *Don't put the candlesticks there.* It works. He stands up—which is to say, he slurps his way off the chair and oozes out of the room.

Time ticks by: seconds, minutes.

"Do you know her?" Dennis asks.

Caroline is sitting, stiff as a wood plank. She stares at the empty glass she is holding. Absolut vodka, mixed with a little seltzer. No lemon. I would have put lemon in it.

"No," she says shortly.

"I'm sorry, Mom." Minna reaches out and tries to place a hand on her mother's knee. Caroline jerks away.

"We haven't been married for ten years," she says. "It's only to be expected, isn't it? Even when we were married . . . " She trails off.

"I don't remember an Adrienne. Do you?" I say to Alice.

"No," she whispers back. I don't know why she's bothering to keep her voice down.

"There was an Agnes," I say. "Terrible name."

"Be quiet, Sandra."

"And an Anna . . ."

"I said, be quiet."

Minna stands up abruptly and leaves the room. Caroline is staring out the window. For a second, I feel sorry for her. Caroline gets a bad rap. But she does her best.

"Have you contacted her?" she asks. She still doesn't look at Dennis.

"He gave an address," he says. "We've written. Evidently, she lives in Toronto . . . ?"

If he's hoping for a response, he doesn't get it. Caroline doesn't move. She continues staring out the window.

"How much?" she asks.

Dennis jerks his head to the left again, like he wasn't expecting her to ask. "What?"

"How much did he leave her?" Now Caroline does turn her eyes to him, eyes as big and blue as a child's drawing of a sky.

"A million," Dennis says quietly.

Caroline closes her eyes, and then opens them again. "More than he left his own children" is all she says. Then she stands up, unsteadily, bumping the chair as she makes her way to the door.

I'll tell you the nicest thing my dad ever did for me: croaked before he could drain away all his cash and left me a bundle to buy a place of my own. Made sure I'd never have to come crawling back to Georgia.

It's funny. I have only one really clear memory of my parents. Alpharetta, 1957 or 1958: before my mom and dad split, before my father's weekends with his good pal Alan. Early summertime, June bugs clinging to the screen doors, the smell of freesia, cow dung, grass clippings, petrol.

They were having a dinner party, and I remember the preparations: cream cheese balls rolled in chopped walnuts; Jell-O salad in the shape of a fish; cubes of yellow cheese beaded with condensation, toothpicks standing proudly like flags from their ranks. I remember helping my mother iron limp white napkins and getting in trouble because my fingers were dirty and left smudges. I remember my dad standing in front of the bathroom mirror, shirtless, moving a razor over his jaw.

I wasn't allowed inside to play so I spent the evening in the backyard. The air was full of fireflies, and when I'd tired of watching, I ran around trying to catch them.

"You know what they are, don't you?"

I turned around, surprised by my mother's voice. Standing on the cement patio, backlit by the kitchen light, her face was unreadable. She held a lit cigarette but she wasn't smoking it. She looked thin and frail, like a kind of bird.

When I didn't answer, she came down the steps into the grass. "Fireflies," she repeated. "You know what they are?"

"Bugs," I said.

When she took a drag, I could see she was smiling a little. But she wasn't looking at me. She was staring out into space.

"They're spirits," she said, in a low voice. "Souls. When a heart breaks, a firefly is born." She reached out a hand as though to catch one, then let her hand drop and took another drag of her cigarette. "They fly forever, sending out secret signals to their lost loves. See? Watch."

We sat very still. I held my breath. In the darkness, the fireflies flared suddenly and then went out, making random patterns in the air. It was the first time my mother had ever told me a story that wasn't out of the Bible; the first time, too, I ever felt sorry for her, or for any grown-up.

"That's what a broken heart looks like," she said, and stood up. "Like a haunting." She turned to go inside, but at the last second she looked back at me. "It isn't worth it, Sandra. Remember that."

Well. I wish I had. Things might have turned out a whole lot different with me and Martin. And who knows. My brains might have stayed where they belonged.

M I N N A

It took Minna forty-five minutes to get Caroline into bed after she polished off three-quarters of a bottle of vodka in under an hour. Caroline's face was swollen and streaked with makeup, and there was a little dried vomit on her lower lip.

Minna rolled her mother over, onto her side, pushing against the warm fat flesh of her thighs and stomach, thinking of a documentary she'd seen once where a half-dozen men had strapped a beached whale with hooks and ropes and pulleys and tried to haul it back to the water. She wished she could sink a hook straight into her mother's fat ass and heave. At some point, Caroline had taken off her pants, and Minna was disgusted by the sight of her cheap nylon underwear, full seated and worn thin in places, clinging desperately to her thighs like lichen to the side of a rock.

Minna was tired. Something kept twisting in her stomach, an alien pain; she should never have come back. She thought of calling Dr. Upshaw but knew it would just make her feel worse. She couldn't even make it two days in the old house without cracking. Pathetic.

There had to be someone else she could call, but she couldn't immediately think of anyone. She was half tempted to call Greg, Amy's father, just so she'd have something to pin her anger to: nail it down, give it a name, the way she had enjoyed shoving thumbtacks into the corkboard map she'd had as a kid. *Find Sweden.*

But Greg was still at work, and she'd never get past his secretary. She was only allowed to call him between the hours of 7:00 and 8:00, when he was commuting back to his home in Westchester, back to his wife and his *real* kids, as he'd once slipped up and referred to them, and half the time he screened her phone calls, anyway. The checks still arrived regularly, though, thank God. She'd burned through four jobs in three years. Fired from two, laid off from two. She had less than two thousand dollars in her savings account.

Amy believed that her dad was a firefighter, a hero, and dead.

There was Alex, whom she'd been fucking recently, and Ethan, who still wanted to fuck her. But they never actually talked, not about real things. Some bullshitting over dinner, flirtation in the back of a cab, and maybe some back-and-forth in the morning, just so it didn't feel too cheap.

She didn't have female friends. For the most part, she didn't trust other women, and other women certainly didn't trust her. There had been Dana—Minna was still sorry about how that ended. Stupid. Dana's boyfriend hadn't even been good in bed. Kind of soggy and spongy and bland, like wet toast. She didn't know why she had done it.

She never did.

She went downstairs to get her cell phone from the study, where she had left it, and found Trenton suctioned like a giant starfish to the carpet, dominating almost all the free space in the room, staring at the ceiling. He sat up on one elbow when she opened the door.

"What are you doing?" Minna was in the mood to get angry at someone.

"Listening," Trenton said, and returned to his back. "Do you hear that?"

He'd probably gotten into their mom's booze. Or maybe he was stoned. This might normally impress Minna—if Trenton had weed, it meant he actually had friends, or at least a friend, to buy it from—but today she felt nothing but a sharp surge of resentment.

Fucking Trenton. The house belonged to him now. And Trenton would go on believing their dad was some kind of misunderstood saint, and feeling superior to Minna for hating him. Maybe she should tell him about Adrienne Cadiou; she had found at least one card with Adrienne's name on it from the stash Trenton had located earlier, and though the messages weren't romantic, the fact that her father had kept them obviously was. She'd been hoping, after the reading of the will, that there might be some other explanation, like maybe her dad had mowed Adrienne down with his car and now she was paralyzed. Hush money.

Stupid.

She had stuffed all the cards and that disgusting lock of hair deep into a trash bag and taken it out immediately to the garage, as if it might contaminate the whole house.

"I don't hear anything." Minna stepped over him, nudging him in the ribs accidentally-deliberately with her foot. But he didn't even flinch.

"I think—I think this house might be haunted," Trenton said.

"Are you high?" Minna said. "Or just dumb?"

When Trenton blushed, even his pimples got darker. He sat up clumsily, and Minna remembered what the doctors had told her mom: that he would never have the same range of motion as before.

"Sorry," Minna said. "Mom's blotto. I'm a little stressed out."

Trenton nodded, but he wouldn't look at her. He picked at a spot on the carpet with his thumbnail. Minna, realizing that the ache had spread from her stomach into her whole body, sat in the chair the lawyer, Dennis, had vacated. The chairs were still arranged in a little circle, like the room had recently hosted a group therapy session.

After a long minute of silence, in which Minna ran an inventory of everything that hurt, from her shoulders to her knuckles to the small, calloused little toe of her right foot, Trenton looked up.

"So you don't believe," Trenton said.

"Believe in what?" Minna said.

Trenton looked embarrassed. "Ghosts."

Minna couldn't tell if he was joking or not. "What is this about, Trenton?"

"We don't *know,*" he said, and then she knew he wasn't joking. "Nobody knows. You said yourself someone was murdered here."

"That's just a story I heard," Minna said. "I don't know if it's true. And I never said she was murdered."

"And Dad—" Trenton began.

"Dad died at Presbyterian Medical," Minna said.

It was like Trenton hadn't heard. "But he could be," Trenton insisted. "He could be, I don't know, stuck somehow—"

A sharp pain went straight through Minna's head, like a flash going off. "If he's stuck anywhere, it's somewhere hotter than this," she said, and then regretted it.

Sometimes, it felt as though the words came out of her mouth without looping in her brain first. Trenton looked so pathetic, and she had a sudden memory of little Trenton, baby Trenton, before his bones had distended his body and made it gawky and puppet-like. She remembered him crawling into her lap, accidentally putting his knee in the soft space between her ribs, just below the two mosquito-bite boobs newly formed, wrapping a fat fist around her hair, saying "Mama." And Minna, nearly thirteen years old, had not corrected him.

"You hated him, didn't you?" Trenton looked up at her. His

eyes were still the same as they had been then: a blue that was startling against his other features, like coming across a lake in the middle of an expanse of concrete.

Minna pulled her right foot into her lap and began to knead it with her fist. "I didn't hate him," she said.

"You didn't love him, though," Trenton said.

"I'm not sure," Minna said. "Probably not."

She didn't know anymore whether she had ever loved her father. She must have. When they lived in California, he had taught her to swim—remembered the feel of his rough warm hands around her waist as she paddled through the water, the sting of chlorine, the high sun and the vivid grass, and dim, watery sounds of her mother calling to them to be careful.

She had been furious when they first moved to Coral River, midautumn, after the leaves had already gone down, when the whole place was nothing but grays and browns, mud and smear. She'd hated it: the colorlessness. The sky crowded by trees. The trees themselves, huddling in their long shadows, letting off the smell of death—so different from the improbable-looking palm tree with its perky crown of leaves, a practical-joke tree, like something designed specifically to make people smile.

The trees in Coral River didn't make people smile.

And the wind and the fingers of cold that reached past the window frames and thumbed up through the floorboards, the bubbling and hiss of the radiators and the banging of the rusty pipes—all of it was strange and ugly and old.

Then one night, her father had shaken her awake—it must have been two, three in the morning—his face so close she could feel the tickle of his beard, so close his smile was like a half-moon. "Wake up, Min," he said. "You gotta see this."

He had picked her up even though she was already too big, just so her bare feet would not touch the cold floor, and he'd carried her downstairs and into his study. He'd held her at the window, where the cold came through the glass and lodged straight into her heart, like a razorblade.

"Look," he whispered. "Snow."

She had never seen snow before, except in TV shows and movies. It had looked to her like the stars were flaking out of the sky. It had looked like thousands of fireflies in the moonlight; like breathlessness, like time stopping, like the most beautiful thing she had ever seen.

Then, she had loved him.

It was unfair that people could pretend to be one thing when they were really something else. That they would get you on their side and then do nothing but fail, and fail, and fail again. People should come with warnings, like cigarette packs: involvement would kill you over time.

When the phone rang, she jumped; she'd forgotten there was a house phone, and for one confused moment she thought she was hearing an alarm.

"Are you going to get that?" Trenton said, watching her, and making no attempt to get up.

It took her a minute to locate the working phone since there were a dozen telephones from different eras crowded on a shelf next to the desk. Finally, on the fourth ring, she found it. It was only when she went to pick up the phone that she realized her hands were shaking.

"Walker," she said past the tightness in her chest.

There was no response. Minna thought at first the line was dead, but then she heard a rustle, the unmistakable sound of someone breathing. She was suddenly on high alert. Instinctively, she angled her back to Trenton, clutching the receiver. Outside the window, the yellow coneflowers were waving in the grass.

"Hello?" she said. And again: "Hello?"

"Who is it?" Trenton said, from the floor.

Nothing but the sound of breathing. Minna felt the up-and-down roll of nausea. It had been here, on this spot, that her father had held her all those years ago and shown her the snow, which fell like a secret between them. Now he was dead and she was getting old.

"Hello?" she repeated one more time. The wave of nausea had brought with it a sudden crystallization of anger. And she knew. Knew it was a woman on the phone—knew it was *that* woman. Adrienne.

"Who is it?" Trenton said again.

Minna ignored him. She gripped the phone so tightly her knuckles ached.

"Listen," she said, and swallowed, wishing her throat weren't so dry. "Listen," she tried again. "Don't call here anymore."

"Who *is* it?" Trenton grunted a little, sitting up.

"He's dead," Minna said. Was it her imagination, or did the woman suck in a breath? She wished she could tunnel down the wires and watch the words take their effect, spitting like small barbed things directly into the woman's flesh. "He's dead, and he left nothing for you. So don't call anymore."

Then she hung up, slamming the receiver, feeling the impact all the way to her elbow.

A L I C E

At night, the house falls into silence. It's a relief. It has been many years since I've shared the house with so many people, and I've forgotten how exhausting it can be: to be filled with so much motion and so many needs, so much sound and tension. It's like the arthritis that swelled my joints in my old age and brought painful awareness to the parts of my body I had always safely ignored.

Do we dream? No. We don't sleep. There isn't any need for it. The body is solid, its corners intact—it doesn't need to be restored.

On the other hand, and especially at night, there are certain times of *drift.* There are moments when the house, the body, has gone still, when we are full of empty air, when nothing needs our attention. Then, sometimes, ideas converge: memory and present, wish and desire, silhouette shadows of people we have been or have known. This is the closest we come to dreaming.

What is now the study was once the sitting room, which became the living room, as times and fashions changed. There was a yellow-and-white loveseat that Ed hated. He traded it, later on, for a couch in green plaid we covered in plastic, so the upholstery wouldn't fade. There was a wireless set we eventually moved into the cellar, to make room for our television, and a faded rug we replaced, when Ed retired, with nubby gray wall-to-wall carpeting:

the newest thing. I used to walk it in my bare feet when he wasn't at home, pacing all the way to the corners, kneading my toes against the fabric, marveling at the look of it.

This was progress. This was modernity: you could cover over the past completely. You could bury the old under a relentless surface of new, stretched from corner to corner.

That's what I return to again and again, no matter how many times I think about it: how naive we were, how we believed in the promise, how we believed the past could be kept down. No. More than that—how we believed in a future that was distinct from the past.

We had bookshelves. Ed liked books, although he didn't read them. He was sensitive about his background, and careful, in public, never to betray the fact that he hadn't finished high school. He liked to collect things that made up for his childhood, as though the weight of his possessions would somehow hurtle him forward into a new life.

Maybe that's why he was obsessed with the railroad. Ed liked to talk in front of company about the *architecture of our country,* and the way it was written in railroads and highways: pistons moving forward, spokes and wheels rolling over a landscape of natural obstacles, chugging headfirst into the future. That was what Ed did his whole life: push, and push, and push.

Ed kept a slim volume of nineteenth-century railway maps, which he had bought for ten cents at an old flea market in Buffalo, displayed proudly on the top shelf. He insisted it not be moved, touched, or even dusted.

This was one of the first secrets I kept from him: when he was gone, I would move the little footstool, climb up to reach the top shelf, take down the book, and read it.

At first it was simply rebellion. But it quickly became more than that. There was something sad about the illustrations, the tracks stitching the land, like a body that had been sewn up after a terrible accident: it was the very attempt to connect that made it ugly.

Thomas and I liked to look at maps together. Even now, when I see the large-bundled volumes on Richard Walker's shelf, or the cardboard map that leans against the bookshelf, I can't help but think of Thomas, and the way we used to trace our fingers over the contours of the pages, following suggested routes, and feeling in our fingertips the possibility of escape.

I suppose, in some sense, wills are like maps: they are the imprint we leave, the places our affections have been entrenched; the work we have done; the money we have burrowed away; the furrows and the paths that lead back to spaces we have gone, and marked, and loved.

I left everything I had—which wasn't very much—to Maggie. In the end, my map was a dry place, a single road tethering me to my only child. In the end, my map was lonely.

I know that that's how it seemed to others. I know what I looked like: a devoted wife, despite everything, and then a cautious, solitary widow; a mother, perhaps too strict, perhaps too careful in her loving. A dry, dusty, throwaway woman, like many others: a woman made to fade, and dry out, and die shaking in her hollow skin.

This is the map I left. I know this. I knew it even before I became old.

And yet there were times when I felt my life full of such richness, such fullness, I couldn't express it, couldn't speak or breathe a word because I feared the disruption—even a single breath could ruin it, like wind over a pond. I didn't want even a ripple.

There were times when, exhausted, I held Maggie, in the dark, to my breast, and her tiny hands clutched at the air, and nobody in the world might have been awake but us. And then the small rosebud mouth, so needy, would find its object, and every mistake and blemish in my life was absolved: there was only giving, there was only the rhythm of life restored: the small pull against my breast, regular and ingrained, like a second heartbeat.

There were times with Ed—in between the storms, in between the distance—when for a miraculous moment, we seemed to wash up on a shore together, and for that moment (an hour, a day, a week), everything that had happened seemed like the long, littered road on the way to happiness. There was a picnic in Saratoga; there was the Fourth of July in Maine, when he surprised me with the ice cream cone.

There was watching Maggie waddle across the kitchen; there was the box turtle she found, and named, and insisted on attempting to keep in a cardboard box filled with long grass and nubby pebbles. Norman. She named it Norman.

There was the Christmas when Ed filled the house with tiny, winking lights and insisted I come downstairs with my eyes covered; there was snow piled deep and quiet in the woods, and sun turning slender cones of ice to diamond.

These are my secrets: roads branching, endlessly branching, each turn leading to a hundred others. When Sandra first came, I was tempted to share, to explain. But now I know: certain stories must remain mine, so that there is a me to remain.

Thomas wasn't mentioned in my will. How could he be? He was by then a phantom.

It's funny—I knew him a little less than two years. Even in living terms, that hardly amounts to anything. And in time that is not-living, in the endless, chalky sweep of eternity, which wears years to sand and blows everything back, dustlike, into void, it is nothing.

But that's the beauty of life: time is yours to keep and to change. Just a few minutes can be sufficient to carve a new road, a new track. Just a few minutes, and the void is kept at bay. You will live forever with that new road inside of you, stretching away to a place suggested, barely, on the horizon.

For the shortest time, shorter than the shortest second's breath, you get to stand up to infinity.

But eventually, and always, infinity wins.

Sandra is talking to herself, going on about the morning and the will in particular. She's still delighted by the mystery of Adrienne Cadiou. I wish she would be quiet; the Walkers have exhausted me, left me with a shivery sense of discomfort, like a body gripped with fever.

"New bet," Sandra says. "What are the chances that Minna will bed that—?"

Just then, something *moves*. A disturbance—a rippling feeling, a passage through spaces, like coming up to the surface when you've been submerged and holding your breath. For a second there is only confusion: a rush of sounds; a blur of brightness, painful and unexpected.

I think of penetration: Ed and the sound of the hyena; Thomas exhaling; a high belly, full with strangeness.

"What in the devil . . . " Sandra's voice is high, strained. She feels it, too. "What *is* that?"

And then I know, all at once, what is happening. It has happened to me before, many years ago, when Sandra first arrived.

Now comes the nausea, and a sense of swinging; then the world breaking apart, as it did when I was small and would spin and spin until I fell backward, watching everything dissolve into color.

Just like that, there it is. A third presence.

Another ghost.

The nausea subsides, leaving me gasping. Sandra lets out a mangled cry. For once in the history of her death, Sandra is struck dumb. I have a brief moment of panic: Richard Walker has, after all, come back.

But then it speaks.

"It's dark," she says simply. Her voice is faint, barely audible. She must be young. She is small; she takes up hardly any space. A child.

"God help us," Sandra says.

PART III

THE BASEMENT

A L I C E

Who is she?

There have been no deaths in the house since Sandra's, and that was in 1987. There have been no deaths on the property, either, not since the incident with the kitten and the old well.

Now a girl! Unfathomable.

She might easily tell us. But she chooses to remain silent. Since yesterday she has not said a single word beyond "It's cold." How old is she? I should say: how old *was* she? Twelve? Fifteen? No matter what I ask her, she refuses to be drawn out. And suddenly I find that I'm remembering things I haven't thought about for ages. Lost children, cowering in the dark. Little Annie Hayes, who disappeared from her parents' farm. I even remember the date the search party was assembled: March 6, 1942. A Tuesday.

Strange, the things that stick.

A M Y

Amy wasn't allowed to go in the basement. Mommy said it was dark and Amy would be scared. But she knew that Mommy was the one who was scared.

Amy thought she might find a doll down there. Once she had found a doll in the basement of her nana's house. It had a wide white face and curls of brown hair and floppy arms and legs but a hard body. She had kept it for a while, but then Mommy made her throw it out after one of the arms got torn off by Brewster, the dog that lived across the street. Amy wanted to perform surgery, but Mommy said *no people will think we're poor I'll buy you a real doll for Christ's sake.* Then she said: *Sorry.*

Amy liked her new doll, but not as much as the one she had found.

She wondered if Penelope from *The Raven Heliotrope* had ever had a mom, maybe the kind of mom who didn't let her do certain things. Amy thought the basement might look a little like the Caves of Werth, which were filled with treasure.

Uncle Trenton was no fun anymore and wouldn't read to her. Mommy said Uncle Trenton was dead and then they went to the hospital to see him and he was white and he wouldn't get up or talk. But then he did get up, but he still didn't talk very much.

Amy was glad they had come to Grandpa's house. She wished she could talk to Grandpa in the Garden of Forever and ask whether all the people from the book were there.

The house was full of white fluff stuff. Mommy said cottonseed. Amy collected it all and placed it in a cup in her room.

It looked just like snow.

S A N D R A

Like the world's worst case of constipation: that's what the basement is like. Like stopped-up bowels and a fat case of gas.

It's even worse now that we've got an intruder. Small as she is, she doesn't belong. It feels like I'm trying to get my stomach around a whole Thanksgiving turkey. I wish I could digest her and spit her right back out where she came from.

The new ghost likes the basement, God knows why. Rolled-up carpets, dismantled televisions and old radios, cartons and cartons of books, and the old boiler: it's all down there. The piano like a kidney stone we can never quite manage to piss out. Burned-out lights and Christmas ornaments. The Walkers have been home for three days now, and even Minna hasn't braved the basement.

And of all places—out of all the dozens of rooms in the house—the basement is where Trenton's got it in his head to kill himself.

My question is: Where'd he get the rope?

I knew a hanger once. Christina Duboise: everyone called her Cissy. She was over six feet tall and so skinny her ribs and cheekbones looked like they were trying to bust out of her skin. I liked Cissy. She was two years older, but we were friends. She was pretty much my *only* friend in school. Everyone ignored me because of where I lived and how I had a fag for a father. I don't blame them, really. I would have hated me, too, if I'd been someone else.

It took me a long time to realize that Cissy was only nice to me because she had no friends, either. In some ways she was even more hard up than I was, even though her stepdad owned three sporting-goods stores and was probably the richest person in town. No one knew anything about her real dad, but I had the idea he'd died tragically when Cissy was young, probably because she *seemed* tragic—big eyed and stoop shouldered, like she was always waiting for disaster to strike. I found out later it wasn't true, that her dad lived a few counties over with a new wife and a new daughter, and I was never sure why I'd always imagined him getting flattened by an oncoming train or slowly wasting to bones in a hospital bed.

Her mom seemed like she belonged in Hollywood: thin and blond with a smile so big I always worried her mouth would split open. She wore about a half pound of makeup and had a habit of wearing high heels everywhere as though she was expecting to be photographed. I knew she didn't like me, but I didn't give two shakes of a rat's ass for her, either.

Cissy lived in a nice big house in the white part of town. Everything her parents owned—the carpets, the sofas, the dining room chairs, the curtains—was white, like they wanted to be sure there could be no mistake about whose side they were on. You had to take your shoes off in the house. I'd never even heard of that before I met Cissy. Every time Cissy went home she had the desperate look of a dog trying not to piss on someone's carpet, and you could just tell she was dead afraid she might spill or smudge something.

They had a housekeeper, an old black woman who came daily to clean and cook. Her name was Zulime, and she had moved from Louisiana and still talked with a heavy Creole accent and, Cissy claimed, practiced voodoo on the side. Her hands were like bits of gnarled wood. I remember how she slathered me in mud one time when my arms were blown up like balloons from poison oak. It worked, too.

Sometimes Cissy came around every day, and on weekends I'd find her leaning against the front door, squinting in the sun, looking like an oversized grasshopper. For weeks she'd trail me like a dog on a scent, babbling about this and that, making plans, daring me to knock on Billy Iversen's door and give him a kiss or to skinny-dip in the creek. (That one I did and came out with a leech practically sucking off my nipple; I had to burn it off with a cigarette.)

Then she would disappear. She'd skip school for days at a time and wouldn't come to the phone when I called. Her mom would turn me away at the door with a voice like sugar in the throat of a vulture: "Cissy's not feeling well, sweetie. I'll have her give you a call when her strength's up." I'll always remember: her long red fingernails on the door, a Virginia Slim smoking in a crystal ashtray behind her, and Zulime moving silently along with the vacuum, refusing to meet my eye.

The summer after freshman year was when Cissy first showed me her spiders. It was June, still those early days of summer when the flowers were in riot and the clouds puffed up and full of themselves, before the heat caused everything to wilt and droop. By the end of the summer, all of Georgia was like a bad watercolor: melting pavement, melting tires sizzling on the streets, and even the sun crawling its way up the sky in agony, as if it couldn't stand the effort.

Cissy said she wanted to show me something down by the old train tracks and I was hoping she'd scored some beer or found a cache of money like Dirk Lamb had the summer before, a whole sack of old coins stashed underneath some rotting floorboards of an abandoned house.

Instead she took me to the Barnaby Estate, an old wreck beyond the swamp that was supposed to be haunted, leaning so far to the left it looked like a drunk trying to keep on his feet. I hadn't been there since the time when I was seven or eight, and this girl Carol Ann dared me to cross the swamp and put my hand on the front door for a full five seconds. I did it, too. I remember the suck of my shoes in the mud and the smell of wood rot and an old icebox on the porch, brown with rust. I stood there with my palm on the wood frame, fear vibrating through me, imagining I heard the creak, creak of footsteps inside the house . . . imagining I saw a ghost moving like a shadow beyond the screen . . .

And then I did see a shadow—a grinning shadow, with teeth like carved ivory.

Before I had time to scream, Old Joe Higgins, resident crazy, stepped into the light: trouserless, grinning, his dick wagging between his legs like a pale fish.

After that I didn't believe in ghosts anymore.

So when Cissy took me back there I wasn't scared, just disappointed and maybe a little curious. She led me down into the basement. I had to duck and Cissy was practically doubled over. A little sunlight came trickling in from a broken window high in the wall, and I saw she'd stocked the place with flashlights, an old beach chair, and some moldy-looking books stacked on a rotting shelf. And jars. Dozens of jars, plus glass terrariums like they had at pet shops for the lizards and snakes. At first I thought they were empty.

She switched on a flashlight and did a sweep. Then I saw beyond all those thin panes of glass: spiders, some of them as small as a speck, some of them bigger than the palm of my hand. I've never been squeamish about bugs, but it turned my stomach.

"What the hell is this?" I said.

"Spiders," she said calmly, as though I couldn't tell.

"But . . . what for?" Maybe it was just my imagination, but I thought the darkness was full of glittering eyes. She kept doing the back-and-forth with her flashlight, and I saw knitted clouds; webs sewn tightly against the glass; small dark blurry shapes, bound in pale thread. I wondered whether she hand-fed them.

"I like spiders." She shrugged and clicked off the flashlight. She seemed disappointed, like she'd been expecting me to cheer. I was relieved when she turned back toward the stairs and I could follow her up and out into the sun. "Spiders are *prophetic,* don't you think?"

That was another thing about Cissy. Even though, like me, she thought school was a load of bull and was nearly flunking her classes, she was smart. She was a reader, too, and always using words I didn't know.

"Spiders are nasty," I said.

We sat outside looking out at the swamp. I smoked a cigarette, and Cissy had three in a row. She smoked like she wished she could eat the cigarette instead.

"There's something else I want to show you," she said, after a while. She transferred her cigarette to the corner of her mouth and started unbuttoning her blouse, squinting a little. I thought maybe it was some lesbian thing, like she was going to show me her tits and ask me to rub them. I'd never heard her talk about a guy, never seen her primp or fix her hair or worry about whether she would get a date to such-and-such dance. She knew she wouldn't, anyway. She was too tall, too skinny, and too weird.

She was wearing a white cotton bra, I remember, and her tits were small and pointy and proud, like the stiff-backed peaks of whipped cream. It wasn't until she inched her blouse down her shoulders that I realized I'd never seen her without her clothes on. Never in a bathing suit, never changing in the locker rooms before gym class, never even on the rare occasion we had a sleepover. She always went into the bathroom and came out in her pajamas.

Her spine was so pronounced it reminded me of sketches I'd seen of certain dinosaurs. She leaned forward, hugging her knees, still puffing away on her cigarette with no hands, and I saw her back and arms were blotchy with fat bruises, blue and black and purple as a twilight sky, and ragged red holes like where she'd been burned with a cigarette.

"What happened?" I said, or something idiotic like that. Funny how in really serious moments people always say the stupidest things.

"My stepdad," she said, straightening up again and almost immediately shrugging her blouse back on over her shoulders. She seemed like she was going to say more, but then she stopped herself.

It was clear enough what she meant. Her stepdad had done this to her—twisted butts out into her skin, paddled her with a belt or a switch or maybe just one of his big, meaty hands. I thought of the local TV advertisements that showed his face, big and red as a balloon, smiling in front of a room full of baseball mitts and footballs, and felt like spitting.

"Why doesn't your mom do something?" I said.

Cissy ground her cigarette out carefully in the gravel. "My mom hates me," she said matter-of-factly.

"That's not true," I said. Another stupid thing. How the hell could I know? All I knew about the woman was she smoked Virginia Slims and wore high heels to the store.

Cissy didn't say anything, just lit another cigarette and inhaled deeply, closing her eyes against the sun. Wreaths of smoke went up around her hair, and I thought of the webs I'd just seen inside, the way they obscured the glass, made it difficult to see.

I kept pressing it. "What are you going to do about it?"

"I'm not going to *do* anything," she said, keeping her eyes closed. "I just . . . I felt like showing you. That's all."

"Why don't you split?"

She opened her eyes and looked at me.

"Run away," I continued. "Just pack up and leave. I'd go with you. We're old enough. There's nothing for us here, anyway. New

York or Chicago. Las Vegas even. Leave everything behind." It wasn't just talk. I'd been planning my escape for years. I figured as soon as I could get together cash for a train ticket and first month's rent, I'd be out. That's pretty much what I did, too. Left three months shy of graduation and spent my eighteenth birthday crashing with a bunch of junkies in a freezing tenement on Grand Street watching a guy even younger than I was puking up his guts in the single working toilet.

Cissy smiled. She looked old: her skin stretched as tight as a corpse's, already crisscrossed with faint lines. "You can't leave it behind," she said. "It doesn't work like that." She stood up. "It's like the spiders," she said, and even though I didn't know what she meant, I let it drop.

I was angry at her, I'll admit it. She wasn't a great friend but she was my only friend, and she wouldn't stand up for herself or do anything.

I wasn't the one who let the friendship drop. After that day with the spiders, Cissy acted like nothing had happened, and I was happy enough to pretend with her. But something had changed. She was never the most talkative, but when I saw her after that, she was even quieter than usual, more prone to long stretches of silence and to disappearing for days at a time. There were fewer dares, and more cigarettes. I couldn't help but feel like she was judging me for something I'd done.

Or something I hadn't done.

By junior year she was hardly coming to school and I'd got my first boyfriend—a dipshit named Barry, but he had a Chevrolet Impala and a decent laugh and a nice way of touching my lower back when we were walking—and Cissy and I barely saw each other until we didn't see each other at all.

One time I passed her when we were driving in Barry's Chevrolet; she was walking on the side of the road away from town, away from her house, toward nothing I could think of: just swampland and crowded forest, fat mosquitoes and wild hogs as big as heifers. Maybe on her way to get more spiders. Our eyes met for a second, and on impulse I raised a hand to wave. Maybe she was going to wave back—but Barry had just finished his beer and chucked the can, and instead she flinched and had to sidestep to avoid getting hit. I reamed him out for that one.

The last time I saw her was just before Christmas, 1969. I came home and found her standing on the porch, leaning against the door with her long legs crossed at the ankles, just exactly like she had so many times before. In her coat she looked even skinnier, like she was being swallowed by the fabric.

"Hey," she said, peeling away from the door, like it hadn't been almost a year since we'd actually hung out. "I wanted to give this back."

She was holding a red sweater of mine. I'd loaned it to her once when we'd been caught in a downpour and then forgotten about it. It was ugly as shit, a gift from my mother's mother, who I saw once a year.

"You didn't have to do that," I said, taking it from her. Even standing right next to her it was like there was a big barrier between us, hard as an elbow.

She didn't seem uncomfortable, though. "It's yours," she said.

For a second we just stood there. It was cold for Georgia, near freezing, and the sky was low and white-gray, the same color as Cissy's skin. Her eyes looked like two bits of chipped ice, and she looked like she'd aged a hundred years since I'd last seen her. Her hair was fine and cut real short, and I could see patches of her scalp.

I was trying to remember what to say, how to talk to her. *How you been?* I was about to ask, when she smiled and said, "Take care of yourself, Sandy."

"You, too," I said.

Would it have made a difference? If I'd said, "How you been, Cissy, come on in, why don't you sit down?" Probably not. Still: something to feel awful about.

She was found by Zulime on Christmas Eve morning. Cissy's parents had gone north for some reason and weren't expected back until that evening. I can still picture it: the bloated purple face against all that white, her skin puckered around the rope. Cissy had obviously planned it that way. She'd left a note with Zulime's name on it, which Zulime recognized, although she couldn't read a single word but that one. So a frantic Zulime took the letter to a neighbor, and that's how the information got out, finally.

I'd had it all wrong. Cissy's stepdad wasn't hurting her, at least not in that way. He'd been crawling into her bed at night since she turned six and her mom had been punishing Cissy for it since she found out. All of it in that house as white as snow.

A few days after I heard the news, I woke up in a panic about the spiders, and what would happen to them. It was just barely dawn when I set out, all quiet except for a dog that started up in the distance. I don't know what the hell I thought I was going to do when I got there, but I kept thinking how Cissy would be so sad if all her spiders froze to death over the winter. But when I got to the Barnaby Estate, I found the basement totally empty. The books, the flashlights, all the terrariums and jars—everything was gone except for that awful beach chair, and a single spider spinning a web between its metal legs.

Want to know something nuts? I took the damn thing. The spider, I mean. Cupped it in my palms and carried it all the way home and into my bedroom and put it on the windowsill where it could watch the world outside and spin. I figured it would eat flies and ants if any dared to come in, and, besides, it was almost kind of like a sign from Cissy. I know, signs are bullshit. But that's how I felt—like maybe she didn't blame me after all.

All of January it stayed by the window, and I was careful not to let my mother in the room since I knew she'd freak. She was pretty much always at church, anyway. And I watched it spin this enormous web that looked like frost on the pane, and finally I knew what Cissy had meant when she told me you could never really get away, just like the spiders.

Because it wasn't just spinning, it was forced to spin, and so it was just as trapped as any of the bugs it managed to catch.

In early February, I came home and saw my mom scrubbing the kitchen, and without looking over her shoulder she said, "I cleared out a spiderweb in your room. I don't know how it got so big."

A week later I got a train to Raleigh, and from there to New York City. I don't know what happened to any of the rest of them—Zulime, Cissy's parents. Alls I know is I hope that Cissy isn't stuck in that godforsaken place, trapped like residue on the lip of a glass.

That's what we are now, me, Alice, and the new ghost, whoever the hell she is: smudges, crusty bits, fingerprints, like stains left over from a faulty dishwasher.

Who knows. Maybe this is the price we pay. Penance, like my mom believed in.

You want to know what we're paying for?

Like that old song says: Go ask Alice.

T R E N T O N

Trenton hadn't thought that it would be so *quiet*. Whenever he'd pictured his suicide—which he had, many times, although he especially liked picturing the parts that came after: Minna thudding to her knees beside his body and wailing; the police swarming the house and filling the rooms with crisscrossed police tape; Caroline bloated with grief; everyone at school humbled, shaken, and girls crying in the halls, hugging themselves—he'd always imagined an accompanying soundtrack.

Now, as he fumbled and sweated in the basement and tried to figure out the fucking knot, he wished he'd thought to bring down his iPod dock. But maybe it was more tragic, more authentic, in silence. Like that old quote about the world ending with a whimper, not a bang.

Still, the silence was getting to him, because in the silence, he could *hear*.

Whispers. Mutters and coughs and the occasional hacking laugh, like a smoker was caught somewhere behind the walls.

Sometimes he thought he heard his name. *Trenton*. A bare, faint rustle, but definitely a *word*. Other times he heard, with sudden clarity, whole phrases, as though someone had turned up the volume in his mind. For example, he had very clearly heard a woman say: *I* tried *talking to her already. Why don't* you *try talking to her?* Then the voice faded abruptly, as if whoever had spoken had passed out of earshot.

He'd spent an hour last night on his laptop, signing in again and again to the shitty Wi-Fi, researching different mental disorders. He was a little too young for schizophrenia but not that young; he thought it was probably that. Good thing he was never going back to school. Or he'd be Schizo Splooge.

He'd decided, finally, on a rope. He was still curious about the gun he'd found in his dad's study, but he didn't even know how to tell if it was loaded. Plus he kept thinking about what Minna had said, about the woman whose brains got splattered on the study wall.

That was the second possibility: that he wasn't crazy. That the house was haunted. But ghosts didn't exist, everyone knew that. Which meant that the fact he was even considering it was crazy.

Back to square one.

It was Thursday, almost twenty-four hours since he'd found out his dad had left him the house, and the first time he'd been alone since they arrived back in Coral River. His mom, who still could hardly look at him—not that she ever really looked at him—had gone with Minna and Amy to do something involving his dad's body, which Trenton did not really want to think about. He didn't like the idea of cremation, although he disliked the idea of burial more. Stuck forever in a box.

He guessed his body would probably be burned. He wondered whether his mom would try and get a two-for-one deal. His dad wanted his ashes buried on the property. Trenton couldn't think of a single place he'd like to be buried. Not Eastchester, Long Island, for sure.

Maybe up here, in Coral River. He had only been six when his parents separated and Caroline moved downstate, but in some ways he'd always thought of it as home. Even though his dad never invited them up to Coral River—even though Trenton had forgotten where the cups were kept, and whether the downstairs bathroom was the first or second door on the right of the hallway, and that the study was painted a deep hunter green—other memories remained, totally vivid.

He remembered struggling behind Minna through deep snow, and breaking up ice on the creek with the blunt end of a blackened stick. He remembered summer days when he went screaming through the fields to startle the birds, and how Minna showed him how to catch toads by making a cup with his hands. He remembered: the kitchen warm and smelling like rosemary; his mother's favorite tablecloth spotted with red wine; early spring evenings on the back porch, bundled in a blanket, raw wind on his face, and candles dancing in small conical holders.

So. Definitely here. With his dad.

He was having trouble getting the rope to knot. He'd looked this up online, too, but most of the instructions seemed to be written for people who already knew a lot about ropes. Like mariners, or people in the army. His hands were shaking a little, which wasn't helping.

Finally he got it. Now he just had to tie off the rope to one of the pipes overhead. The back of his neck had started to sweat. He could practically *feel* another pimple growing there. He wondered how long it would be before Minna and his mom came back—they'd been gone at least an hour and a half. He'd heard the phone ring at some point. Maybe they were trying to reach him on the house line.

A small part of him was stalling. He thought that if he were interrupted or miraculously discovered, maybe it would be a sign that he shouldn't do it.

But nobody came.

He found a dirty stepstool crammed in among the clutter of boxes, old trunks, and discarded furniture; he positioned it directly under one of the sturdier-looking pipes. It took him a while to maneuver onto its seat. He'd never been athletic—he'd been practically forced off his Little League team in fifth grade—and the accident had fucked with his balance. Something to do with damage to his inner ear because of all the shards of glass. He was lucky, his doctor had told him, that he wasn't deaf.

"I'll bet . . . won't go through with it . . ." He heard suddenly, the words fading in and out, like a bad radio frequency.

He removed the note from his back pocket, which he had written out carefully before thinking he should have typed it, since no one could ever read his handwriting.

The voice came in again, sharp and clear, as if it was speaking directly into his mind: "He wrote a note! Little Shakespeare. Let's hope he has better luck than . . . " It faded out again.

"Shut up," he said. Then again, a little louder. "Shut up."

His heart was beating dry and frantic, high in his throat, like a moth's wings.

It was weird. He had hardly felt anything in six months, except for a brief, gut-tearing desire to puke when his mom had come into the basement, where he'd been playing *World of Warcraft,* and announced that his father was dead. Since the accident he could barely even jerk off—although he did anyway, approaching it with grim determination, like a soldier in front of the firing squad, bracing for the inevitable explosion.

After two fumbling tries, he managed to sling the rope over the rusted pipe. He realized belatedly that he should have fixed the rope to the ceiling before making the noose, and he felt briefly annoyed with himself for screwing up something as simple, as elemental, as suicide. He should have used the gun after all—or better yet, just swallowed some pills. But that had seemed like a cop-out, somehow, even more than the act of suicide itself. An overdose was something that could be mistaken for an accident. He was hoping that his final act would *mean* something. That it would make Derrick Richards sit up and say, *Jesus. I never knew Splooge had it in him.*

Upstairs, the front door opened and closed with a loud bang. Trenton slipped. For a teetering second he was both falling and imagining that he had fallen—imagining his damaged ankle hitting the ground and snapping like a twig, imagining lying prostrate on his back underneath the noose until someone came and found him. He reached out and grabbed hold of an old wooden wardrobe, managing to right himself at the last second.

The basement door opened and Trenton's heart stopped. It had to be Minna. He yanked the rope down from the ceiling pipe and thudded clumsily to the ground, feeling the impact of the short jump all the way to his teeth. He sat down on the stool just as an unfamiliar pair of sneakers came into view, pounding down the stairs.

"Oh!" The girl stopped short, still halfway up the stairs. Trenton felt the blood rush to his face.

She was pretty. Even with her face flaming red (which it was—at least she was embarrassed, too) and her hair cropped short and dyed some weird artificial black that was practically purple, she was pretty. She didn't have a single pimple anywhere on her face.

"I'm sorry," she said. "I didn't think . . . well, I didn't think anyone was home."

Trenton was doing his best to look casual, but he was also aware that he was sitting in the middle of a dark, dingy basement, under a single functioning lightbulb, holding a noose in his hands.

For a second the girl looked like she was going to bolt. But then she came two more steps down toward the basement. "Are you a Walker?"

Her smile was big and friendly and full of teeth that weren't very straight. It had been a long time since a girl had smiled at him. "How did you—?" he started to ask.

"It says so on the mailbox." She put her hands on the banisters and swung herself down the last few steps, landing neatly on the basement floor. She was no longer blushing. Trenton still felt like his skin might melt off at any second.

"Christ," she said. "You guys ever clean down here?"

Trenton finally thought of something to say. "Um . . . who are you?" His voice was a croak. He cleared his throat.

"Katie," she said, as though that answered his question. She waded right into the piles of old furniture and books and rolled-up carpets. While she had her back to him, Trenton coiled the rope quickly and stuffed it in between two cardboard boxes, hoping she wouldn't see it.

"I'm Trenton," he said, even though she hadn't asked.

"Cool." Katie bent down to scoop up a soccer ball and toss it to him. "You play?" Trenton was temporarily distracted by her butt, which was not so round as Angie Salazar's but pretty close, and by the small hole in her jeans, which revealed that she was wearing cute red underwear beneath them. He barely managed to catch the ball.

"No," he said. Then he blurted, "I can't play anymore. I was in a car accident."

"An accident, huh?" She was looking at him the way Dr. Sawicki, the shrink he'd been forced to see after his parents had finalized their divorce, had looked at him when he said he was doing fine—as if he were lying and she knew it, and he knew it, but she was too polite to point it out directly. Except Dr. Sawicki had normal brown eyes, nice eyes, like the eyes of a cow. Katie's eyes were hazel, practically yellow. More like a cat's.

Trenton wanted to ask her where she had come from, and what she was doing there, but he couldn't find his voice. Katie turned away from him again.

"Look, Tristan—"

"Trenton."

"Yeah, that's what I said." She nudged a roll of wrapping paper out of the way with the toe of a beat-up green Converse sneaker. "I didn't mean to barge in on you. I can see you're busy. Sitting on stools, playing with ropes. I get it." So she had noticed. Trenton felt a rush of humiliation so strong it was almost like anger. She was laughing at him. "So I'll just, you know, say good-bye and see you later—"

"Wait," Trenton said. His voice sounded very loud, and the girl—Katie—paused at the foot of the stairs.

"Wait." Trenton licked his lips, which felt very dry. "Why did you come? If you didn't think there'd be anyone home, why'd you come?"

Katie hesitated for a fraction of a second. "Fritz," she said, making a face. Her two front teeth overlapped a bit, and one of her incisors was very, very pointed. It gave her a lopsided look that was almost reassuring. "My cat. He got out."

"What does he look like?" Trenton said.

Katie blinked. "Like a cat," she said. She turned to go and then stopped, pivoting slowly back around to face him, seemingly struck by an idea. "Wait a second . . . Richard Walker . . . I saw something about a funeral."

The word *funeral* sent an unpleasant vibration through Trenton's chest. "He's my dad," he said, and then quickly corrected. "Was."

"Shit. I'm really sorry." She was staring at him in that way again—like she was trying to decode him.

"Thanks," Trenton said shortly, crossing his arms. He turned away, slightly, letting his hair swing forward; he was aware that he had a particularly angry pimple on his left cheek, and he didn't want her to see it. "We weren't that close," he added, so she wouldn't feel sorry for him. "We're just here for the funeral. And to clean up." He paused. "The house is mine now." Immediately, he didn't know why he'd said it.

"Oh, yeah? That's pretty sweet."

Trenton jerked his head up to look at her and she blushed. "I mean—sorry. Sorry for your loss," she said. "That's what you're supposed to say, right?" She shook her head, and her short spiky hair shook with her, like alien antennae. "I'm the worst at this stuff."

"It's all right," Trenton said. He was relieved, actually, that she wasn't pretending to be sad and solemn and knowledgeable. Like Debbie Castigliane, his mom's next-door neighbor, who'd come over bearing a tray of take-out lasagna like it was myrrh, sitting wide-eyed in the kitchen and patting Caroline's hand, and all the time counting the vodka bottles in the trash, feeding on the grief like a human mosquito.

"I mean, here I am, just running off at the mouth and you're in the middle of some big family tragedy . . . " Katie was still talking, still moving around the room, poking things.

Trenton had a sudden memory of the time when he was eleven and his dad had come out to the island. They'd met at Walt Whitman Mall and stopped in front of the Macy's for a bit and watched a woman with a tight red apron and a smile as white as plastic demonstrate the latest advances in nonstick pans at a big booth. She flipped and slid and swirled and all the time, she never stopped talking or smiling. His dad had bought a complete set of eight pans.

Katie reminded him a little of the woman with the pans. It was dizzying to watch her, even harder to keep up with what she was saying.

"Hey." She bent forward and, before Trenton could stop her, snatched up the rope from where he'd stashed it. "What's with the noose? You weren't about to kill yourself, were you?"

"What? *No.*" Trenton realized, too late, that the note to Minna was still sitting out.

"Come on, 'fess up. You were."

Trenton felt a flicker of irritation. "Even if I was, do you think I would tell you?"

"I don't see why not. Can't see what difference it would make." While she was looking down at the rope, studying it, Trenton quickly shoved the note to Minna in his back pocket. "Hey—you know what you could do with this?"

"No," he said.

"Autoasphyxiation." She reached up and coiled the rope once around her neck. As Trenton took a quick step back, horrified by the look of it, he stumbled on a box and had to sit down to avoid falling. Katie laughed again and unwrapped the rope from her neck. "Don't tell me you've never heard of it. People choking themselves while they . . . Oh, man. There I go again. Sorry. God forgot to give me an off switch." She reached out and punched him in the arm. "You don't mind if I keep it, right?"

This was why he never talked to girls: it was like following a maze where the walls were always shifting. "Keep what?"

She rolled her eyes. "The *rope*. I mean, you weren't using it, right?" Her eyes flashed on his again—eyes that held a challenge—and he looked away. "Didn't think so. Besides, if you wanted to off yourself, you could do a lot better than hanging. I mean, if you break your neck, that's all right. Otherwise you could be swinging there for ages. You know how many suicides end up clawing their fingernails to shreds, trying to take off the noose?" He didn't think she really wanted an answer so he didn't give her one. She plunged on, "So you sure you don't mind if I keep it?"

Trenton did mind, kind of. But he didn't see how he could say no, and what she'd said about suicides clawing their fingernails to bits had turned his stomach. He would probably have screwed it up with a rope, anyway. He shook his head.

"Awesome." Katie smiled, showing off her crooked teeth. He wondered, just for a second, what it would be like to kiss her and whether she'd taste like cigarettes. "Hey, listen. You gonna be sticking around for a while? I'm having a few friends over on Saturday. You should come."

Trenton couldn't tell whether she really meant it. "Thanks," he said carefully. "But I'm not really . . . I mean, parties aren't really my thing."

"It'll be fun, I promise." For a second, she looked much younger.

"What about your parents?" Trenton said, and then he immediately hated himself.

"My parents are away," Katie said. "They don't care what I do, anyway." Trenton nearly contradicted her but realized it might be the truth. "It's the big-ass farmhouse at the end of County Lane 8. Only house on the road. You can't miss it. Just go around to the back."

"I haven't said I would come," Trenton pointed out.

"You'll come," she said. "There's nothing else to do." She smiled; she knew she had him. "Just don't tell anyone. The cops are insane around here. You are old enough to drink, right? You're not like, fifteen?"

"I'm seventeen," Trenton lied. He'd be seventeen in a few months.

Katie waved a hand. "Close enough. I'll be eighteen next month. So . . . Saturday?"

"Yeah." Trenton could feel himself relenting. "Yeah, okay."

"Great. Eight or nine or any time after." Katie took a step toward the stairs, and Trenton had to call her back.

"I'll let you know about Fritz," he said.

"What?" She had the rope coiled around her wrist.

"Fritz," he said. "If I see him, I'll let you know."

She smiled wide again. "Careful," she said. "He bites."

Then she turned and darted up the stairs.

A L I C E

In my day, people knew how to keep secrets. They minded their mouths and their manners.

If you don't have anything nice to say, don't say anything at all. I remember my mother repeating that like a mantra—remember the *taste* of the words, like curls of soap and an ache in my jaw—remember my mother's hands wrapped thickly around my neck, and the light of the bathroom, bright as a halo.

I learned to swallow words back, hold secrets on my tongue until they dissolved like soap bubbles.

We kept our secrets for confession. For the priests.

The new ghost is praying. She is whispering to herself, repeating Psalm 23, over and over: "The Lord is my shepherd, I shall not want."

I never told anyone, not even Father Donovan, about Thomas.

He died very young. Aneurysm: a burst bubble in the brain. I read about the funeral in the local paper. It had been fifteen years since we'd last spoken, but I went and sat in the very last pew. I'd told Ed that I was going to the store and had to change into my good black dress, and a pair of heeled black shoes, in the woods that stretched along the road to Coral River, planting my stockinged feet in the soft dirt, feeling the wind touch my armpits as I wrestled the dress over my head.

I hardly remember the memorial, the speeches, the wreaths of flowers. I do remember his widow: pale and pretty, though heavy around the jaws; dark-eyed with grief, sitting in the first pew with her children. With Thomas's children. Ian and Joseph.

Halfway through the service, a woman next to me whispered, quite loudly: "Who was it who died? I can't hear." And I realized she had only come to watch, that she hadn't known Thomas at all.

I left early. I couldn't bear it. The church smelled like a basement, like things locked up and forgotten. And perhaps they *should* be.

Bless me, Father, for I have sinned.

Trenton hasn't moved since the girl—Katie—left. He sinks down on a sealed cardboard box as though exhausted by the exchange.

Go away, I want to tell him. *Leave, and never come back.* I want them out. All of them. Even Trenton, who isn't Trenton anymore, but some horrible version of a boy, twisted and deformed like in some Frankenstein story. Playing with ropes and guns, whispering to us in the darkness.

I don't care what Sandra says. It's obvious he can hear us.

"I knew he'd never go through with it," Sandra says. "That boy's got the balls of a bunny rabbit. What does he have to be unhappy about, anyway? He's—what?—sixteen? Seventeen? He just came into money, for Christ's sake."

"Money never solved anything," I say.

"Spoken like a true rich kid," Sandra says, even though she knows I turned my back on my family to marry Ed.

"He maketh me to lie in green pastures," the new ghost whispers.

"For Christ's sake, I'm begging you," Sandra says to her. "You'll drive me up the wall."

"What about you?" I say. I don't know where the anger comes from but it's there, immediate and overpowering. I'm sick of Sandra, sick of the way she acts and has always acted—as though everything, all of life, is there to be shrugged off, shaved away, ridiculed and minimized. She's like a person looking through the wrong end of a telescope, complaining that everything looks small. "What did *you* have to be so unhappy about?"

Sandra says shortly, "That's different."

"He leadeth me beside still waters."

"You drank a bottle of rubbing alcohol." I know I'm overstepping my bounds. "You lost your job—"

"That's enough," Sandra says. Then, to the new ghost, "Will you kindly shut the hell up?"

But the new ghost keeps going. "Though I walk through the shadow of death, I will fear no evil . . . "

Now I can't stop. Part of me knows that I'm not really angry with Sandra. I'm angry with Trenton, and Minna, and Caroline, and even Richard. I'm angry with the whole stumbling, fumbling world, which we're forced to watch, a sick repetition of the same tired hungers and needs. I'm thinking of Richard's body, bundled in white; and Sandra's face half spread across the walls; and Trenton standing beneath a rope. I'm thinking of bodies hauled up from the funeral parlor next to St. John the Divine when I was a kid, and the smell of smoke and skin in the air, and how there will never be an end to it.

"You lost your friends," I say. "You nearly lost your house. And what about the man—Martin? If you hadn't died in time—"

"I said, that's enough."

I feel a spark of anger, a quick flash, like a match striking. *Surely goodness and mercy will follow me all the days of my life.*

Trenton cries out, and everything goes dark.

CAROLINE

Caroline heard glass breaking, and a short cry, as soon as she walked into the house. The sound cut through the "muffling": that's what the awful woman at Sunrise Center had called the effect of alcohol on Caroline's brain, the time she had been forced to go to a rehab center after accidentally tapping another car on the way home from a dinner. No one had even been hurt, but the other woman, who'd had a baby in the car, had been hysterical about it and insisted on calling the police.

Muffling—the woman at Sunrise had said it as though Caroline should be ashamed. But afterward, whenever she'd had a couple, Caroline always imagined her brain nestled in a kind of hand-knitted mitten, warm and protected.

But now the muffling split apart, and for a short second everything was sharp and painful.

"Trenton," she said, turning to Minna, feeling a sudden panic. "That's *Trenton*." She turned blindly in the hall; she didn't know where the sound had come from. "Trenton? Are you okay? Are you okay?"

"I'm fine." His voice was faint. She still couldn't tell where he was. She had always hated that about the house: how it sucked up sound and voices and footsteps, as though they were all being absorbed, slowly but surely, into the walls.

"Where are you?" she cried out, still unable to quell the panic. Her chest felt as though it had collapsed, as though a big fist had reached out and punched backward in time, back to that awful night of Trenton's accident—the two-hour drive through the dark; the dingy hospital and the ugly woman who'd barred her from going into the operating room, staring at her as though she was some species of insect; the long wait without anything at all to drink.

"He's in the basement, Ma. Stop shouting." Minna opened the basement door with a foot, as though it was the door to a public restroom and she was worried about germs on the handle. Amy made a rush for the stairs, and Minna grabbed her arm.

"What did I tell you, Amy?" she said. "You don't go down there. Not unless Mommy takes you."

Amy began to wail.

Caroline moved past both of them and angled her body so she could squeeze down the narrow staircase. Her head was pounding. "What are you *doing*?" she said, moving carefully down the stairs. Each step sent a small tremor of pain through her body: *ankles, knees, hips*. The doctor had said she should lose some weight. Cut out the booze. She had nodded and said *oh, yes, absolutely*, as she had done so many times with Richard, when she had no intention of listening.

If the doctor had her estranged husband, or her children, he would drink, too.

"Nothing." Trenton was standing in the middle of the vast cluttered space, looking guilty about something. "I was just—cleaning up."

It was obviously a lie. Trenton hadn't helped at all in the three days since they'd been back in Coral River. Caroline realized that he'd probably been looking at pornography. He must have found his father's collection.

Several months after Trenton's birth, Caroline had gone looking for Minna's old stroller in the basement and found a stack of magazines, stashed unself-consciously in a trunk that also contained several baby items and the hat Caroline had bought Richard on their honeymoon. She'd sat on the ground for hours, unable to look away, unable to stop turning the pages—the way she'd heard that a bad electric shock caused you to hold on.

"What was that awful noise?" she said. "Did you break something?"

"I didn't do anything," Trenton said. "The lightbulb just . . . exploded."

"The wiring in this house was always screwy," Minna said. Caroline turned and saw she had come halfway down the stairs. Amy was trying to get around her, and Minna shuffled side to side, like a hockey player protecting a goal.

Of course. Minna was taking Trenton's side. Anyone could see he'd been fiddling around where he wasn't supposed to—maybe he thought he had the right, now that the house was his. Caroline felt a rush of anger that replaced the fear and obliterated it.

The house had been a constant point of contention in her marriage. She had not initially wanted to move from their sprawling, sunny home in California, on its small trim lawn on a small trim street in a nice gated community not far from the ocean. She had liked the guardhouse, where an ever-rotating cast of polite young Mexicans stood watch and checked names against a list—as though each time she returned home, she was accessing an exclusive party.

And then Richard had decided he wanted to be back in New York, close to where he had grown up. He had dragged her across the country and installed her in a vast, dark, drafty house, plagued by mice and termites, erratically heated, prone to leaks and pipe freezes and toilets backing up onto the floor.

Caroline had declared war, first on him; she had refused to sleep with him for two months. When she realized that her tactics only amused him, and that he was getting it elsewhere, anyway, she declared war instead on the house. She ripped out wallpaper and replaced it with patterns of her choosing. She scrubbed the cabinets, rearranged the furniture, shopped, and shopped some more. She put lights everywhere, as many as twelve in a room. She'd never been good with her hands and never before cared to do work herself; in California, there had always been gardeners, and decorators to match the cushions with the couch, and Caroline had to do nothing but approve it all. She was surprised to find she had taste. She could get things done.

She spent a spring building up a garden—her very first—carting soil and fertilizer and new bulbs, small as presents, weeding and trimming and rooting oxalis from the soil, cursing the blue Veronica that wouldn't bloom, and sweating into the soil beds.

And slowly, without her noticing, she had begun to love the house. She loved the way her bedroom filled up with light in the mornings, like a glass filling with rich cream. She loved the smell of the gardens after a rainstorm, and the smell of the woods in the autumn, rich and full and deeper, somehow, than anything she'd ever known in California. She even loved the creaking floorboards, and the pipes that shuddered and banged, as though they had a voice.

She loved the first freeze, which patterned the windows with lace, and making coffee in the kitchen wearing thick socks; she loved the cottonwood trees and their fluff, drifting through the weak spring light.

But she had continued to pretend to hate it. She had pretended, still, that Richard had brought her there against her will, because it gave her power over him. She had pretended that she was happy to leave him and move to Long Island with Trenton, even though it broke her heart. She had lorded it over Richard, the fact that he had made her unhappy for years and years, even though she *was* happy; at least, the house had made her happy.

But Richard won in the end. Maybe he'd thought the house would be a burden on her. During one of their last communications, he'd apologized at last.

"I should never have moved you from California," he'd said, sounding small and old. "You always hated it here. I should have been a better listener."

She had almost told him then. She had almost said *No, you're wrong. I miss Coral River. I've missed it every day.* But it was too late to give up the lie, which she had clung to for so long, which had become as much a part of their relationship as either of the children.

And now he was dead, and he would never know, and the house belonged to Trenton.

Had Richard done it to punish her, because she hadn't come back? Or had he really thought she wouldn't want it?

"You shouldn't be down here," she said. Her headache was getting worse. "You shouldn't be messing around."

"I told you, I was cleaning up, okay?" Trenton said, drawing out the last word so it suggested vast indifference. The anger came in short, sharp pulses now and seemed concentrated directly behind Caroline's eyelids. She, Caroline, had been slaving away since she'd arrived in Coral River. And Trenton, as usual, had sulked and brooded and made everyone's lives miserable, made enjoyment impossible, like a fly in a bowl of soup.

If anything, he'd gotten worse since the accident. He sat for hours in front of his computer, doing God knows what (more porn, probably). He answered her questions in monosyllables, was cagey about Andover, and complained about having to return there.

"This afternoon I want you to help Minna," Caroline said. Every so often she remembered that as his mother, she could tell Trenton what to do. Most days he seemed like some far-off constellation, ever present but mysteriously out of her orbit. "I want to see you packing boxes. I don't want to hear a single complaint. And clean up that glass."

"I told you, it wasn't my—"

"Just do it," she said, cutting him off.

Trenton mumbled something that Caroline couldn't hear. But she didn't care. She was done; she had handled Trenton, and now she could go upstairs and sit down, take the weight off her feet, have a drink in peace.

She was irrationally angry with Richard for dying and leaving her alone. Even though they had been separated for ten years, and divorced for four, he'd been a constant in her life. His phone calls, his moods, his pleas for her to return; he had grounded her.

Minna was still standing on the stairs, and Caroline couldn't move around her.

"Oh my God." Minna's eyes were fixed on the far side of the basement. "Oh my God. Are you kidding me? He fucking kept it?"

"Minna!" Caroline said. Amy put her hands over her ears and began to hum.

Minna obviously didn't hear. She moved down several steps, still fighting to keep Amy behind her. Caroline realized she was looking at the piano.

"It doesn't even play anymore," Minna said.

Caroline was losing patience for the basement, and for her children. "How do you know?" she said.

"Minna whacked it with a baseball bat," Trenton said. "You don't remember?"

Caroline definitely did *not* remember that. "When?"

"I was fifteen, Ma."

"But . . . " What Caroline did remember was a young Minna, her hair coiled and pinned neatly to her head, her long, slender fingers skating over the keys like a shadow passing over water. She didn't know why Minna had stopped playing. "But you were going to go to Juilliard. And Mr. Hansley said . . . "

"Don't," Minna said sharply.

"Mr. Handsy?" Trenton said.

"Hansley," Caroline correct him, before she realized that he'd been making a joke. Then she had another memory, less pleasant: coming into the piano room on a hot summer day with a pitcher of lemonade, and Mr. Hansley scooting quickly away from Minna. Hansley smiling, fiddling nervously with his glasses, talking too fast. Minna silent, staring at the keys, refusing to make eye contact.

Gripping the banister, Caroline began to climb, forcing Minna to squeeze herself against one wall so that she could pass. When Minna shifted, Amy ducked around her and barreled past Caroline.

"Amy!" Minna reached for her and then stared, exasperated, at her mother. "See what you did?" she said.

But Caroline didn't care. She was glad to have caused Minna some minor irritation. Minna chose not to remember all the things Caroline had done for her: the calamine lotion Caroline had applied to Minna's bug bites; the Band-Aids she'd put on Minna's cuts; the scrambled egg soup she'd made for Minna whenever she was sick.

She didn't remember that Caroline had tried to buffer her from the worst of Richard's moods—his rages, definitely, but also his indifference, which seemed to fix onto an object just as strongly as his anger. Caroline could still remember thirteen-year-old Minna curled up under her blanket, shivering, blue-lipped, after Richard forgot to pick her up from a dance lesson and she'd been forced to wait for an hour and a half in the rain.

"It would be better if he hated us," she'd said. "But he just doesn't care."

"He does," Caroline had said. But even then she had felt uneasy; Minna had hit on something that for years Caroline had tried to deny. That was why she had left Richard, ultimately: she'd realized that he had loved her only because she belonged to him.

The short climb had left Caroline winded, and she paused just before the final step, trying to catch her breath. Her feet were so swollen she could see the skin swelling around the contours of her flats. She rested her head against the wall, which was cool. Her heart was going wild in her chest. Recently she had been imagining, more and more, that it would simply stop.

"Careful of the glass," Minna was saying below. She had followed Amy down into the basement. "Don't touch that. It's rusty."

"What is it?" Amy said.

"Who knows. Garbage. Trenton, a little help, please?"

"What the hell do you want me to do?"

"Don't curse in front of Amy," Minna said.

Caroline could feel their voices through the wall. She lifted her head. She was so tired. She didn't know how she would make it up the last step.

"In *The Raven Heliotrope,*" Amy was saying, in a high, pleading voice, "the Caves of Werth are filled with treasure. Can we play pretend, Mommy?"

Caroline spoke up before Minna could answer. "There's no treasure down there, Amy," she said. Her voice was unexpectedly loud. "Just garbage, like Mommy said."

She hauled herself up the final step and went to the kitchen to get a drink.

A L I C E

"Are you proud of yourself?" Sandra asks.

"What do you mean?"

"You did that," Sandra says. The new ghost whimpers—a low, animal sound. "Congratulations on a nice little show."

"I don't know what you're talking about," I say, even though of course I do.

She means the lightbulb—the explosion. And I *am* proud. I'm ecstatic. It has been many, many years—decades—since I've felt that kind of power.

And it gives me hope.

I've only seen one bad fire. I was seven or eight when a conflagration spread through our neighborhood in Boston and leaped across several houses before attacking St. John the Divine and the funeral parlor next to it; by morning, the houses were gone and the church was blackened with smoke and ash. The air stunk like melted glass and something chemical I couldn't name, and volunteers were enlisted to bring coffins out of the wreckage. My sisters and I went down to watch the action, and in particular, to see the bodies come out: coffins covered in a layer of silt and ash, bodies bundled in tarpaulin and half burned away, bits of hair and fingernail.

The fingernails keep growing, my sister Delilah told me. *The hair, too.*

Someday you'll be dead like that, my sister Olivia said. *You'll be nothing but bone and fingernail, and no one will miss you.*

Ashes to ashes, and dust to dust.

Sandra doesn't know about my plan for the fire. How could I tell her? If I'm right, it will be the end of us. That's the whole point. In fiction, ghosts remain because of some entanglement with the living world, something they must do, resolve, or achieve.

I assure you that isn't the case for me. The world has nothing to offer me, no single shred of interest. I'm a woman trapped on a balcony, watching a passing parade, a blur of noise and motion that eventually turns to a single point on the horizon, a gutter full of trampled and muddy cups, and the sense of wasting an afternoon.

There was Maggie. But even she might be dead by now. I like to think I would have known, would have felt it, but I know that's fantasy. Maggie was a stranger to me in her adult life, a stiff-backed, short-haired woman with tastes and habits I hardly recognized. *Tofu,* she told me, the last time I visited her in San Francisco, when she served me a plate of vegetables and brown rice and some lumpy, milk-white substance that reminded me of curdled fat. *I'm a vegan now.*

Amazing, isn't it? That hearts that once beat in sync could be so perfectly and forever separated. That's the whole process of life, I think: a long, slow process of separation. It can be cured only by the reabsorption into everything, into the single heartbeat of time.

It's my time to go home.

PART IV

THE GREENHOUSE

TRENTON

Trenton hadn't been inside the greenhouse in years and was startled by the bird: as soon as Trenton closed the pantry door it rose, flapping, to the sky, so close that Trenton could feel the air shredded beneath its big, black wings.

Several of the glass panes in the roof were missing—shattered, Trenton assumed, or blown away during the last big storm. A rusted ladder was still leaning against the exterior wall, as if someone had abruptly decided the repairs weren't worth it. There was a covering of fine green grass embedded in the dirt, so his footsteps made a crunching sound.

The greenhouse he remembered was a jungle, a riot of flowers as big as a child's head, trembling with moisture, humid and exotic and totally off-limits. He remembered the emerald light, the alien-looking orchids, the summer roses climbing trellises all winter long.

There was no longer anything green in the greenhouse, except for a dozen fake plants—squat Christmas trees with plastic bristles, fabric lilies, improbable plastic orchids, and even a miniature palm tree—crammed into one corner of the rectangular space. What plants did remain were dry, brown, and brittle.

It was Saturday, 10 A.M., and Trenton was, for all intents and purposes, alone in the house. Amy was in the den, all the way on the other side of the house. His mom was still sleeping. She'd gotten drunk in her room last night, doing whatever the hell she did, and would probably stay up there until at least noon. And from his bedroom window he'd spotted Minna skirting the edge of the woods, a felt cap pulled low over her ears even though it was already probably sixty degrees, wearing an old pair of waders.

Getting up onto the shelf was difficult; the old wood groaned underneath him as though it might collapse under his weight. But he managed. When he stretched out on his back, he was mostly concealed by the fake planters and the intersection of their manufactured leaves, and thus invisible from both the pantry side and the door that led out toward the lawn.

He had one joint left from the stash he'd bought from an older guy who worked at the Multiplex in Melville, Long Island. He sparked up, took three hits in quick succession, and stamped out the end of the joint so he could save it for later. He lay back, feeling a delicious heaviness in his legs and arms, a sudden wave of calm.

He couldn't stop thinking about Katie and the party. He was dreading it. He shouldn't go. He would have an awful time. Most of Katie's friends probably knew one another. They would stare at him and whisper behind his back.

But a small part of him was eager to see her again. Did that mean he wasn't ready to die?

No. The plan was the plan, and he would still go through with it.

The sun was weak and the sky above Trenton was full of scudding clouds, breaking apart and re-forming. Like a kaleidoscope. His thoughts, too, broke apart and re-formed.

Light flickered. Shadows skated across the shelves, and Trenton shivered. He thought about the accident. He had memories, fragmented and strange, of a hundred shadowlike hands carrying him down a dark tunnel.

And then he felt it. Or heard it. He didn't know which but he *knew:* someone had just entered the greenhouse. He sat up, suddenly alert, his mind sharpening.

Trenton's throat closed so tight he couldn't even scream.

She was there. And yet she was not there. A *thing,* an unmistakable presence. He knew it was a girl—or a woman—because of the way it moved, shifting in the sun, watching him from behind a shadow of hair.

It didn't occur to him that he was just high, and seeing things. He'd smoked plenty of times before—weed was the only thing that helped him float through his months at Andover—and once had even seen a bathroom wall pulsating in and out.

But never anything like this. She was *real.* He felt it, too, in the stiff terror that seized him, the desperate desire to cry out, and the dryness of his mouth.

The longer he looked, the more she materialized: shoulder blades cut from shadow and green eyes flashing like dark leaves. Hair teeth mouth, breasts small as two bare flower buds.

Go away, Trenton tried to say, but couldn't. He felt like he was back in the hospital again, paralyzed, arms and legs useless and unresponsive. *Leave me alone.*

She spoke. The words came to him, a faint, dry rustle on the wind that lifted and turned the leaves scattered on the greenhouse floor.

"What am I?" she asked. "What happened to me?"

The terror left Trenton at once, replaced by a sadness so cutting and deep he felt like he wanted to cry. It was worse than anything he'd felt in years—worse, so much worse, than the lack of happiness he was used to, a hollow negative space of no feelings at all. This was a dark, black pit of sadness, like staring into a well and seeing a child trapped at its bottom. He knew, without knowing how he knew, that she was scared.

Almost without realizing it, he sat up and extended a hand to her, the way he would have done with a stray animal.

There was a loud crack, then the sound of splintering glass. Trenton ducked, cursing. His first thought was that another lightbulb had exploded, but then he remembered there were no lightbulbs in the greenhouse.

"Shit!" Minna's voice, muffled through the thick glass walls, came to him; then she was shoving into the greenhouse from the garden, using her shoulder. That door had obviously remained unused for years and was practically rusted shut.

"What the hell?" Trenton was shaking, furious. The girl—*the ghost,* he thought, and then knew that it was true—was gone. Where she had been was nothing more than a narrow rectangle of light, and dust mites revolving slowly. He felt an unaccountable sense of loss.

"Oh." Minna had finally managed to get the door open and entered, red-faced, pushing her hat back from her forehead. "Hey. I didn't get you, did I? That fucking thing fires to the left."

"Get me?" Only then did Trenton understand what the cracking noise had been, just as he noticed a bullet wedged into the wooden shelf two inches from his left knee. Distantly, he heard his mom calling for them, her voice high-pitched, hysterical.

He was so angry he could hardly speak. "What the hell, Minna?" He was screaming; even he was surprised to hear it. "What the fuck were you thinking? You could have killed me."

"I said I was sorry," Minna said, even though she hadn't. She plunked down a pistol; Trenton recognized it as the one from his father's desk, and he was even angrier that she had figured out how to load it. "It wasn't my fault, anyway. I'm telling you, that thing—"

"Pulls to the left. Yeah. You said." Trenton's head was pounding. He hadn't imagined it. He knew he hadn't. Minna said someone had been murdered in the house. Had he really just seen her?

"I was trying to get that goddamn coyote." Minna was still wearing the thermal shirt she liked to sleep in.

"What?" When Trenton tried to stand, he realized how stoned he was. He got a rush of black to his head.

Minna wasn't looking at him, thank God. "It's the size of a frigging pony. It was sniffing around the house this morning. I was worried Amy would try and pet the damn thing."

Caroline burst through the door that connected the greenhouse to the pantry, wearing nothing but a thin bathrobe, open, over her nightgown. For one horrifying second, Trenton had a perfect view of his mom's breasts, each shaped like the flap on an envelope, swinging loosely beneath the thin silk. He looked away quickly. "What happened? I thought I heard a shot."

"There was a coyote," Minna started to explain, but Caroline cut her off.

"A coyote? What about the police? Did you call them?"

Trenton looked up sharply. "The what?"

Minna stared. "What are you talking about?"

Caroline had obviously just gotten out of bed. The sheets had left faint creases, small webs, across her chest and cheek. "The police," she said. "There's a squad car coming up the drive."

CAROLINE

"I don't want them in the house," Caroline said. "Don't let them come into the house." She knew she sounded hysterical but couldn't help it.

She felt a panic attack coming on. That happened to her sometimes. Her mouth would go dry and she couldn't breathe and her heart would beat like a dry moth in her throat, and she would know, absolutely know, that she was dying.

There had been streaks of blood in the toilet this morning—her lungs, maybe, or her liver. Ever since the doctor had lectured her about the possibility of cirrhosis, she had imagined her liver like a dying fish, gasping in the middle of a toxic oil spill.

She needed a drink. But she couldn't drink with the police in the house. She still remembered the cop who had arrested her after she'd rear-ended that stupid woman, the way he'd hauled her roughly to the car, not caring that she was sick, not caring that Trenton was in the backseat. And the cop who'd called to tell her about Trenton's accident—a woman, that time. *He might not make it,* she'd said casually, like a grocery store clerk explaining that a coupon was no longer valid.

Minna stared. "Why not?"

"I just don't. Make them go away." She heard the sound of car doors closing, and voices, muffled, from outside. "They have no right. We didn't do anything. They can't come poking around."

"What are you afraid of? They'll turn up a dead body?" Minna said.

Caroline couldn't tell her daughter that she had a sense that the police were here about the woman—Adrienne, to whom Richard had left all that money. She couldn't stand to hear the woman's name spoken out loud again.

Late last night, Caroline had taken Minna's laptop into her room and spent hours clicking through links and search bars, looking for pictures, articles, anything related to an Adrienne Cadiou in Toronto. The weight of the darkness, the weak blue light—it had made her feel comforted, somehow, like being in a bubble.

And yet at the same time, she was terrified Minna or Trenton would wake up and find her, and every time the house moved or the radiators hissed, she froze, hands hovering over the keyboard. She wondered if this was how Richard had felt reading porn, or watching it, later, on their shared computer. But no. He had not been embarrassed. Sometimes he even left the videos up, so that when she sat down to type an e-mail—painstakingly, with many errors, because she had never been a fast typer—she was surprised by the sudden vision of labias as pink as orchid blooms, or breasts like Minna's were now, hard as bowls. She suspected he did it deliberately, to punish her.

She found five Adrienne Cadious in Toronto. One was a college student, nineteen, with a mouth full of braces. A second woman, seventy-four, was mentioned in several articles as being one of the first female runners of the Boston Marathon. The third woman was probably Caroline's age, with red hair too long for someone in her late fifties. Caroline couldn't figure out whether she was still alive—several articles mentioned she'd been the victim of a recent hit-and-run and showed her with her arms around a girl, presumably a daughter, with the same pattern of freckles and wide-spaced eyes—but it didn't matter, anyway. Richard hated redheads.

There were two others: a mother of four, a little fat but not as fat as Caroline was now, and with a pretty smile, who ran a cooking blog called TheGoldenSpoon. Caroline had spent nearly an hour scrolling through recipes, reading about techniques for peeling tomatoes and how to make a perfect omelet, searching all the time for a code layered beneath the surface of the words, a message to her, to Richard.

There were dozens of pictures, not just of meals but of Adrienne herself, and, often, her children: fat-faced, grinning, holding up chocolate-covered fingers toward the camera.

Would Richard have done it? She wasn't sure. But she couldn't rule it out.

The last Adrienne was forty-two, and there was a single article that appeared about her on the second page of search results. She had spoken at the Ottawa Regional Breast Cancer Benefit; she was a breast cancer survivor, and she worked as a lawyer at the Canadian Immigration Bureau. The photograph was disappointing—head only, and slightly blurry, and moreover taken from an angle that made it difficult to see her features clearly. Whether she was pretty or not, it was hard to say.

Caroline spent another hour searching for more information about this Adrienne, looking for a better picture, but had found nothing. By then it was two A.M., and she was very drunk and she knew she would sleep, finally. Still, it had taken her another half an hour to figure out how to clear the history so that Minna wouldn't know what she was doing; Caroline knew about clearing the history because Trenton had spoken about it after she went on his computer looking for evidence that he was developing normally and wasn't reading about assault weapons or how to make a homemade bomb, which had been suggested to her by a magazine she'd read at the dentist's. He had caught her, and said, in the annoying smirking way he had recently perfected, "Ever hear of deleting history, Mom?" Then, of course, she was left to wonder whether he'd deleted history *because* he'd been researching bombs.

Caroline heard footsteps coming up the front path; she could see two men, distorted by the glass.

"Go and see what they want," she told Minna. "Even better, make them leave."

Minna rolled her eyes. "Fine." She left through the garden door.

Caroline heard the doorbell ring once, sharply, and then fall silent. She heard Minna's called greeting and a burst of overlapping voices, then footsteps, crossing back toward the greenhouse.

Minna hadn't gotten rid of them.

For the first time since entering the greenhouse Caroline saw, suddenly, what it had become: the sad plastic simulacrum, the withered plants crying out for water, the boxes of old Christmas decorations and dirty wooden shelves, still imprinted with watermarks and ghostly rings where flowerpots and planters had once stood. This had been her place, the only spot in the house that had really belonged to her. She could make flowers grow, could coax even the most difficult orchid to life and make thick coils of plumleaf azalea overspill their planters.

Richard had left the greenhouse to die. Now Richard was dead.

There had been blood in the toilet this morning.

A L I C E

The new ghost is nervous. Sandra, too. She hates the police, probably because of her many unpleasant run-ins with them. There was, for example, the time she accidentally drove her car onto a neighbor's property and parked it nose-first against their mailbox; the time she played the Grateful Dead on full volume until four A.M. while consuming an entire bottle of Maker's Mark; the incident of the stolen goldfish from the restaurant in Dover Plains . . .

"I don't believe it." Minna reenters the greenhouse, flushed, excited. "I can't believe it. My mom won't, either. You know I still have our prom photo somewhere?"

Two men trail after her, like marine animals riding the wake of a boat. The first is about her height, broad shouldered and balding, with a big smile and a stomach. His uniform is dark blue and looks rumpled, as though he stores it in a corner.

The second man is wearing a bright red windbreaker, dress pants, mud-encrusted leather shoes. He is tall, thin, and unsmiling.

Minna stops when she finds the greenhouse empty. "She was just here," she says apologetically. "Mom!" she calls out. "Mom!"

The tall man frowns and checks his watch.

"I'm right here." Caroline emerges from the pantry door, holding a cup so tightly the veins on her hand stand out. She has fastened her bathrobe, at least, although the mottled surface of her chest is still visible. "No need to shout."

"Mom, look." Minna gestures to the shorter man; he is still standing there, beaming, while his partner shifts impatiently. "You remember Danny Topornycky, don't you?"

Caroline frowns. Minna charges on impatiently, "Toadie, Mom. We called him Toadie. My prom date?" Minna nudges Danny's arm. "My very first boyfriend."

"Somehow, I doubt that." Danny laughs. "Nice to see you again, Mrs. Walker."

"I go by my maiden name now," Caroline says. "Bell."

Minna looks happier than I've seen her in all the time she is home, except for brief moments with Amy: tickle wars and raspberry kisses, and when they lie entwined, sleeping. "I had no idea you were a cop."

"Yeah, well, the old man was a cop," Danny says, shrugging. "You remember he busted Richie for DUI on prom night?"

Caroline says, "Why are you here?"

Minna glares at her, then turns back to Danny. "Do you want coffee or anything?" She starts toward the pantry door. "We can sit down and catch up—"

"No!" Caroline bursts out. Everyone turns to look at her. "I—I'm sorry," she says. "The house is a mess . . . I'm sorry. It's embarrassing."

"That's all right," Danny says. He's stopped smiling, at least, and looks less like an overstuffed teddy bear and more like a cop. "Sorry to barge in on you like this. This is Detective Rogers, from Suffolk County."

"Suffolk County?" Minna frowns. "In Long Island?"

"Massachusetts." The taller man speaks for the first time. He has a voice to match his face: worn down, stretched thin.

"You're a little far from home, aren't you?" Minna's eyes keep returning to Danny. But now he's keeping his eyes on his feet, playing his part.

"I'm investigating a disappearance," he says, and for just one second, Minna and Caroline, the greenhouse, the whole house—us, me—seem to vanish, and all I feel is that tiny pulsing presence, the new ghost, drumming like a heartbeat. "Vivian Wright. Sixteen."

Rogers reaches into his back pocket and extracts a photocopied picture of a girl. Long blond hair, dark smears of eye makeup, rings in her lip, ears, nose. The picture quality is terrible: she is half turned away from the camera, grinning at something offscreen, her features charcoal-smudgy.

The new ghost stirs. I can sense her fumbling to see, to learn her way into the air currents, to see with her no-longer-eyes and taste with her no-longer-tongue. She does not know how to be, yet.

"It's an awful picture," Minna says. She leans close to Danny to look—so close her breasts nearly end up on his elbow. But he doesn't seem to notice. She draws back. "Don't you have anything better?"

"We're waiting," he says. "The parents are on their way back from Cape Town now. Apparently they were on safari. No phone, e-mail only once in a while. It was the babysitter who filed the report. Said she showed up for the job and Vivian"—he tapped the photo—"was just gone. Vanished. At first she thought Vivian had just blown out of town for a few days, for a joke. She'd done that kind of thing before. But . . . "

"But what?" Caroline says.

Detective Rogers blinks. "It's been over a week," he said.

"And you think she came all the way up here?" Minna says.

"We're not sure," Rogers says. "She used her credit card to buy a ticket—one way, no return—on a Greyhound heading to Buffalo. And a 7-Eleven in Milford has her on surveillance tape, buying chips and some sodas. She's wearing a baseball hat, but it's definitely her. The cashier remembers asking about the piercings. We've been hitting the towns on the line, asking around."

"I'm just helping out with the locals," Danny jumps in. "Disappearances aren't our typical gig."

Sandy mutters, "He turned out just as stupid as the rest of them."

"You think she was alone?" Caroline is slightly calmer now, but she's still gripping her glass. "When a young girl runs away, there's usually *somebody*. Right?"

"We're not sure she did run away," Rogers says. He's good. Noncommittal. "She could have been compelled to leave. Or lured up here by someone. There was no one with her on the tape, but that doesn't mean she was alone."

"Do you think she's . . . ?" Minna trails off.

For a moment, there is silence. The clocks seem to pause; the pulse stops in this ticking, groaning body. Even Sandra doesn't dare make a sound. The word, unspoken, hangs like a mist. *Dead.* Do you think she's dead?

The new ghost trembles.

"We're investigating every possibility," Detective Rogers says, which I know means yes, he does. "She hasn't used her card again. Hasn't used her cell phone, either. She used to have Facebook, Twitter, all that, but her parents made her shut it down a few months ago, so no help there. Problems with an ex-boyfriend—that's what her friends said, anyway."

"Maybe she's with her ex-boyfriend," Minna suggests. She nudges Danny, smiling. "It's always the ex, isn't it?"

Danny glows as red as a fire poker. "I don't know about that," he says. He pats his shirt down over his stomach.

Rogers doesn't smile. "It isn't this time. The kid hasn't spoken to her in months. He moved to Austin with his family in November."

"Well, then what *did* happen to her?" Caroline's voice is shrill.

There's another beat of silence. This time Rogers comes out with it. "She might be hiding somewhere. She might have been kidnapped, although there's been no ransom. And she might be dead. But we hope not." He takes the photograph, folds it, returns it to his pocket. "Sorry for barging in. Here's my card, and Danny will leave you his, too."

Danny's already working his card over with a pen. "I'm leaving you my cell, too, Min," he says. "We should catch up while you're here."

Rogers looks faintly annoyed. "If you see anything suspicious, please call right away."

"You expect us to trip over a dead body in our garden?" Minna says. No one laughs, and Caroline says, "Minna, *please,*" and presses one hand to her head.

"Anything suspicious," Detective Rogers repeats.

Then they're gone, and Caroline and Minna are left standing together in the greenhouse, surrounded by dead and rotting things.

I'm expecting Sandra to make an idiotic comment but instead she simply mutters, "Bad business." I can feel her withdraw, curling into the walls, into the wood shavings, small, hard, and impregnable, as she always does when she's in a bad mood.

The ghost, the new ghost, is still shaking.

"Vivian?" I whisper. "Is that you?"

But she doesn't make a sound.

The search party for Annie Hayes was organized two days after her parents first noticed she'd gone missing; I heard about it as I did almost all my gossip, from Dick Harte, who ran a dairy farm in Depew and delivered the milk. It had been a bad winter, and the ground was just beginning to thaw from the latest assault: fissures appeared on the blue-veined rivers, still slickly coated with ice; the ground was patchy and raw, the trees had their hackles raised to the wind. On some mornings, with the wind howling and the gas sputtering under the kettle, I even missed Ed. I sweetened my coffee by drinking it through a sugar cube. There was a war on, and at home we felt it this way: in the cold-bed mornings, and sugary grit between our teeth.

Dick Harte had a truck embossed with a cow and the name of the farm, but for most of the winter he made his rounds in an old-fashioned sleigh, hitched to two of his horses. I remember he had the sleigh the day he told me about Annie Hayes and the search party, because he complained that the remaining snow was so slushy and full of muck he'd practically had to turn around; and the horses stood there, breath steaming in the dawn, and I thought of how cold Annie must be, wherever she was.

We were to meet at noon in front of the church in Coral River, a walk of just over four miles. The sky was dense and knotted with clouds, like a gigantic, fleecy eyebrow.

All this has stuck with me.

I don't remember receiving instructions, or the early part of the search. I don't remember seeing Thomas among the volunteers, although he must have been there, and it seems strange that I shouldn't have noticed, since so many men were away. I do know at some point we were fanning out across a field and it had begun to rain. Black expanses of mud grinned up at us between the snow; I was freezing again and had called Annie's name so often my throat was raw.

How awful, I was thinking. How unbearably awful to lose a child.

I got separated from the group—there was movement in the forest at the edge of the trees; I was sure it was Annie, scared, hiding in the shadows. The rain was rattling hard through the branches, and I could hardly see, my eyes were watering so badly; my fingers were swollen to uselessness.

A few feet into the woods, my foot drove straight through a fine surface of gray ice, down into a pit of mud and pulpy leaves—some kind of animal hole. I pitched forward onto my hands and knees. Immediately I knew I'd twisted or sprained my ankle, and the pain cleared my head. I realized I'd been following some animal, a fox or a deer. There was no child out here, in these woods. If there were, she was no longer alive.

I tried to stand, and suddenly there was a hand guiding me firmly to my feet.

"Are you all right?"

Glasses, beaded with rain; a beard, not too closely trimmed; the smell of damp wool and tobacco; a fine, straight nose, with a bead of moisture hanging from its end.

Those were my first impressions of Thomas.

Afterward he claimed to have noticed me even earlier, standing in the crowd, though I never believed him. I've relived that moment so often in my head, I can never be sure what really happened and what we only embellished afterward. But does it matter? We make reality our own, handle it until it is as soft as pressed butter.

There was the offer of a ride; the polite resistance, his insistence—*you can't make it back on your own, not on* that *foot*—and, finally, the *yes, thank you, if it really isn't too much trouble.* He kept calling me *Miss* Lundell, even though Lundell was my married name. I didn't correct him.

There was his arm around my waist as he supported me across the field through the endless sheet of rain. There was feeling as though we were alone, with a sky of glass above us.

Thomas had a Hudson touring sedan, which felt novel and very luxurious to me, even though it was corroded with rust and the engine turned over several times before it would start. Ed and I didn't own a car.

Thomas told me he was a professor of classics at St. Aquinas

University, in Buffalo; I asked him several questions, and I thought he was ignoring me until he apologized and told me he was deaf in his right ear. He'd lost his hearing as a little boy, after his older brother stuck a pen in his ear, as an experiment, to see how far it would go.

It was then—in the car, as he explained about the pen and why he wasn't at war, when he had to tilt his left ear toward me so that I could give him directions to the house and twice made the wrong turn, anyway—that I began to love him.

Do you think that's unrealistic? That this, too, is a story I made up after the fact? To justify and excuse, perhaps—to make sense of everything that came after? Maybe. But it happens—every day, for someone.

Take little Annie Hayes, for example. Two days after the search, it was discovered that she'd been hiding in the cellar of the local pharmacist. His eight-year-old son, Richard Kelly, had been sneaking her chestnuts and milk from the kitchen all week, and they were plotting to run away together. A month earlier, he'd given her free ice cream at the counter of his father's shop, and she had decided it was love.

Both children were whipped, of course. But Annie did, finally, grow up to marry the pharmacist's son, and in the spring of '52, when I had not spoken to Thomas in nearly a decade, I threw handfuls of rice at the new Mrs. Annie Kelly and tilted my face up to the sun to watch it scatter.

S A N D R A

Memory is as thick as mud. It rises up, it overwhelms. It sucks you down and freezes you where you stand.

Thrash and kick and gnash your teeth. There's no escaping it.

Down.

In Georgia, the mud was thick and dark as oil.

Down.

I remember my dad scraping his shoes on the rusted shoe box he inherited from *his* father, who I met only once, and who had chins like fat rolls of sausage; and my mother, vibrating like a plucked string, hitting high notes of rage, whenever he forgot and tracked mud across the floor.

And further down:

My friend Cissy's housekeeper, Zulime, smearing cold mud on my arms swollen with poison oak, telling me to *hush, now.*

The flood of 1987, and the wash of water and silt thundering down the lawn from the river, and the poor turtle on the front porch.

Down and down, until all that's left is the memory of ghosts.

Trenton's been slinking around outside, spying, because the cops aren't gone three minutes before he sticks his head back into the greenhouse. Caroline has gone inside, probably reloading on the sauce. Minna is just standing there, leaning against the shelves, eyes closed, birds twittering through the broken ceiling, sunlight slanting hard as knives.

"What did they want?" Trenton says, trying to act casual.

"Some girl disappeared," Minna says, without opening her eyes, "from Boston."

Trenton's a little less wound up than he was before. His face isn't so cigarette-ash gray. "Boston? So what're they doing out here?"

"I don't know." She straightens up. "Hey—do you remember Danny Topornycky? Toadie?" Minna waits for Trenton to respond, which he doesn't. "Forget it. You were too young."

"What about him?" Trenton says.

"Nothing. He's a cop now, that's all. We just ran into him." She picks at her thumbnail with her teeth. "I always really liked Danny."

"Don't," Trenton says, shoving his hands in his pockets and making for the pantry door.

"What's that supposed to mean?"

"Just don't." Then he stops, suddenly, and pivots. "Wait. He's a cop?"

"Yeah. So?" It's Minna's turn to play sullen.

Trenton licks his lips, which are dry, full of flaking skin. "You . . . you have to do me a favor."

"Do I?" But then: "What is it?"

"That person . . . " he says. "The person who was shot in the house . . . ?"

Minna rolls her eyes. "That's just a story, Trenton. I don't even know if it—"

"Just find out, will you?" he says. "Just find out when, and, and . . . who. I'm just . . . curious, okay? Just ask him. For me."

Minna sighs. "All right," she says. "I'll ask. But that was years and years ago. He may not know."

"He saw her," Alice whispers, awed. "I told you. He saw her."

"But he thinks she's me," I say. That gives me a nice, long laugh.

Martin better be ready.

I wonder whether he still fiddles with his watch when he's nervous, whether he still wears socks to his knees, whether his laugh still sounds the same: like a quick explosion.

I wonder whether he kept the letters. Probably burned or shredded them. He knew what I could do, what I *would* do, if I'd had the chance. He'd fed me nothing but lie after lie until I was choking on them, like one of those geese that gets cream shoved down its throat.

I wonder whether he still does his shopping at Gristedes, and whether it even still exists.

I first met Martin over the watermelons. That's not one of those expressions, either, that means something dirty even though it doesn't sound like it. I used to like going to the grocery store, even when I didn't have two nickels to rub together.

I liked the way the vegetables were all laid out like jewelry in a velvet-lined case: cabbages tucked neatly next to shiny red peppers next to cucumbers next to lettuce, all of it misted over, regular, with a fine spray of water. Sometimes on hot days I'd go to the store just to bend down and put my face over the lettuce and inhale, let the water hit the back of my neck and shoulders, and pretend I was nothing but a cabbage, or a flower in a greenhouse—with nothing to do but be cared for.

Maybe that's why Caroline was so crazy about her greenhouse. Maybe she liked pretending, too.

I'd seen Martin once or twice in passing. He had the kind of face you remember: broad and flat, with eyes as round as gumdrops, like a little kid's face that's just been stretched and pulled a little by the years. He was tall, too: six foot two, and sturdy as a bulldozer. That's just how I like my men: if I wanted someone I could knock over, I'd start going in for women.

It was July and a heat wave and I'd come to the store to cool off, stick my face in the freezers and under the mist, pick up a refill of tonic and maybe some ice cream to eat for dinner. And there in the center of the produce aisle was a huge display of watermelons: a pyramid of them, stacked halfway to the ceiling, and several of them cut open to show off their insides, juicy and red, winking at me like a promise.

Of all things, it made me think of my mother, how she greased one up in lard before the church social every June, and how the kids would fight to catch hold of it; and spitting watermelon seeds off the front porch and watching the birds swoop down to eat them; and the first bite, letting juice run all the way to your elbow. The heat was making me loopy. It nearly made me start crying to think of how long it had been since I'd had a watermelon.

So I went poking and squeezing and looking for the perfect one, like I'd seen my mother do hundreds of times, working my way around the pyramid and taking my time. I never saw Martin come up. But just when I got my hands around a watermelon, his hands landed on it, too.

"It's mine," was the first thing I said, not taking my hands off it.

"I don't think so," he said. He didn't take his hands off, either, so we were standing there, two strangers, holding a watermelon between us.

"Ladies first," I said.

He laughed. I have a thing for teeth, and he had nice ones. "That's old-fashioned," he said.

"I'm old-fashioned," I said.

"I doubt that." The smile stayed in his eyes. "I've got an idea."

"What's that?"

"How about we share it?" he said.

So we did. We drove back to my place, and we polished off the whole damn watermelon and a bottle of Glenlivet he picked up on the way. It was the most fun I'd had in a long time, and I was flattered, too. Martin worked on the Buffalo City Council and had his own business selling medical equipment. He wasn't some lowlife I'd picked up in a bar.

That first night was great. One of the best of my life, I'd say. I pretended not to notice his wedding ring the whole time.

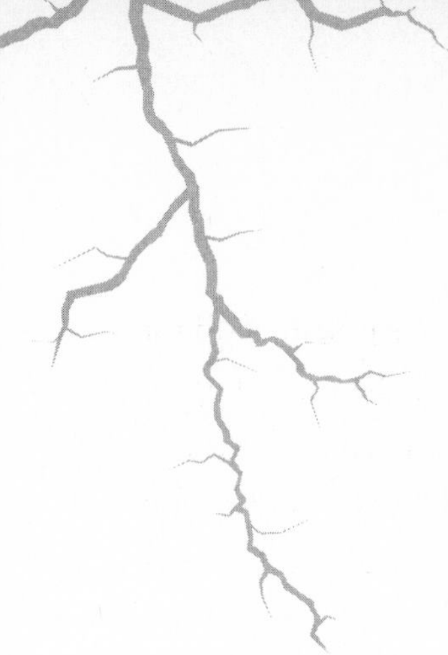

PART V

THE BEDROOMS

A L I C E

"Well, she didn't waste any time, did she? Couldn't have been quicker if she'd tripped and fallen on his—"

"Please, Sandra. Not today."

I'm trying to ignore Sandra's voice. I am trying to ignore what is happening in the Yellow Room entirely, but the rhythm of grunts and groans, the tapping of the headboard, like a periodic spasm, keeps drawing me back.

There is no way to get around this fact, and no point beating around the bush: Minna is bedding the undertaker in the Yellow Room.

The room smells sweet and slightly rotten. It brings back memories of nausea, makes long-ago echoes in my head—Ed's hand gripping the headboard, eyes squeezed shut in concentration, a bead of sweat tracing its way from his forehead to the tip of his nose. *Knock, knock, knock.* Iron and hardness; as though he could pound away all the past disappointments.

Ed closed his eyes and saw railroads. I, too, learned to escape. Maybe that's why I was able to adapt to this new body so quickly. I severed the connection to the old one long ago.

"Do you know what her problem is? Nymphomania. Sex addiction."

Sandra fancies herself an amateur psychologist because she did office work for a Dr. Rivers before he fired her for stealing pills. She has the names of over two hundred phobias memorized, as she is fond of reminding me, including the word *geniophobia,* which is a fear of chins. For the most part, I think that psychology is no better than phrenology.

However, in Minna's case, Sandra might have a point.

The man was in the house less than twenty minutes before she had him stripped down to his socks and he was mounting her like a dog. That is, in fact, exactly what he looks like: his pale, mole-speckled back reminds me of the shaved, ridged spines of a greyhound.

Minna is closing her eyes. I can tell she doesn't want to look at him. I used to close my eyes, too, with Ed. The undertaker is speaking, a low murmur of babble words, curses, and exclamations. Impossible to ignore, however disgusting it is.

I try to think my way into the tangle of wiring behind the radiator. Just a little spark . . . a little friction is all I need . . .

"I think I've underestimated the girl," Sandra says. "It's impressive, really. Just think about it. Urns to underwear in thirty minutes or less! It could be a TV series, don't you think?"

For two days, Danny Topornycky has been ignoring Minna's calls; she's been walking around with her phone plastered to her palm, checking it constantly. Today, she has had better luck.

Are you really here to talk urn styles? Don't you find it depressing? I could never do what you do for a living. I'm pleasure oriented—that's what everyone says. I love to have a good time. Do you *like to have a good time, Chris?*

Now Minna is quiet—surprisingly so. Her face is perfectly composed—a look of relief—as though she has finally, after a period of exhaustion, been allowed to sleep. Christopher Deber, of Deber & Sons, does all the work, and I can't help but see: the animal haunches rising and falling under the tented sheets.

Then: a gust of air, of Outside. A twinge in our side: the kitchen door opens, and Amy runs into the house.

"Oh, no," I say. "No."

Sandra says, "Here comes trouble."

"Do something," I say, as Amy heads for the stairs.

"Mommy!" Amy calls, but not loudly enough—not so loudly that she can be heard over Chris's grunting.

"This is terrible," Sandra says, but I can tell she doesn't mean it.

Amy is on the stairs. Chris is saying *justlikethathuhyoulikeit-likethat* and Amy is running, running. I try to think myself past the steps, out of the banister, into her feet. *Turn around,* I want to scream. *Go back.*

"Mommy!" she singsongs. Not loudly enough. She is almost at the landing. Two more steps. One more minute. Chris lifts and thrusts, lifts and thrusts.

Then: a miracle. Amy trips. She stumbles on the last stair and falls flat on the landing, hard, on an elbow. Instantly, she begins to wail.

Minna snaps her eyes open. She launches Chris off her; he practically flies off the narrow bed, hitting the ground with a thud.

"What the—?"

"Shut up," she says.

"Jesus, I was just about to—"

"I said shut up." Her voice is low and urgent. She is looking not at him, but at the door, which is open a crack. "Get under the bed."

In the hall, Amy picks herself up, sniffling. "Mommy," she wails. For just a second, I have the overwhelming urge to reach up through the floorboards, to wrap myself around her.

"What?" Chris climbs to his feet, covering his *Thing* with one hand. His body is long and pale and lumpy, and his chest glistens with sweat. "I'm not going to—"

Minna looks at him. "Get under the bed," she says calmly. "And don't say a word. Don't cough. Don't fucking breathe. Do you understand me?"

"Christ," he mutters. But he gets on the floor, lying down on his back. He has to uncup himself, and though I don't want to see It, I have no choice: there it is, socklike and pathetic, already shriveling, the animal that leads men, hot and panting, through their lives. Then he wriggles, wormlike, under the bed, seeping his sweat into our floorboards, pricking us with the sparse constellation of hairs that grow from his shoulders to his waist. His heart stutters against the floorboards—staccato, irregular, bringing memories of other heartbeats. Ed, pounding; Maggie, sucking; Thomas, fitting his body to mine. Sandra, lying naked on the bed, and a small brown spider traveling her neck, her chin, her open mouth, and disappearing finally into the darkness of her throat, where I could no longer see it.

For a second, I truly hate Minna.

"In here, sweetheart!" Minna is rearranging the duvet, so it pools over the side of the bed, concealing Chris from view. She tugs the sheets to her chin, sweeps a hand through her hair.

Amy comes to the door, sniffling. She stops when she sees her mother in bed. "What are you doing?" She wrinkles her nose. I wonder if she can smell it.

"Headache, precious," Minna says, with an exaggerated sigh. "I was taking a nap."

"I want to nap, too." Amy bounds toward the bed.

Minna shoots out one hand. With the other, she keeps the sheets at her chin. "Don't come in here," she says, too sharply. Then, in a normal way, "I might have germs."

Trenton comes in after Amy. He leans—or rather, collapses—against the doorway. "What's up with you?" he says.

Minna flashes him a dirty look. "Migraine." She reaches out and touches Amy's chin. "Princess? How about you wait downstairs so I can talk to Uncle Trenton, okay?"

"I want to nap," Amy insists.

"Come on, Amy." Trenton takes a step forward and puts a hand on Amy's shoulder, drawing her away from the bed. "I'll meet you downstairs, okay? It will only take a second."

"What the hell?" Now that Amy is gone, Minna doesn't bother controlling her anger. "I thought you were going for more boxes."

"Forgot my wallet." Trenton shrugs. "We got all the way to Oakbridge, and—"

"Jesus Christ, Trenton," Minna explodes. "What the hell is wrong with you? I ask you to do one goddamn thing—"

"What's wrong with *me*?" Trenton backs out of the room. "It was a mistake. You don't have to be such a bitch about it."

"Don't you dare call me a bitch." If Minna were not stuck in bed, naked, I'm pretty sure she would get out of bed and slap him. She lies stiff, white-faced, for several long minutes, until she hears Trenton pound downstairs again, until she hears the front door open and then slam. She keeps her sheets at her chin. She leans her head against the headboard. Otherwise, she is frozen.

"Can I come out now?" Chris's voice is muffled.

"Yes," she answers.

He wriggles out from the bed and stands again. This time, he doesn't bother cupping. His Thing has returned, now, to its normal, shriveled state, and again I think of an animal that has retracted, burrowed away to nurture its hunger.

"Phew." Chris sits heavily on the bed. "I had no idea you had a kid. God, that could have been awkward. Well, all's well that ends—"

"Get out." Minna closes her eyes.

Chris starts. "Hey," he says softly, after a long pause. He reaches out and touches her face. She doesn't withdraw. She doesn't open her eyes. "Hey. Look, I'm sorry about that. But I thought you wanted to have a good time. That's what you said, right? And we were just getting started . . . "

"Please leave now," Minna says simply. "The kitchen door should be open. Or you can leave through the hall. It's up to you."

For a moment, Chris watches her. Then he stands abruptly, searches the floor for his shirt, and angrily wrestles on his pants.

"Crazy," he says. Just as he did during intercourse, he lets out a volley of curses, a string of half-muttered words: "Fucking insane. I just came here . . . and I had no idea . . . you were the one who wanted . . . That's fucked up, you know?"

Minna says nothing.

When he has laced up his shoes, and cinched his belt, he stands, staring down at Minna. She must sense it. Still, she doesn't open her eyes.

"Fucked," he says, one last time, and then bursts out of the room, and down the stairs, and out the door, leaving his small black folio, full of urn styles, sitting on the hall console. I think he may remember and come back for it, but he doesn't.

For a long time, Minna lies there. I can't help but remember the way her father sat for a whole day after Caroline had taken the children, while the milk curdled in his coffee.

"Good-bye," she says finally, into the empty room.

Then she pushes off the sheets and stands, and goes into the bathroom, and turns on the shower.

I wanted Amy to trip. I wished for it. I willed my way up through the stairs. And then she tripped.

First, the lightbulb in the basement. And now Amy.

I'm working my way back: into a real body, into feeling.

Touching, pushing, blowing.

Power.

I wasn't always as helpless as I am now. When I first died, when I found myself here, in this house, I could still feel my old body—hands, legs, arms. And I could still go blundering, occasionally and blindly, and find that I had accidentally upset a vase or rattled a table or bumped against the washing machine and turned it on. The Killigans were in the house then, and they used to joke about it: *the house is haunted,* they'd say at dinner parties. *I swear, just the other day, the TV turned on by itself.*

It's like the men who came home from the war missing limbs. Afterward, for a long time, there were the agonizing itches in long-lost toes, the cramps in amputated calves. Ed lost his left pinkie finger to an artillery blast, and until the day he died he claimed he could feel a hangnail there. One time, I came downstairs in the middle of the night and found him, half drunk, hacking away at the air with nail scissors. *Phantom limb syndrome,* they called it.

When your whole body is gone, it's the same thing, just on a larger scale—phantom body syndrome. You feel it, you sense it, and somehow this keeps you grounded in the physical world and allows you to knock elbows with the TV and bump shins against chairs.

But as time went on, as I learned to see by touch, and hear by echo, as air does, and smell the ways walls do, by absorption, the old body receded further and further into the past, and so did my ability to affect things in the physical world.

Is that why Trenton can see her? The girl, Vivian—if it is Vivian—is still so new. She hasn't forgotten how to be alive.

That's the trick: to remember the old body as closely as possible, to feel my way back into it. The narrowness, the needs; the exhaustion and hunger; the pains and the explosions of pleasure. If there's any hope of escaping, I must.

The bed in the Yellow Room isn't so very different from the bed we bought for Maggie once she had outgrown the cradle—from Woolworths, of course, delivered to us sheathed in plastic by men as solemn-faced as pallbearers. For the first six months after we moved her from the cradle, Maggie would wake up screaming. I would climb into bed with her and gradually she would calm down, while I whispered into her hair and kept one arm locked tightly around her waist, to show her I was there.

I remember: the frantic fluttering heartbeat winging through her back, against my breasts and rib cage.

I remember: her sputtering, sniffling breaths, the feel of sweat seeping through her pajamas, and the smell of raspberries in her hair.

I remember the ramrod terror, too, when I heard her crying—the fear that she would never calm down, the fear that I could never pull her back from that black dream-space, the yawning nightmare mouth. Even after she calmed down, the fear would keep me awake: this fragile shell-person, this strange miracle of bones and blood, so easily ruptured and broken.

I wanted to absorb her back inside of me. I would have taken off my skin like a snake and folded her away, to be my secret again.

But she grew, and grew, and grew; and our bodies took us farther from each other. Did she remember those nights? Did she remember how I used to hold her, and rock her to sleep, and sing lullabies into her hair?

Probably not. Most likely, those memories were swallowed up in the long, tangled dream of childhood, swept back into the darkness that used to surround us, thick as syrup, when we slept side by side.

I've had to come to terms with that.

But who knows? It's *possible*. It's possible that underneath the layers and layers of resentments and fights, of distance and criticism, some memory of those early days was preserved, in some rarely used place, the way that a body stores memory of motion and rhythm. Perhaps, later in her life, she was able to excavate the feel of my arms around her, the repetition of my voice saying *I love you, I love you*. Perhaps it brought some comfort to her.

The body restoreth, and the body taketh away.

I remember:

Ed's fist; an explosion of pain, like a sudden burst of color.

I remember:

A mosquito bite on my knee; scratching until I bled.

I remember:

Thomas's chin bumping lightly, once, against mine, the first time we kissed.

S A N D R A

What does Alice remember about the turtle?

We've never talked about it. We've never even talked about how Maggie and I were buds for one afternoon. Tit for tat. God knows there's plenty Alice has never discussed with me. If secrets were stuffing, the woman would be done up like a Thanksgiving turkey.

For example: the suitcase in the bedroom wall.

The funny thing is it never would have come out if Martin hadn't made that idiotic comment about Jimi Hendrix.

It was January 1987. Martin and I were lying in bed, drinking wine, watching the snow come down. Snow was falling soundlessly outside, piling in heavy drifts against the doors and windows, softening the fields and wrapping the world in silence. In all the years I was up north, I never got tired of watching the snow.

We'd been at it for a few hours—the drinking, I mean—and were already pretty wound up when the Doors came on and Martin said, out of nowhere: "I don't see what the big deal about Hendrix is. I think Krieger's just as good."

We started going back and forth, and I got up to pour a drink, and just because I was distracted and busy calling Martin an idiot, I tripped over the lip of the carpet and wound up on the floor.

Instead of helping me up, he said, "Don't you see, Sandra? Don't you see what you're doing to yourself?" And he looked at me like I was some smelly, homeless beggar—like he wanted to turn away but was too polite.

I kicked him out before he had time to put his pants back on. The sight of him hop-skip-jumping over the gravel on the driveway, barefoot and ass shining like a moon, almost made it worth it.

That was when I put my foot in it. Literally. Back in the bedroom, furious, I sank my foot halfway through the wall before I realized what I'd done—and realized, too, that instead of support beams and drywall I'd kicked straight through to a narrow rectangular laundry chute made of hollow pressed tin. And there was something inside it: a large box, I thought at the time, wedged in at an angle.

I had to rip my wall open even more to get it out. It was a small leather suitcase, layered with dirt. I was hoping for something scandalous, a skull or a pile of stolen jewels, and I have to say I was pretty disappointed when I opened it to find a brown tweed jacket, a single black sock, a St. Aquinas University pin, and a length of pink ribbon, like a child's hair thing.

To this day, Alice won't tell me why she hid the suitcase, or when. Of course I have my theories. But I don't press. When you're up each other's asses all day long, you really have to draw the line somewhere.

For three months the suitcase sat in my bedroom, in front of the hole in the wall, safe on its mound of plaster. I didn't think of trying to return it. I didn't know who to return it to. I knew it wasn't the Killigans'—one look at the peach wallpaper, and I knew Mrs. Killigan would never let that piece-of-shit luggage in the house. I vaguely remembered an old lady and a daughter who lived in the house way back in the day, but so what? Mind your business, that's my motto, or at least it was before everybody else started traipsing their business across my rooms.

All that changed after the rains. For weeks in May the skies opened up, bringing a glut, a gut-spilling onslaught of rain, vomiting leaves onto the windows and driving surfs of mud down the hill and onto the porch and pushing a tunneling rush of water from Lackawanna Creek into the basement. For days the water rose in the house, creeping up toward the staircase, floating cans of paint and revealing little drowned frogs, bloated, pale, belly-up.

I remembered sitting with the little creased bible on my knees in Sunday school, listening to stories about the Flood, and thought for the first time that maybe there was something to it. But finally the weather broke. The sky turned clear as summer bluebells, and the sun sat high and fat, smug as a cat, curled up on a drift of clouds.

The rains brought everything up. The lawn was a trash heap, a beach littered with the dead. The mudslides had unearthed men's shoes and washboards, eyeless dolls and socks stiff with mud, lost mittens and old Coca-Cola bottles and hats reeking of mildew.

And on my front porch, unblinking, mouth open like it had been calling for help: a goddamn turtle. A strangely human face, puckered and tragic. It was a big sucker, too, the size of a dinner plate. And the words: bright red, barely chipped, obviously painted painstakingly by a child on the turtle's dark, patterned shell.

Please return to Maggie Lundell.

Like I said: everything comes up in the end.

TRENTON

This time, Trenton did not smoke weed, but just lay very, very still—so still his lungs ached from the effort of controlling them. He had left the window open in his bedroom, then partially lowered the blinds, trying to replicate the quality of the light in the greenhouse.

He wanted to see her again, but he was afraid, too.

"Hello," he whispered.

He thought he heard a snicker, or an echo of a snicker. The voices were still there—sporadic, often indecipherable, like footsteps that stop as soon as you pause to listen.

Was it her?

The memorial for his father was in just six days and Trenton had not anticipated being alive to see it. But the ghost had changed things. He could not—he *would* not—kill himself until he knew the truth about her.

He lay there, listening to a fly buzz somewhere, watching bits of cottonseed float in through the half-open window on long fingers of sun. He was tired and hungover. He'd drunk too much at Katie's stupid party.

He should never have gone. Trenton had thought it would be a high school thing, and everyone would know one another, and he would feel out of place. Instead it was just a bunch of random people floating between the kitchen and the basement. He wondered where Katie picked her friends: they looked like refugees, or people who might work in a shitty dollar-for-a-pound thrift store, if they worked at all. Trenton was positive he recognized one of the boys from the butcher counter at Mick's Deli. Even Katie hadn't seemed to know anyone very well. Several times, she had confused a girl's name, calling her Megan instead of Melissa. And when Trenton had asked how she knew everybody, she had responded vaguely that she liked having people around, which of course wasn't an answer to his question at all.

Katie took him out to the back porch and sat so close to him their thighs touched all the way from hip to knee. She was impressed that he could name a few constellations—thanks to an astronomy elective at Andover he'd taken for the easy A—and together they'd counted the fireflies floating through the dark.

"I used to pretend that fireflies were fairies," Katie had said, her voice a little thick. "I'd imagine I was a fairy cursed to live in human form, and someday I'd transform back." She turned to him. Her breath smelled sweet, like raspberry vodka. "Do you ever wish you were someone else?"

And he had answered truthfully, "All the time."

But then Marcus had showed up with more alcohol. Marcus. What a sleazeball name. He looked like a sleazeball, too, with a goatee thin as a rat's tail and dirty jeans and a tattoo on the back of his hand of a girl in a bikini using his pointer finger as a stripper pole. He must have been at least twenty-five.

Trenton had been so close to kissing Katie.

He was just starting to doze off when he felt it—a change in the atmosphere. His lungs tightened in his chest and he was temporarily paralyzed, as he had been the moment he'd first woken in the hospital, encased in plaster, unable to move or even cry out, because of the tubes in his throat.

He kept his eyes closed, afraid that if he opened them, it would prove to be just his imagination. Or she would get scared. He squeezed them together so he wouldn't cheat, feeling his heart beat deep in his chest, and found himself praying that this was real. That she was real. That he wasn't crazy.

Trenton felt her sit down on the bed. The mattress didn't sink, the headboard didn't groan, but he felt it nonetheless: a change next to him, as though a sudden wind had sprung up. Now he didn't know whether to open his eyes or not.

Don't go away, he thought. *Don't go away.* But he was terrified. He could no longer feel his fingers or toes.

The thought occurred to him: maybe she was coming for him, to take him over to the other side. And he remembered the moments after the accident, and the feeling of soft shadowed hands all over.

"Are you asleep?" Her voice, too, was like wind across the sheets.

"No," Trenton said, and he forced himself to open his eyes.

He tried not to scream. Or maybe he tried to scream and couldn't. The desire was there, a hard pressure in his chest and throat and terror deep in his guts; but he kept breathing, in-out in-out, and made no sound.

Once, in seventh grade, Trenton had come down with a bad migraine just before basketball tryouts. Standing on the court, he'd seen holes in the boys charging at him, holes in the floor, great swirling pits of darkness in the air and ceiling. He'd spectacularly missed a free throw before puking right in the middle of the gym. But nothing was worse than the holes.

That's what this was like: parts of her were there, and parts of her weren't, but he couldn't exactly tell which was which because the holes, the dark spaces, seemed always to be moving, eating up first her jaw or the left part of her cheek, then her shoulder and elbow or half her chest or a leg. The more he looked, the worse it became—dizzying, immobilizing, like entering a house after staring directly at the sun and fumbling blindly for familiar shapes.

"Who are you?" she said.

"I'm Trenton," he said. "I live here." It was far better when Trenton didn't look at her directly. He scooted up on his elbows, leaning back against the headboard, and stared instead at the wall, where he could see the faint outlines of posters he'd had tacked there when he was a boy—places where the sun had bleached more or less, and small nicks in the wall from the thumbtacks. In his peripheral vision, she seemed far more solid. "Who're *you*?" he said, although he thought he knew.

"I'm nobody anymore, am I?" she whispered. Then: "The others told me I was dead. They told me to get used to it."

"The others?" Trenton said. His throat was dry.

"They're always fighting," she said simply.

For a minute, there was silence. Trenton was waiting for the girl to ask him for help—to avenge her death, or something. Wasn't that why ghosts hung around? But she said nothing. Would anyone believe him? No. Of course not. He wasn't even sure *he* believed him. Maybe he was imagining this whole thing, hallucinating. Maybe he'd finally cracked.

Or maybe the accident *had* killed him, and the past four months had been one weird dream, and he'd been dead the whole time, and he was only just discovering it. There was a movie like that.

"What's your name?" Trenton asked.

"Does it matter?" she said. Then: "Why am I here? What *is* this place?" Her voice broke and she began to cry. The holes became even deeper and darker. He quickly looked away. "I miss my mom," she said.

Trenton felt the sharp wrench of sadness again, an emotion so strong it seemed to bring his stomach to his throat. He wished he could reach out and put a hand on her shoulder. But she would break apart, he was sure of it. And he wouldn't be able to handle it—if his hand passed through her. He might throw up.

"You were killed." He swallowed. Jesus. It was hard to break the news of someone's death. He sympathized, a little, with the nurse who had called his mom with the news of Richard's death, even though she'd been a bitch about it. "A long time ago. You were shot here, in the house—"

"That's her," she said. "One of the others. Sandra. *She* got shot. Some guy stole a letter from her . . . " She flickered briefly and Trenton thought she might vanish. But then she was back: a small dark curve in his peripheral vision. "The others don't like me very much."

Trenton closed his eyes and opened them again. The voices he'd been hearing . . . he must be hearing all of them. The ghosts. One of them had been killed in the house, *his* house. But there were others . . .

It was crazy. He hadn't even believed in ghosts, at least not until the accident.

The thought returned to him: maybe he was already dead. And even though this was what he had wanted, and been planning for, he felt sick.

"Do you remember anything?" he said.

There was a pause. Trenton shivered. He felt as if a wind had come in through the window and tickled the back of his neck, before realizing that the ghost had shifted, that they had briefly touched.

"I remember Ida," she said. "She lived next door. But there was something wrong with her bones. They grew all crooked. She always wanted me to play cards, but I didn't like to. Does that make me a bad person?" Before Trenton could answer, she went on, "And the church—we lived down the street from the church. The bells drove Mom crazy. But I liked them. Especially at Christmas, when they played the hymns." She fell silent again.

"I meant about what happened," he said, because he had to say something, to take control, to keep her from crying again. He had to do something to fight the feeling that *he* was about to cry.

And he suddenly remembered what Minna had said about the cops; they'd come looking for a girl who'd disappeared. He felt a tingling in his spine. It might be her. It must be.

She hesitated. "I remember a car," she said quietly. "It was raining. I think—I think I screamed." She broke off. Trenton could feel her tense, gather together; she was suddenly as still as the sky just before a storm. "Someone's coming."

"Wait," Trenton said, but it was too late.

There was a loud bang, then a grating noise outside Trenton's window. He cried out as a large red blob came into view. Next to him, the ghost disappeared. She simply evaporated, like a mirage when you approach too close; one second she was a brushstroke of shadow, and then even that was gone.

It was Katie, wearing a hat far too hot for the weather. She got an arm over the windowsill. She was red-faced from the climb.

"What the fuck?" Trenton crossed over to her and grabbed the back of her jacket—his jacket, he realized, which he'd left at her house last night—too angry even to be impressed by the fact she'd managed to drag the ladder all the way from the greenhouse.

"A little help?" she panted.

He hauled and she pulled, and finally she managed to get her legs over the windowsill. Then she snaked herself headfirst into his room, banging her knees on the floor. Trenton almost asked if she was okay, then decided against it.

"What the hell are you doing here?" he said, backing away from her so that there was at least ten feet between them.

She sat back on her heels, whipping off her hat, which was too large. Underneath, her hair was wispy and obviously unwashed. Trenton wished he didn't think she looked cute.

She unzipped her jacket—his jacket. "What's it look like I'm doing?" She tossed the jacket on his bed. "Return service. You don't have to thank me."

"Thank you," Trenton said.

"You're welcome."

She stood up, wincing as she bent and unbent a knee. Underneath the jacket, she was wearing a T-shirt with a faded rainbow logo, so small and tight he could see the silhouette of her bra straps when she turned around. It was the same thing she'd been wearing last night, and Trenton wondered whether she'd been to sleep yet. He thought of that guy, Marcus, and the stupid tattoo—pictured that hand working its way across Katie's thighs—and then tried really hard to think about something, anything, else.

"So these are your digs, huh?" she said, walking the small room, forcing him to step aside and around her.

"We have a front door, you know," Trenton said. Every time she came close, he smelled her: the same mix of lemon, Marlboros, chemicals. He *felt* her, too. He could feel the warmth of her skin but also the blood flowing underneath it, the pulse working beneath her skin, her lungs expanding, all those countless valves shutting and opening. She was so alive, it frightened him. He didn't feel half so alive as she seemed.

"I like to make an entrance." Katie said it lightly, but she wasn't smiling. She seemed anxious—hopped up, maybe. "Besides, I'm allergic to parents. Your parents are home, aren't they?"

Trenton decided not to correct her use of the word *parents* by pointing out, once again, that his father was dead. "My sister is," he said.

"Same thing." She spun around in a circle, still scanning the walls, as though trying to learn some secret from them. Trenton was suddenly embarrassed that his father had never removed the cluster of sports decals from one corner of the room. But Katie didn't comment on them. "So why'd you pull an Irish exit last night?"

"A what?"

"You left without saying good-bye."

"You looked like you were busy," Trenton said, before he could stop himself.

She turned to him at last. Her eyes were bright. "You're mad about Marcus."

"I'm not *mad,*" he said, crossing his arms, then realizing it seemed like he was trying too hard to look casual and dropping them again. "Why would I be mad? I don't care what you do. I don't even *know* you."

"Okay." Katie exhaled. She sat down on his bed and drew her knees up to her chest without asking whether she should take off her shoes. Trenton noticed the way the bed sagged under her weight. He wondered whether, even now, the ghost was watching. Weirdly, he felt guilty. "I just thought you might be upset, because . . . " Katie trailed off.

"Because why?"

She looked up at him from underneath the heavy fringe of her bangs. "Well, because it kind of seemed like you wanted to kiss me last night."

Trenton wanted to laugh, but his face was frozen. A high whine, like the noise of a cornered animal, worked its way out of the back of his throat.

"I wouldn't have stopped you," she said quietly, so quietly it was practically a whisper, and Trenton thought he might have misheard. He couldn't think of a response. He could do nothing but stare. Then he heard footsteps coming down the hall toward his room.

Instantly, Katie rocketed off the bed.

"Trenton?" Minna's voice came through the door. "It's me. Let me in."

Katie dropped to her knees, as though thinking of trying to crawl under the bed, where Trenton had shoved his suitcase and a load of dirty socks. She drew back.

"What are you doing?" he whispered, and then said, louder, "One second."

Katie crawled across the floor and opened the closet door. This was mostly empty: his only suit and nice dress shirt, which his mother had insisted he bring, hung forlornly on an otherwise empty rack. Katie backed into the closet, put a finger to her lips, and then closed the door. Metal hangers clinked together faintly.

"Trenton?" Minna said again. "Today?"

Trenton crossed to the door, feeling a slight thrill in his stomach: there was a girl, a pretty girl, hiding in his closet. At Andover, girls snuck into boys' rooms all the time—but never his room.

"What is it?" he said, opening the door, hoping he wasn't blushing.

Minna was wearing a hooded sweatshirt, cinched tight around her face, which made her look even thinner than usual. "Look, I'm sorry about yelling earlier, okay?" she said, not looking at him.

"Okay," Trenton said. He almost preferred when Minna was a bitch, because then he didn't have to remember how close they had once been. "Is that it?"

She turned her eyes to him. "I asked Danny—my friend, the cop, remember?—about that woman who died. Here." She passed him a piece of paper, folded in half. "He e-mailed me the details. So if we see him again, be sure to thank him."

Trenton unfolded the piece of paper. It was a short e-mail, subject: SANDRA WILKINSON. Trenton felt dizzy. Sandra. The ghost had said something about a Sandra, and a stolen letter.

That means he couldn't have invented it. He couldn't have made her up.

> Sandra Wilkinson, aged 41, was found at home on the morning of March 14, 1993 by Joe Connelly, roofer. Single shot to the face, removed two of her teeth. There were no prints on the gun but her own, but the door was open and there were signs someone had been with her the night before. Inquest returned inconclusive verdict.

Then, after several spaces:

> This is the kind of thing you wanted, right? Looking forward to seeing you. Danny.

"Happy now?" Minna asked.

His hands were shaking. He folded up the piece of paper and put it in his back pocket. He was surprised to feel that there was already something folded up there and then remembered, with a jolt, his suicide note. "What about the girl—the disappearance. Have they found her yet?"

Minna had already started to turn away.

"No. No, they haven't found her," Minna said. "She's probably hacked up to pieces and buried in a well somewhere."

"That's disgusting," Trenton said loudly.

Minna shrugged. "Sorry," she said, not sounding sorry. "You asked."

Trenton closed the door and locked it. His heart was beating very fast. He was remembering, then, the time their new kitten had gone missing and they'd found it after a week, fur matted, frozen stiff with cold, at the bottom of the old well.

His closet door opened, and Katie crawled out.

"It smells like my grandma's bathroom in there," she said. She stood up, slapping the back of her jeans.

"You can go now," Trenton said. He was tired, and he was sure she was making fun of him. *I wouldn't have stopped you* wasn't the same as *I wanted to*. Maybe she'd come all the way here *just* to make fun of him.

"Don't be like that," she said. She came close to him, and it seemed as if she might say something else. Instead, she reached out, snatched the piece of paper from his hand, and started to read. "Cool," she said. "So someone was murdered in your house?"

"Maybe," Trenton said, taking the paper back. "It was never proven."

"The good crimes never are," she said, as if she had some great knowledge of it. He'd liked her better last night, in the darkness on the porch, underneath a black tarp sky that made everything seem small. She had seemed more real to him then. "Hey, you know what we should do?" She didn't wait for him to answer. "A séance."

"A what?" Trenton said, although he'd heard. He couldn't help it; he thought how nice it was to hear her say *we*.

"You know, a séance. Ouija board and candles and all that. We'll call up the ghost, make her tell us who did it."

As she said the word *ghost,* Trenton thought he heard an echo voice in the walls, in the room and floor, a response too faint to make out. "I don't think that's such a good idea," he said.

"It's a great idea. Come on, let's." She took a step closer to him. Her eyes were the exact color of good weed—like something you could fall inside to get high. "*Please*. You and me. Tomorrow night?" She made her eyes big, and even though he knew it was the kind of trick girls did, it worked: he felt his body responding, felt a sudden ache through his fingers, like they wanted to touch her all on their own.

He took a step away from her. "I'm babysitting my niece tomorrow," he said. He was glad for the excuse—and also a bit disappointed.

Katie shrugged. "Can she keep a secret?"

Trenton felt himself relenting. "As well as any six-year-old." He added: "She goes to bed early."

Katie smiled. "So we'll be alone," she said. She stared at him for a second, and her smile faltered. "Hey, Trenton?"

"What?"

"I really am sorry. About the party last night. It's complicated, with me." She touched her fingers to her lips and then brought them to his cheek.

Trenton jerked away instinctively. He hated people touching his face.

"See you tomorrow," she said, and then she climbed out the way she had come, through the window.

A L I C E

Next to the bookshelf in the Blue Room is a place in the wall gouged at various heights: three foot ten, four feet three, four foot four.

This is where Trenton marked his growth, year by year, picking and chiseling with the Swiss army knife Richard bought him for his fifth birthday—briefly confiscated by his mother, who thought he was too young, but then commandeered by Minna from Caroline's underwear drawer and returned to Trenton, as a bribe, to keep him from telling when he caught her smoking from the bedroom window.

This is how we grow: not up, but out, like trees—swelling to encompass all these stories, the promises and lies and bribes and habits.

Even now—*especially* now—it is hard to say what is true.

One thing I do know: it was Thomas's idea to run away.

I ran away once when I was a little girl. That was the year I got a suitcase for Christmas, after I'd begged my parents for a briefcase like the kind my father took with him to work. I loved my father's briefcase, with its dark velvet interior and recessed compartments, and places for his pipe, his eyeglasses, and his papers. It was as clean, as ordered, as regular as my father himself.

My suitcase was small and powder blue, with brass latches and a fleecy soft interior and little pockets for putting in whatever I liked. It wasn't my father's briefcase, but I liked it even better, especially the small lock that kept it closed and the accompanying key, which I wore like a necklace. Inside, I kept my prized possessions: three silver barrettes; a snow globe my grandparents had brought me from New York City, featuring a tiny bridge and even the miniature figure of a girl standing on it who looked just like me; a small china doll named Amelia, missing one arm, which I'd rescued from the trash after my older sister got tired of her.

For months I carried that suitcase with me everywhere, even though my sisters ridiculed me endlessly about it. I even insisted on taking it to school, and my teacher, Mrs. Hornsby, let me keep it by my desk, instead of among the jumble of overcoats and rubber boots and mittens dripping snow by the radiators in the back.

One night, I came out from the bath and found my sisters in my bedroom. They'd broken the lock, just snapped it in half, opened the suitcase, and laid everything out on the rug. Their fingerprints were all over the snow globe. Poor Amelia was discarded facedown on the floor. They were laughing hysterically.

I lunged at Olivia, my middle sister, first. She'd had bad pneumonia as a kid and was weaker than Delilah. I managed to wrestle her to the ground before she kneed me in the stomach and Delilah hauled me backward. She pinned me and sat on my chest.

"You know why Mom and Dad bought you that stupid suitcase, don't you?" Delilah leaned forward so that her hair tented around me. Her face, mean and gloating, was all I could see. "They want you to run away."

"You're a liar." I was doing a bad job of trying not to cry.

"They told us so," Delilah said. "They never wanted you in the first place."

I spit at her. She slapped my face, hard, and finally I couldn't swallow back the tears anymore, and I started to cry, huge heaving sobs that nearly made me throw up. Later, they must have felt badly; Olivia made me warm milk with honey and Delilah braided and pinned my hair so it would curl in the morning. But I didn't forgive them.

I had my revenge. The next day, a Sunday, I snuck away through the crowd congregating after church and circled back around to the stairs that led into the basement, where the church held socials and doled out soup on Easter. It was colder than I'd expected, and darker. For hours I shivered alone, listening to the distant echo of voices, praying both that I wouldn't be discovered and that I would.

Eventually, when I couldn't feel my fingers and my toes had gone numb in my boots, I went home. The sun had set, and I remember the strangeness of the streets in the dark: the gray crust of snow over everything, the rutted sidewalks, the Christmas displays behind vividly lit windows.

I saw my sisters even before I pushed open the gate: both of them pressed face and palm to our front windows, the glass fogging with their breath, watching for me. Behind them, my father was pacing and my mother was sitting on our small cream-and-yellow-striped sofa, white-faced, with her hands in her lap.

Standing in the dark, knowing that I would go inside and everyone would fuss over me, was one of the happiest moments of my life. It was like staring into a snow globe and knowing I could shrink down and pass through the glass, that we would all remain forever suspended, safe, even as the world continued, dark and vast, outside our little boundary.

My sisters squeezed me until I thought my breath would run out. My mother cried and called me darling even as my father made me lie over his legs so he could spank me. I went to bed with a backside red as an apple, but my mother brought me soup so I wouldn't catch pneumonia, and Olivia and Delilah piled in bed with me and read from my favorite book, *The Wind in the Willows*.

Thomas and I should have had an ending like that. We were to take his car to New York City, and from there a bus to Chicago, where Thomas had a cousin who would help us get set up. I imagined several jewel-colored rooms filled with books, a fire in the grate, and snow falling softly on dark streets outside our windows. I imagined lying with Thomas under a blanket filled with down, talking late into the night, waking up with the tips of our noses cold and the windows patterned with frost.

I imagined that we would be happy together, that together, we would be home.

CAROLINE

Caroline had now learned how to make a lemon tart, and that you should never actually boil an egg. She couldn't stop reading Adrienne's blog, TheGoldenSpoon, and refreshing the page in the hopes that more pictures would appear.

And yesterday, due to some happy accident, a series of maneuvers that she would never be able to replicate, she had found a profile that listed a hometown and even a zip code; and then, from there, after paying the ridiculous sum of $14.95, she had a telephone number. She had stared at it, stunned, for a good five minutes. She almost wished she could tell Trenton, who was always accusing her of being hopeless at computers. Trenton and Richard were amazingly alike, for people who had spent hardly any time together.

Look what I did, she wanted to say.

She told herself that she only wanted to hear the woman's voice. Just once. She felt she would know then; she felt everything would become clear. Whether or not she was the one. Why Richard had done it. Why he'd done all the things he had done.

She picked up the phone and listened for a moment to the dial tone. How many times in her life had she reached Richard here, in this house, on that number? She always imagined their voices entangled somewhere in the wires when they spoke, caught up in a grid she didn't fully understand, passing back and forth. Once the calls were disconnected, she imagined the echoes of old conversations would be trapped there, floating back and forth with no exit, like ghosts.

Caroline's hands were shaking so much that she misdialed the number the first time, reached an Italian restaurant, and had to hang up and start over. The second time, she managed it.

The phone only rang once before it was snatched up. "Don't tell me you've gotten on going *west,*" a woman said, her voice hurried, impatient, and lower than Caroline had expected from the photographs.

Caroline was seized with sudden panic. She had not expected the woman to pick up so soon—or even at all. She had not thought of what she would say. But she needed Adrienne to speak again. Was she the one? Caroline didn't know, couldn't decide.

Too many seconds had elapsed. "Hello?" Adrienne said—it was Adrienne, that Caroline knew—dragging out the last syllable already. "Are you still there?"

"Hello," Caroline croaked out.

Instantly, Adrienne's tone changed. "Who is this?" she said carefully.

Caroline didn't answer. One second, two seconds.

"Who is this?" Adrienne repeated. "Hello?"

"Wrong number," Caroline said and hung up. The blood was thundering in her ears, and the room was spinning. She tried to think herself down the phone line, into the kitchen—because she was sure Adrienne had answered in the kitchen, no doubt interrupted in the middle of making lemon soufflé or chicken soup from scratch—tried to imagine the mouth pressed to the phone, the hands with their neat nails, the jeans dusted with flour. Had she and Richard met in hotel rooms? Had he gone to visit her and sat with his shoes and socks off at her kitchen table, shirt unbuttoned, drinking wine, laughing, eating the food she had cooked him?

She didn't know. Already, she could hardly remember Adrienne's voice. She'd been too nervous.

She redialed, pressing the phone so tightly against her jaw it hurt. This time she would say nothing.

Adrienne picked up again almost immediately. "You did it again," she said. This time, she sounded bored.

Despite her intention to say nothing, Caroline was so startled, she spoke up. "What?"

Adrienne cleared her throat. "You dialed the wrong number again. Who're you trying to reach?"

Caroline couldn't think of a single thing to say. She was listening so hard, she wished she could squeeze herself into the receiver and travel the line herself.

"Is this one of Bella's friends? If this is one of Bella's friends, I don't care what your parents do, but in my house prank calls get you a good old-fashioned grounding."

"It's not . . . I don't know Bella," Caroline said.

There was a short pause. "Listen," Adrienne said. Her voice had turned fearful. "Listen. Whoever you are. Don't call back."

Then Caroline was listening to the dial tone again.

S A N D R A

It took me nearly two weeks to track Maggie down. Back then, there was no e-this and online search—just columns of identical names, and lots of dialing and dead ends and finger cramps.

At last, I got her. She was a low-voiced woman who paused before every sentence as if she was debating whether to speak at all. Even when she picked up the phone, she paused, and I counted several seconds of heavy breathing. By the time she said hello, I was about to hang up.

Why did I call her? Why did I think it was important?

Up and down, up and down, a ladder of choices leading to the next choice, and the next, until suddenly you've run out of choices, and ladder, and you find time as rare and thin as air on a mountain. Then it's oops, sorry, turn's over.

"Are you Maggie Lundell?" I said. "From Coral River?"

"Not anymore" is what she said. Then: "How did you find me?"

"I found a turtle with your name on it," I answered.

There was another pause. And then a sound like she was overcome with the hiccups. It took me a moment to realize she was laughing.

"I'll be damned," she said. "I knew he would come back."

Maggie arrived two weeks later. How could I have known it

wasn't a good idea? That even then, Alice was waiting, watching, twitching in the walls like an overgrown cockroach?

It was a day that made me glad I'd left New York and the Lower East Side and its crusty people, with faces like moth-eaten cloth. Here it was all bluebells and honeysuckle, climbing roses and birds chasing each other across the sky—a place where nothing bad could happen.

A bit of golden dust unwinding like smoke in the sky announced her; then a wide, boxy maroon Mazda came bumping up the drive. The owner matched the car: wide and squat, with a square jaw and a thatch of bright red hair, cut short. I pinned her for queer right away.

She moved slowly, deliberately, the same way she spoke. It was only eleven A.M., but when I asked her if she wanted a soda or something to drink, she said, "Got any gin?" I liked her right away.

We sat on the deck and bullshitted for a few hours—she told me about the way the house had changed, and about the turtle she'd named Norman, and how she suspected her mother had deliberately turned him out of the house, and I told her about how I'd ended up in the middle of Buttshit, Nowhere, USA, and how glad I was. She was interested in the New York scene. She'd been living in San Francisco for three decades but had grown tired, she said, of all the "faghags." She'd followed a job to Philadelphia after she found her last girlfriend cheating with her ex-husband—"an engineer," she said, as if disgusted.

I didn't blame her. I'd been with an engineer once in my life, and every time we were screwing around I felt like I was some kind of mechanical model he was trying to deconstruct or decode. Pull a wire here, twist a nob, oops, that's not working, how about pressing this button? It's like he expected me to start beeping and flashing a green light.

She did installation art and worked in TV production to make ends meet.

As we got deeper into the bottle, she started pausing less, talking a little freer, telling me about some of the stuff she did—trash cans inverted and made into toilets, that kind of stuff, but I've never been much of an art lover, and I certainly don't know why someone would pay fifty grand for a piece of rusted metal, but whatever floats your boat. She told me, too, about the commercial work: regional stuff, mostly, although I had seen one of her TV advertisements for toilet bowl cleaner and thought it was very well done.

The afternoon lengthened and sharpened, too, like a microscope had been adjusted; the sun, the drinks, the coolness of the house every time I went inside to pee. I told Maggie about where I worked, the Rivers Center for Psychiatric Development, and about the kooks and the weirdos my boss researched: phobics, neurotics, psychotics, freaks of all shapes and sizes.

"It's the liars I'd be most interested in," she said. "What do they call it? Compulsive liars."

"What about them?"

She stared out over the back lawn; sloping down toward the woods, it dropped suddenly into shadow where the sycamores and the oaks began. "Aren't we all, in a way? Liars, I mean. Unable to help it."

"Not me," I said. "I've always been a straight shooter. What you see is what you get."

"But that's the whole point." Her voice had softened as she got drunker. She wasn't slurring, exactly, but where before she spoke in short staccato, now her voice was all melody. For a quick second, I thought of Georgia, and even missed it—the tip of a hat, the drawl of the postman saying *hey there, little lady*. "We don't know we're lying," she went on. "Not about ourselves, anyway. Everything we see, everything we remember—it's all just made up, isn't it?"

A fly was drowning spectacularly in her half-empty glass. She went to take a sip, grimaced, and then fished the insect out with an unsteady finger.

"Looks pretty damn real to me," I said and laughed.

We'd finished most of the bottle of gin before I got around to showing her the suitcase. I was sorry almost as soon as I did, because just like that the good times were over, and I realized—with the kind of bottlenecked clarity only a solid afternoon of drinking brings—that she was very, very drunk. Later that night, I would come upstairs and see her passed out in my bedroom, clothes on, spread-eagle, mouth open in a puddle of drool.

She was quiet as she examined the objects one by one, like she was puzzling over a crossword. I started getting impatient and made a joke about it, but she didn't seem to hear me.

I started thinking about food, and whether I should eat something and risk killing my buzz, or whether I should just open the whiskey, which I didn't particularly want to share. Would she notice if I refilled my glass in the kitchen? Was she too drunk to notice?

"This isn't my father's jacket," she said abruptly. Her eyes were red and her mouth wet, like a wound in the center of her face. "It's too small. Not his style, either."

I was bored already—wishing now that I had asked her to leave, so I could open the whiskey and drink it in peace, while the shadows swallowed up the hill.

"I never really knew her," Maggie said. A little bubble of spit had formed at the corner of her mouth.

"Who?" I asked automatically.

"My mother," she said. "My father, either." She was quiet for a bit, and I thought this might be a good time to excuse myself, take a pee, sneak some whiskey into my glass. She wouldn't even notice.

But then she blurted out: "Did you know your parents?"

I knew what she meant, but I didn't think it was the right time to tell her: about my dad playing tug-of-war with his buddy's privates, about my mom babbling to Jesus in nonsense words behind the chipped white doors of the Holy Light Pentecostal Church, and bleaching the walls until plants withered in their vases and cats asphyxiated on our doorstep.

So I just said, "Parents are a bitch."

That's more or less how I've always felt about it, anyway. Parents teach you a lot of things, but the most important thing they teach you is this: how people will fuck you up in the future. If they're any good, they teach you to get used to it.

"She never said she loved me," Maggie said. She didn't bother to try and wipe her nose or eyes, just sat there with her thick arms useless in her lap, one hand still wrapped around her drink. "Never once."

Something in my stomach tightened, like she'd sunk a fishing hook just below my belly button and started to pull. I never could stand the sight of crying—hadn't cried myself since I was a little girl and Mom walloped me ten times over the head with the King James Bible after she heard me tell my cousin Richie Rodgers to "go to hell."

And maybe it was because I was thinking of that—the old home in Georgia, and Richie, and what had happened to him—but when Maggie looked up at me, eyes big and pathetic and desperate as an animal's, I had a sudden memory of this time when I was twelve and my uncle Ronnie took me hunting. Richie was there, too: by then fourteen, with a face like an open sore and teeth too large for his mouth and a laugh like a donkey getting kicked.

Ronnie and I split off from Richie—I don't remember why—and halfway through the afternoon we came across a deer, and Ronnie fired like an idiot, too far to the right. Still, the deer ran for a good half a mile before collapsing. By the time we got to it, it was gasping, kicking in pain, eyes rolling up to the sky. And I remember it fixed on me for a second and I could practically hear it: kill me, it was saying. Please kill me. Ronnie was shooting with shells the size of a thumb and I knew that inside the deer, a hundred sharp-toothed pellets had exploded like shrapnel, burrowing into its organs.

I grabbed Ronnie's shotgun and fired three times straight into the deer's head, until it didn't even look like a deer anymore and I knew it could feel nothing.

That's exactly what Maggie looked like in that moment—like that deer, silently pleading with me. And I knew that those unsaid words, *I love you,* were her own exploded shell: that those hurts were embedded deep, killing her slowly. I guess we all have some of these—memories like artillery shells, fired at close range.

"Well, maybe she didn't, then," I said to her. It may seem cruel, but sometimes, you got to just pull the trigger.

And like I said: I didn't know Alice was watching.

CAROLINE

Three more seconds. Two. That's all she needed.

She had to *know.*

She knew she shouldn't. She tried to stop. But her fingers weren't obeying her brain.

Caroline picked up the receiver and dialed Adrienne's number again.

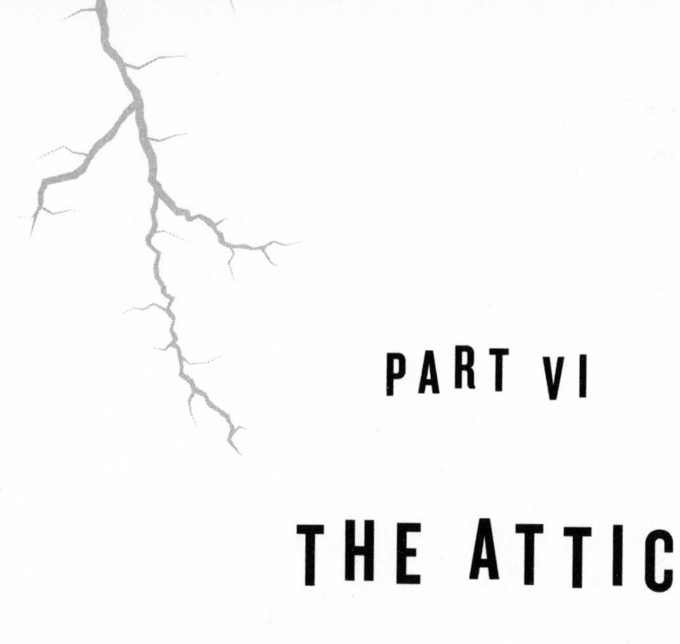

PART VI

THE ATTIC

S A N D R A

Martin loved the attic. Don't ask me why. Until he insisted on exploring the house bottom to top, I'd probably been up there twice in the whole time I lived in Coral River: once, to unload the dump of stuff my dad saddled me with after he died; and once to check for a dead animal after the whole house went rank with a bad smell. (It was a raccoon and I found it after two days of searching, in the old laundry chute; it had crawled halfway up the wall before getting stuck. The plumber had to draw it out with one of those steel wires they use for breaking up matted hair in the drain.)

If you'd asked me—if you asked me, still—I would have said attics are like the spleen of a house. Ignored, forgotten, useless.

But six months after Martin and I first shared that watermelon, we went exploring. It had been snowing for days—that was a bad winter. Even in the ten seconds he stood inside the door, stamping ice from his boots and shaking it from his beard, a half inch of snow gathered on the kitchen floor and afterward melted all over the linoleum. He hadn't been inside twenty minutes when they announced on TV that the road back to town was closed.

"I guess I'll have to spend the night," he said, putting his arms around me. Cheeky bastard. Like there was any doubt.

We were deep into a bottle of cognac (Martell, 1950) when he said it: "I want to see where you live, Sandy."

"You've been here plenty of times," I said. "Besides, I never get to see where *you* live."

He ignored that. "I've seen the kitchen. I've seen the den. I've seen your bedroom." He leaned forward and put his hands over mine—warm hands, but raw from the weather and the cold and rough from long-ago summers spent hauling lobsters at a wharf in Maine, calluses that had never gone away. Funny how the past gets down into the skin.

It was so cold in the attic we could see our breath hanging like miniature ghosts. Martin went back downstairs for a second bottle of cognac and a blanket, and we sat together on the hardwood floor, between the boxes, inhaling the smell of wood and damp and cold.

"Close your eyes," Martin said. "Listen."

"To what?" I said. There was nothing: no sound at all. Even the house was still, wrapped in its drifts like a fat old baby in a blanket.

"The snow," he said.

I opened my eyes. "You can't hear snow."

"You can," he said. He still had his eyes closed. He looked like a different person when he wasn't smiling. Older. Tired. A stranger. "Shhh."

I closed my eyes again, just to humor him.

But the weird thing is after a minute or two, I thought I *could* hear it. Not sound, but the opposite of sound. It was the slow accumulation of silence, the sticky, heavy drift of nothing, like watching shadows grow and turn to dark, or like this time I was a kid and saw a solar eclipse, watched a black disk float over the sun and saw all the light get swallowed up in an instant. Now I was hearing all the sounds of the world get swallowed up.

When I opened my eyes, Martin was smiling again. "The sound of snow," he said.

After that, it became like our thing. Even when he wasn't around, I used to go up there sometimes, because it reminded me of him. I even started to get used to the smell, like an old person's laundry basket, and the spiders spinning silently in their corners. Cissy would have liked it in the attic.

Alice told me later she used to hang around in the attic, too. She had a whole rig up there, a desk and everything. First she was pretending to write because it gave her an excuse to keep away from her husband, and he was too lazy and usually too drunk, so she says, to climb the stairs. But then, after a while, she started really writing, and she churned out *The Raven Heliotrope,* three hundred pages in two years.

It was peaceful up there.

Then, a week before the big *wham-o blam-o*, brains on the wall, the roof collapsed. It had been another frigid turd of a winter, and for months the snow, fine as sifted flour, had been piling up quietly, so I hardly noticed.

I wasn't home. I'd gone looking for Martin. It had been a rough winter on me. We'd been at it, me and Martin; I got canned from my job for no good reason; and on top of everything else, I got the news from my doctor: cancer. A knot on my lung, tight as a web, lit up like a Christmas tree on the scan.

I needed to tell Martin. I called him at home, which was forbidden, and I'll never forget what it felt like when *she* picked up the phone: like standing out in the cold and seeing warm lights off in the distance and knowing you'd never make it.

"Hello?" she said, half laughing; and I heard his voice, too, in the background, like he'd just finished telling a joke. There were other voices too, overlapping, and a song playing in the background. Something with a violin.

I knew where he lived. He was careful but not careful enough, and it was no big secret. He knew I wouldn't show up there unannounced, but that's just what I did. I drove all the way to Buffalo through the funnel of snow and parked right in front of his house, which was bigger than I'd imagined and prettier, like a big cupcake covered in white icing. I could see him moving in the living room, passing out drinks to his guests. And I could see *her,* too: blond and small as an insect, touching his face, his arm; rearranging the chairs, opening the window to let out the smoke; and every time she moved it was like she was saying, *I belong here. I belong here.*

At the last second I lost my nerve so I just sat there. I had a bottle of Smirnoff to keep me warm, and I sat until it was finished and the guests had all gone home, spilling out into the darkness and cold, still laughing, waving scarves like people in old movies leaving on a ship. Martin and his wife stood waving at the door, transformed by the warm light behind them into a single shape.

Driving home, I lost control on the ice and went headfirst into a fence and some idiot cop barely out of puberty threw me in the tank overnight for being drunk. The cell was white and empty and smelled like piss, but in the morning when the sun came up on the walls, it was almost pretty.

When I got home, my roof was gone. Overnight the weight of the snow became too much to carry. What tipped the scale? Think about it: there must have been a final snowflake that did it, a fraction of a fraction of a fraction of a milligram that made all the difference.

Don't think I felt sorry for myself. The way I figure it, life's the sum total of all our small mistakes, little tragedies, bad choices. Addition on top of addition. They pile up and pile up until the cost of keeping up appearances is too high and the weight is just too much.

Then: collapse.

Alice says we got to let go. Maybe she's right.

If you want the plain truth, it wasn't the gun that killed me. What I mean is: it wasn't the gun that killed me *first.*

When I was six, I started having a dream about a long white hallway full of closed doors. It looked like a hospital, except there were no doctors and no nurses, no people at all. Just a long stretch of closed locked doors.

Sometimes it was quiet. Sometimes I could hear people talking inside the locked rooms, voices muffled by the walls. Sometimes there was even music playing. And I knew if I could just find the right door, it would open for me, and I'd pass through into my house, into my room, with the big bay windows where a decade later a spider would sit spinning for Cissy, and the view of the front yard and the big sky and the birds pecking worms out of my mom's garden.

But I never could. Find it, I mean. All the doors stayed locked.

The dreams stopped after a while, when I got a little older and got into boys and dope and music and beer. But I'll tell you something. For a while, I thought Martin was going to be the door.

When his wife found out and he said he was ending things with me, I think I went a little crazy. After thirty years, the dreams came back. Even when I woke up, the dream was there: a long hallway of locked rooms, and people laughing inside of them.

The gun was just the go-between. It was the loneliness that got me in the end.

A M Y

Amy was supposed to be sleeping but she couldn't sleep and there were noises in the attic besides. She couldn't sleep because Uncle Trenton was a bad reader and he'd rushed through her favorite part of *The Raven Heliotrope* and he hadn't given her a good-night kiss plus he'd tucked her in too tight, which made her feel like a giant burrito.

And he smelled weird. Like the kind of clear juice Nana drank, and also a little bit like the big store where Mommy bought her perfumes.

She knew why Uncle Trenton was in a bad mood. It was because of the body in the ground. She'd heard Nana talking about it with Mommy when they were getting ready to leave. *I don't see what all the fuss is about,* Mommy said. *She's six feet under by now and everybody knows it. They should be looking for her with dogs and a shovel.* And Nana said, *Imagine her poor parents.*

Amy was playing in the corner and they didn't bother to be quiet because they thought she didn't understand—but she did. Six feet under was where you went when you were dead like Grandpa or like Penelope in *The Raven Heliotrope.*

Amy wondered whether the girl who was six feet under who was upsetting Trenton would come back, like Penelope had in the book. Innocents don't really die, so after she was buried six feet under beneath a tree, the tree started weeping and its tears spilled on the ground and Penelope woke up. And so she lived happily ever after and the tree was named a weeping willow like the kind they had outside in the front yard. Maybe that's where the girl who was upsetting Trenton was buried.

Amy was thirsty. She would ask Trenton for a glass of water and he couldn't be mad because everyone knew that without water you would die. Her feet felt strange on the floor, like they were full of tiny shivers. Mommy would tell her to put on socks but Mommy wasn't here and it was just Amy and Trenton and maybe the girl six feet under.

In the hall, the noises in the attic were even louder, and Amy knew they weren't just mice or creaks but footsteps and voices. The trapdoor in the ceiling was open, and the stairs were lolling out like a wide wood tongue, and there was light spilling onto the carpet and shadows moving back and forth.

"What about your sister?" someone was saying, and it was not Trenton but the girl.

"She's out to dinner with my mom."

"I meant your younger sister."

"I told you, she's my niece. And she's asleep."

They were talking about her, and Amy felt proud. She wanted to know what a dead girl looked like because she'd always wondered whether Penelope had bugs in her hair when she woke up and kissed Prince Thomas and he was just too nice to say anything.

"Where do you want the candles?" the dead girl was saying when Amy put her foot onto the first stair.

T R E N T O N

Trenton had been hoping Katie wouldn't show—or even better, that she would show but forget about the séance idea. No such luck. He'd just managed to put Amy to bed when he heard the faintest tapping from downstairs, like Katie was using her fingernails to knock.

"I don't think candles are such a good idea," he said, squatting down and trying to fit his arms around a huge oak bureau that Katie insisted he move.

"Of course we need candles," she said. She had two packages of tall white pillar candles and she was busy tearing at the plastic with her teeth. She looked like a deranged gerbil. The roof was so low they were bent nearly double. "I stole these just for you."

"You stole them?" Trenton said.

She shrugged. "I'm broke." She managed to get the first package open. She spit out a small square of plastic and shook a candle into her hand. "Voilà," she said, brandishing it.

He was worried the séance wouldn't work, and he was worried it would. He was worried that Katie would see the ghost and freak out, and also that he would freak out but Katie wouldn't see her so she wouldn't understand why he was freaking out. There were so many different things to worry about, he was having trouble keeping them straight in his head.

Trenton strained against the bureau and managed to move it about half an inch. Christ. The thing felt like it was made of molten lead.

"Put your back into it," Katie said.

"You could help," he pointed out.

"I *am* helping." She was setting up the candles, arranging them in a circle in the middle of the floor, which they had cleared of boxes and trunks by stacking everything together in teetering piles, leaving only a narrow pathway to the stairs. When she was finished, Katie unrolled the blanket, which she'd carried up from the living room. ("It's a séance," he'd said, "not a picnic." And she'd looked at him, head tilted to the side, fingering the side of her nostril where he could still see twin holes that must once have been nose rings, and said, "Ghosts don't know the difference. For them a séance is a picnic. What the fuck else do they do all day?" He was halfway tempted to answer: *I'll ask.*)

It was cold in the attic, and Trenton had the sudden feeling of a finger running lightly down his neck. Watched. That's what it was. It was the sensation of dark eyes on him, concealed, hidden behind the jumble of stacked boxes and furniture. And now it occurred to him, of course, that that's what ghosts did all day—was all they could do.

They watched.

He jammed his fists into the front pocket of his sweatshirt.

"You okay?" Katie asked. She shrugged off her sweatshirt—which was pink, and patterned with grinning skulls—and Trenton looked away quickly, so he wouldn't be caught staring at her too-small tank top underneath, and the stripe of tan stomach above her jeans.

"Yeah," Trenton said. "Let's just get this over with."

"That's the spirit." She rolled her eyes, then sat down on the blanket and crossed her legs. When she leaned forward, he could see her cleavage. She patted the spot in front of her. "Park it."

Trenton hadn't thought about how difficult it would be for him to sit cross-legged. He sat down first sideways, with his legs pointed outward to the candles like the second hand in a giant clock. He bent one knee but couldn't get the other to work. He was too stiff. It had been a long time since he'd done his PT.

The whole time, Katie observed him in silence. "What happened to you?" she asked finally.

Trenton had to settle for leaving one leg extended. "I was in an accident," he said. "A car accident."

"You said." Katie narrowed her eyes. "Were you trying to kill yourself?"

"What?" Trenton stared at her. "No. No, of course not."

"You can tell me," Katie said. Her expression hadn't changed.

"I wasn't even driving," he said, and immediately felt that old pain, a sharp pull of regret that he *hadn't* died, that the warm soft hands hadn't carried him off into the darkness, that instead he had woken up with his broken body straightened out and immobilized and pinned to a hospital bed like an insect pinned to soft cotton. "My friend was driving."

"Was your friend trying to kill you?" she asked, unsmiling.

Trenton couldn't help it. He laughed. The idea of Robbie Abramowicz, who weighed like three hundred pounds and was the only kid at Andover less popular than Trenton was, trying to kill anything was funny. "I hope not. He's my only friend at school." He was embarrassed, immediately, to have said it.

But Katie didn't seem to notice. "I was in an accident once," she said. Abruptly, she spun around and pulled up her shirt. Trenton tried to say something but only managed to gargle. He could see the small, regular knobs of her spine, and a blue butterfly tattoo—a fake—peeling away on her lower back. Running up the length of her back, like a second spine, was a narrow cord of scar tissue, thick as a child's finger. "One time when I was little my parents took me to the zoo," she said. "I wanted to see the tigers. I was so small I slipped right into the pen when they weren't looking."

"Really?" Trenton was relieved when she hitched down her shirt.

"No." She turned around to face him again. "Spinal birth defect. I had, like, five surgeries before I was two."

He stared at her. "Do you make everything into a story?"

"Yes," she said simply. For a second, Katie looked just like she had the night of the party, like the girl who had counted fireflies and asked him to point out the North Star. "That way, I can make up my own endings."

Then she lunged forward and for a second Trenton's heart stopped and he thought, *She's going to kiss me.*

But she just sat up on her hands and knees and reached behind him and started lighting the candles with a lighter. She was so close to him. She was wearing a T-shirt, and the way she was bending over he could see the curves of her breasts, full and soft-looking, like they'd fit perfectly in his hand, and one strap of a faded yellow bra. He had to look away because he was starting to get hard. But even so, he could smell her; and when she moved, she bumped his shoulder, and he wanted to take her face in his and inhale her and taste her tongue in his mouth. She was probably a great kisser.

Trenton was more than a little hard, now, and he shifted and thought of dead things, and old ghosts, and poor, shivery girls, full of holes, trapped behind walls.

Katie finished lighting the circle of candles. "Maestro," she said, slipping her lighter back into her pocket. "Lights off."

Even sitting, Trenton managed to reach the frayed cord that

controlled the only light in the attic: a bare, wire-encased bulb, like something you would find in a prison. With the lights off, Katie's face looked very different, full of strange planes and angles, lit up imperfectly in the candlelight. Dark shadows climbed the walls, and Trenton thought of a lamp he'd had as a kid, which had sent images of zoo animals skating across his ceiling when it revolved. Sitting in the attic with Katie, surrounded by candles, was a little like sitting in the middle of the lamp.

"All right." Katie inhaled deeply and closed her eyes. Trenton kept his eyes open, watching her. For several seconds, she said nothing. She looked thinner in the darkness, and younger, too. Her eyelashes were very long, resting on her cheeks.

She opened her eyes again. "Well?"

"Well, what?"

She made a little gesture of impatience. "You have to talk to them. You have to call them out."

"This was your idea," Trenton said, who could think of nothing he wanted to do less. He still had the sensation of being watched, and he imagined dark eyes growing in the corners like tumors. He wanted to go downstairs with Katie, sit on the couch, put in a movie. Maybe she'd sit right next to him, so their thighs would touch again.

"Trenton." Katie looked at him as though she were a teacher, and he a disappointing student. "I can't talk to them. They won't listen to me."

Trenton felt the small touch against his neck again, light as a breath, and shivered. "Why do you think they'll listen to me?" he said.

Katie leaned forward. Trenton could see small points of candlelight reflecting in her eyes. "You almost died," she said. "You were one of them for a while. Haven't you ever seen a movie about ghosts?"

He knew she was kidding, but he couldn't even fake a smile.

Was Katie right? He had almost died, and now he could speak with the dead. Trenton thought of those moments after Robbie had swerved and for one second the guardrail, and the trees beyond it, were lit up like a still photograph—the feeling of dark hands and of warmth and also of silence, like a kite detached from its string, suspended in still air.

He'd been a ghost. For a few seconds, he'd been a ghost.

Katie must have interpreted his silence for resistance. "Fine," she said. "I'll do it. Give me your hands. And close your eyes. No cheating."

Trenton wiped off his hands quickly on the back of his jeans before allowing her to take them, in case his palms were sweaty. He pretended to close his eyes but tried to look, a little, from under his lashes.

"No cheating," Katie repeated, and so he really closed them.

"Spirits of this house," she said, making her voice deep and loud. Trenton opened his eyes; he was sure he'd heard a stifled giggle. But Katie squeezed his hands urgently, so he closed them again.

"Spirits of this house," she said again, using the same booming voice as a movie narrator or game show host, "we call on you to speak. Announce yourselves to us!"

Silence. They sat with their eyes closed, listening to the gentle creaking of the wood. Trenton was aware of the feel of Katie's fingers on the inside of his wrists, and the soft warmth of her hands.

"What's supposed to happen?" Trenton asked, after a bit.

"Shhh."

He opened his eyes. Katie was very still and very serious and reminded him of a small animal listening for predators.

"I don't think—"

"Shhh." She opened her eyes again to glare at him.

Then he heard it: a rustling sound from one of the corners. Katie must have heard it, too.

"What was that?" she asked excitedly, dropping his hands. "Did you hear that?"

"Probably mice," Trenton said, trying to sound calm. It probably was, anyway; he'd seen a whole pile of mouse shit when he was moving the dresser.

"Close your eyes. Come on." She seized his hands again, before he had a chance to wipe them off. "Spirits of the other realm," she said, assuming that voice again. "We come to you as friends, as fellow creatures of the dark . . . "

This time he was sure he heard a snicker.

"We ask that you open your secrets to us . . . "

Underneath Katie's words, rising to the surface of his hearing, like objects surging up on the tide, he suddenly heard a profusion of voices.

"This is *her* doing."

"Don't be mad, Alice. A little séance never hurt anyone."

"Stop your idiocy, Sandra, please. For once in your death."

"Testy, testy."

"Please. Both of you. Stop it."

They came from all sides, from everywhere and nowhere. Little points of pain exploded in Trenton's head, as though each word were an arrow fired into his brain. He dropped Katie's hands and, without realizing it, cried out. It was worse than a migraine. It was worse than anything.

"Trenton," Katie's voice seemed distant now, muffled behind layers of cloth. "What is it? Are you okay?"

The other voices were real, sharp, finely tuned, louder and clearer than he'd ever heard them.

"Look at him. Just look at him. And you still claim he doesn't hear?"

"Calm down, Alice, don't get your panties in a bunch."

"Everything will be ruined . . . "

There were fists pummeling Trenton's brain, and colored lights blooming behind his eyes. He had to get out. He had to get away. He started to stagger to his feet, on legs that no longer moved the way he wanted, a puppet trying to move its wooden limbs. Katie was still shouting from behind her layers of cloth, but he could no longer hear what she was saying. He managed to stand, finally, and cracked his head on the ceiling.

"Leave us alone. Can you hear me, Trenton? *Leave us alone.*"

Trenton opened his mouth to reply, no longer caring if Katie thought he was crazy. He didn't care about anything but making the pain stop.

But before he could speak, or shout, he felt a motion in the air—as though a dozen windows had been opened at once. At the same time, lightly—just lightly—the pressure of a hand on his back.

He stumbled. And then the candles turned over. Not singly, but all at once, so that in one split second, in a time too quick to register, the blanket was on fire and there was smoke unfurling like ribbons from the ground and Katie was screaming.

"Trenton!" Katie's terror cut through the muffling, through the fog in Trenton's brain, through the *other* voice, receding now but still distinct, repeating the same words, over and over.

"What have you done, Alice? What the hell did you do?"

AMY

It was fun to hide, even though she had to sit in a little ball on the floor, and it was cold in the attic and also smelled weird. She had to be very careful to be quiet because that was how people found you, if you moved a lot or made sounds. That was how Amy always found her mom when they played hide-and-seek because Mommy didn't know how to sit still and also she always hid in the same spot, under the bed.

Mommy wasn't a good hider but Amy was. She could hide for hours without moving hardly and stay quiet as a mouse or even quieter. It was fun to watch people when they couldn't see you, like being God or the Eye of Judgment in *The Raven Heliotrope*, which was invisible but there in the curve of the sky and everywhere at once, so the whole world was mapped on the inside of its eyeball.

Back home, Amy had found a little hole that went from her closet through to her mother's closet and sometimes she hid there when Mommy thought she was doing something else, like napping or watching TV, and then she liked to watch her mom being her mom when she thought she was all alone and Amy wasn't there to be the daughter.

Except one time there was a stranger there with her mom, a man, and Mommy was naked, and he was naked and ugly and Amy didn't like looking at him. But Mommy had kissed him and made little noises like Brewster, the neighbor's dog, when he was about to pee on the floor. Amy didn't like that and she was glad the man went away and never came back, but now she didn't like to watch her mom so much anymore.

Amy didn't understand what Trenton and the dead girl were doing, but she thought maybe Trenton was trying to make Grandpa come back to life like the dead girl did. It was fun to watch even if she couldn't see that good because she was hiding behind a stack of big cardboard boxes and could see only through a little crack between them.

But then Trenton got mad and was holding his head like her nana did in the mornings if you woke her up by talking too loud, and the dead girl was calling out, and Amy started to get scared but she didn't want to move because if Trenton saw her he'd be even madder.

And then there was fire and she knew it was fire because Trenton kept saying it and also because she'd seen it before, in Nana's house in wintertime and also this one time Mommy tried to cook dinner and something happened and then there was fire on the stove. And Mommy screamed *stay back, Amy, stay back,* and pressed Amy back far against the wall while she sprinkled white stuff on the fire to make it go away.

So Amy stayed back and didn't make a sound because that was what Mommy told her to do and because she didn't want Trenton to be mad. She pressed her knees to her chest and stayed small, and quiet.

A L I C E

In *The Raven Heliotrope,* I wrote a scene about a fire: the palace of the Innocents burns down after it's raided by marauding Nihilis. The Innocents outsmart them and flee through a hidden tunnel to safety. They use magic to lock the palace doors, entrapping the Nihilis, and Penelope asks her pet dragon to burn the whole place down, so the Nihilis can't desecrate it. *The fire was like white ribbons, reaching into the sky.* I was very pleased with that sentence, and especially pleased with that image, of the white ribbons.

These flames aren't like ribbons at all. They're like mouths, like greedy fingers, like something alive: leaping, running up the walls, swallowing boxes and broken furniture.

"Are you proud of yourself?" Sandra's voice is like the hiss and pop of the flames. "You'll kill them all."

I can't answer. I can't speak at all. I'm breaking apart on billows of smoke: memories are floating up from distant, buried places. Throwing up, day after day, in the toilet, clutching the porcelain for support; sheets stained with blood and water; the willow tree running its long thin fingers along the ground, as though searching, searching for something.

"What's going to happen?" The new ghost sounds like she's about to cry. "Are they going to burn? Are we going to burn?"

Trenton has managed to extinguish the blanket. But the fire has already spread too far. It jumps from surface to surface, skates across the old wooden bureau, hooks onto the low-beamed ceiling, and starts its climb.

Katie is on her hands and knees, looking for something. Trenton tries to pull her backward, toward the stairs. She wrenches away from him.

"My phone," she says. She is wide-eyed, sweaty. "I need to find my phone."

"Forget about that." Trenton, coughing, grabs her elbow, but she shakes him off again.

"Do something," Sandra is practically shrieking. "You got them into this mess."

I open my mouth; my voice is the sound of smoke. "It's too late," I say.

Murderer. The word reaches me faintly. Sandra's voice, or a voice from long ago, from beneath the willow tree.

AMY

Amy's throat hurt and she was hot, and she wanted to run downstairs and get in bed, and she wanted her mommy. But there was no way out. Everything was on fire, and she couldn't see, and she couldn't make herself any smaller, but the fire was sniffing around her shoes like a mouse except it wasn't a mouse, it was something that would kill you.

Amy was going to die and go in the ground and maybe she would never, ever wake up.

She began to cry. And crying hurt her throat even more, which made her cry harder. She was all alone in the dark and the fire, and she was going to go in the dirt and there would be bugs there. She curled up in a ball on the floor and tried to be so small even the fire wouldn't find her.

She was the best hider. Mommy always said so.

It was very hot, like Mommy had put too many blankets on the bed.

She was tired.

Something moved. Someone shouted.

Amy's eyes were heavy, and it took her a long time to open them. The girl, the dead girl, was looking at her through smoke thick like dark water.

"Oh my God," the dead girl said.

The dead girl went away, and Amy closed her eyes again. But then the dead girl was back, somehow. She'd walked straight through the fire. Maybe because she was dead and she wasn't afraid.

The dead girl was lifting Amy. Amy wanted to ask what it was like to be dead, but she couldn't make her tongue move and her head hurt too bad and she was so tired.

"Shhh," the dead girl said. "It's okay. You're going to be okay."

Her hair smelled like flowers.

M I N N A

It took Minna two days to work up the courage to climb up into the attic and assess the damage; then she did it only because her mom reminded her they would not be in Coral River much longer. When she finally managed it, she thought for one confused second it must have snowed. Then she realized it was cottonseed. Cottonseed and bird shit. The roof was partly gone. Sunlight filtered down over the charred wood, the burned remains of old cardboard boxes and termite-riddled furniture, whatever had been stashed up here, all of it covered in a layer of white. Even now she could see the drift of cottonseed across the blue sky. A raven was hopping around among the rubbish, pecking, turning over scraps with its beak.

"Get out of here," Minna said, aiming a kick in its direction. It startled and went flapping, a blur of dark wings, into the sky.

Toadie appeared next to her a second later, carrying latex gloves and a box of 39-gallon industrial trash bags, like the kind Minna used for raking and carting leaves. "Looks like you got carpet-bombed," he said, toeing a bit of white-streaked wood with a shoe.

She hadn't cried at all since her dad died and didn't intend to. But seeing the evidence of the fire, the birds an occasional black blot against the sun, she felt an incredible, an immeasurable grief. Amy was safe. She knew that. The doctor had told her she would be fine—no asthma even. But Minna couldn't stop thinking about what could have happened, what had almost happened, how close they had come.

Unimaginable tragedy. She'd heard that expression, somewhere, in an article about a mother who lost her child in an accident. But Minna *could* imagine it, in vivid detail, and she had been ever since Trenton called her, breathless, half senseless, two nights earlier. Fire, fire. That's all she remembered hearing, and the sharp cry of sirens in the background. Fire.

When Amy had grabbed the phone and started to sob, Minna's knees nearly gave out. She'd always thought that was just an expression, but it wasn't. She actually felt her legs simply stop working, like they'd been vaporized.

Still, the fear stayed with her. She'd had a dream the night before they were all on a roller-coaster ride, hurtling through the darkness, and sparks kept grinding out from under the wheels. She hated it when her subconscious churned out such obvious metaphors.

She couldn't even masturbate. She'd tried yesterday, in bed, in the shower, even in the study, now empty of everything but furniture, thinking that might be the problem, the source of the horrible tenseness inside of her, a swollen feeling, like she was filling slowly with steam. But she couldn't even get close. Pleasure came in a short initial wave and then petered out. She worked her own hand so hard against her body that she was left feeling raw, with a headache from gritting her teeth.

"You okay?" Toadie said. He put a hand on her arm, so his fingers grazed the inside of her elbow. She tried to pretend it excited her and turned to him, forcing a smile.

"I'm fine," she said. "Thank you. For helping."

"You know I could never say no to you," he said. He had little webbed lines by his eyes when he smiled now. He was a lot larger. But otherwise he looked just the same.

Two weeks ago she wouldn't have said she'd been in love with Toadie in high school—prom weekend she'd ended up fucking his friend Peter Contadino in the bathroom—but now she was beginning to think that maybe he was the only person she had *ever* truly loved. She was remembering all the good times: the gentleness of his touch, as if he was always afraid she might shatter; staying up on his roof to watch the sun touch everything in turn, making each house, valley, and hill real again, like God bringing nameless things out of the dark. While her parents were negotiating the terms of their separation—which was just as complex and entangled as their marriage—Minna had practically moved into Danny's house, sleeping most nights on the pull-out sofa in his basement. She remembered how she had once woken in the middle of the night to find him sleeping next to her, shirtless, one hot arm slung around her waist, his chest pressed to her back. Thinking he finally wanted to have sex, she reached for him. But he stopped her. "You were crying in your sleep," he'd whispered, and for a moment she was rigid with embarrassment, with fear. He had stroked her hair until she fell asleep, as if she were a child; and they had never mentioned it again.

"You got a roof guy?" Danny asked, passing her a pair of latex gloves. "I got a roof guy, if you need one."

That was, Minna thought, the essence of Toadie. He had a roof guy. Some things never changed. She didn't know whether it was comforting or depressing.

Maybe she could be in love with Danny again. Maybe that was it. She could fix whatever was broken, get married, learn how to fold socks and make casseroles or whatever normal wives did. She tried to imagine living with Danny, staying with him, but could call up nothing but an image of his bedroom when they were teenagers—the rumpled NY Rangers sheets and plastic blinds, the mason jar full of sea glass he'd had on his windowsill since he was a kid.

Just like she couldn't really picture screwing him. She'd decided she *would* screw him, she should; it was only right. Like old times, except in the old times they'd never done more than kiss and fumble around. But he wasn't gay. He was recently separated; he had a daughter a little older than Amy. So that was okay; he could obviously get it up.

But she just couldn't picture it. Whenever she tried, she imagined only a blur of flesh, and an amalgam of various men and places and bedrooms: pink fleshy stomachs and sweating hands and the sounds of panting.

"What happened, anyway?" Danny moved away from her. "It looks like something . . . exploded." He craned his neck to look at the hole in the roof. "Nice view, at least."

"I don't know," she said. "Trenton wouldn't give me a straight answer." She felt it again, the steam pressure of anger with nowhere to go.

(*I was with a friend,* Trenton had said, and Minna had said, *What friend? You have no friends.* And he'd shut up and stared at her, wounded and reproachful, as if *she'd* done something wrong.

After a minute, he'd blurted, *It was a séance.*

And she had felt a fist in her chest, in her throat, everywhere. How long had it been building up? She couldn't keep track. *A séance,* she repeated, and he looked away. *For what? For that stupid ghost story?*

It's real, he said, his voice getting high-pitched. *It's real, Minna. You almost killed Amy.*

Well, I didn't, did I? I got her out.

She'd slapped him then. Hard. But it didn't help the tightness, everywhere, like she would explode. Maybe this is what a spark felt like, just before it became fire: like it could destroy the whole universe.)

"Poor guy," Danny said. "He must be lonely up here."

"We're all lonely up here," Minna said quickly, without intending to.

"Hard to believe you're ever lonely, Min," Danny said. He touched her hand quickly. "You were always the most popular girl in town."

Minna turned away from him. She felt nauseated, looking at the ruins of the attic and the sky and all the cottonseed floating down. She was *always* lonely. That was the problem. It was like a hunger.

She'd thought having Amy would help and it did, for a while; but Amy was growing up now.

Danny squatted and began sifting through the mess. His jeans were a little too short, and she could see his socks—athletic socks, a little yellowed—but she pretended not to notice. He looked older than he should have; he was only twenty-nine. But she felt older than she was—she felt so tired.

"Look at this." From the ashes, he extracted something colorful. It was a pink sweatshirt with black skulls all over it. One of the sleeves was burned away. "It isn't yours, is it?"

"No." She thought about what Trenton said, about being with a friend. But where could he have met anyone? He had barely left the house. "It's probably been there for years," she said. "Trash it." But the sweatshirt had reminded her. "Any luck on the girl—Vivian? The one from Boston?"

"Ongoing." He shuffled over, still squatting, and began sorting and bagging, sorting and bagging. It was nice to watch his fingers work. He'd always had nice hands, and long thin fingers that seemed to belong to someone different. "Her parents are back from Africa, so we should have more luck soon." Minna could tell he enjoyed talking as if he belonged to the investigation, as if it were his. All men liked to feel important. Her father had demanded it, insisted on it, squeezed it out of every interaction and conversation like someone wringing water from a towel. "It's no accident she came up here. Her parents spent two summers in this area when she was a little girl. Who knows. Maybe she kept in touch with some people. Maybe a boy."

"How long has it been now? Two weeks?" Minna didn't know why, but she suddenly had a vicious urge for him to say it: she was dead, she was obviously dead. "You don't really think she's still alive, do you?"

He didn't answer, and he didn't look at her, either. There was a long moment of silence. "I remember your dad, you know," he said abruptly. "What'd he do again? Paper, right?"

"Cardboard, mostly," she said. "Cardstock, cereal boxes, things like that. But he sold the company ages ago."

"He was a nice guy," Danny said.

"He was an asshole," Minna said.

He acted as if he hadn't heard her. "I remember sophomore year we were all hanging out in the living room. Your parents were upstairs. And we were being so careful to hide our beers . . . O'Malley was putting the empties in the trunk of his car. Then your dad came down and we freaked. We thought he was going to be mad. But he poured out some scotch and gave us all a try." He laughed again. "He just wanted to be part of the fun."

"He wanted to show off his scotch," Minna said. Everything she saw, everything she was turning over was trash. They would need more bags. Danny was moving too slowly.

"I thought it was nice. He let us sleep over. Like, fifteen kids in the living room. I remember the Miller twins didn't want to crash, so he drove them home. It was probably two in the morning and freezing cold. Remember that?"

"No," Minna answered honestly. She tried to picture her dad starting up the car, breath condensing, wearing his old down jacket over his striped pajamas, maybe an old pair of waders he'd grabbed before starting out the door. Breaking off ice from the windshield in the middle of the night, hands chapped, the wind blowing hard pellets of snow over the yard. So he could drive her friends home. She didn't like to think about it; it made her feel she had missed something critical, something elemental, about him.

"I remember how he showed up at my mom's house every day for, like, two weeks after your parents split and you were crashing with us most of the time. You wouldn't talk to him. But he kept showing up."

She wished she could tell him to shut up. Her hands were shaking.

"And how proud he was at graduation. He must have taken a million pictures. *Look for the most beautiful girl in the room, and that's my daughter.*"

She didn't remember any of it. She felt a sudden wrench of grief. She realized, horrifyingly, she was on the verge of tears.

"Do you think—" Her voice broke a little and she swallowed. "Do you think some people aren't meant to be happy?" She didn't even know what she was going to ask before the words were spoken.

Danny shuffled a little closer. They were still squatting, both of them, among the drift of ashes. It would have been funny if it didn't feel so awful.

"Hey," he said. "Hey. Look at me." She managed to. His eyes were nice and brown and unremarkable, like the rest of him—one hundred percent normal. He might be the only normal person she knew.

"You're going to be happy, Minniemouse," he said, his old nickname for her; then he put one hand on her cheek and brushed away the dampness with his thumb, which was calloused and comfortable feeling.

Suddenly she *could* imagine it, and she knew that this was the answer; and she was kissing him, hard, pushing her tongue onto his, trying to get deeper, to push into him, to find the softness of that big black space where she could disappear.

"Wait," he said, pulling away, gasping a little.

"No." She grabbed his face, straddled him, pushed her breasts against him. Down, she wanted to go down, into a place of quiet and breathlessness and heartbeats, into a place where she was alone and at peace.

"Wait. Wait." This time he put both hands on her shoulders and pushed her backward. He wiped his mouth with his hand, like she was contaminated, and Minna saw pity in his eyes and felt suddenly cold. "Stop."

"What's the matter with you?" Her voice sounded like a stranger's, or like a voice heard from far away: small, strangled. "Are you gay or something?"

"I'm married, Minna." He was still looking at her in that pitying way, like she was a child and he was breaking the news about a dead kitten.

"You said you were separated."

"Minna . . . " He sighed and rubbed his forehead, where he was going bald. "That's not how things work."

She stood up and felt the floor seesaw underneath her. She wanted to crush him, to humiliate him, to let him know how little she cared about him. She wanted to reach inside him and find what was soft and twist, and twist. "It's okay. Everyone thought you were gay in high school, too."

Something flickered in his eyes. Anger. Minna felt triumphant.

But instead of yelling, he simply stood up. "See you later, Minna," he said, in a tired voice, and made for the stairs.

"That's why I fucked Peter Contadino," she burst out. She wasn't thinking straight. It was like being drunk, like falling into a long tunnel of unconsciousness. "At prom. Because you wouldn't. Because everyone said you were gay."

He paused at the top of the stairs. His spine went rigid. Now he would turn around. Now he would come back, yell at her, look at her.

But he didn't. He didn't say anything at all. Minna's whole world teetered on the edge of a long second. Then Danny continued downstairs, leaving Minna alone.

AMY

Secrets were for grown-ups. That's what Uncle Trenton said. And Amy had a secret now, and that meant she was all grown up like Uncle Trenton and like Mommy.

The secret was about the dead girl, who had a name, which was Katie. But Amy couldn't tell anyone about the dead girl, not her name or anything else about her, like the fact that she smelled like flowers and not dirt.

"Remember, Amy," Uncle Trenton had said. "I'm counting on you. This is big-girl stuff."

Amy promised because she liked the dead girl and didn't want to get her in trouble. The dead girl had carried Amy away from the fire and had stood holding hands with her outside while they listened to the *scream scream* of fire engines in the distance and Trenton shouted on the phone, and when Amy's socks got all wet with dew, the dead girl helped her take them off and even took off her own shoes and socks, too, so they could have bare feet together.

"Shhh," she said, when the trucks were so close Amy could see the trees lit up red and white and blue from all the sirens. The dead girl smiled and pressed a finger to Amy's lips, and the finger tasted a little like smoke. "I was never here."

Amy watched her disappear into the darkness, holding her shoes in one hand.

PART VII

THE BATHROOMS

A L I C E

It has been four days since the fire, and since Sandra first decided on the silent treatment. Even though I've spent decades trying unsuccessfully to get her to shut up, now that she has, I find that I miss her conversation.

I went through the same thing when Ed died. I'd longed for his death, prayed for it, fantasized about it the way some people do about tropical vacations. One time, after a bad storm, we were confined to the house for four straight days; we both must have gone a little crazy. Ed was taking shots from our bedroom window at the crows huddled on the bare branches of the sycamore tree across the field, and missing every time but one; later he fell asleep, whiskey-drunk, with his arm still around the shotgun. In the middle of the night I got out of bed and stood above him, staring at that barrel gleaming sharp as a promise, staring at the shadowed blot of his head, thinking, *I could do it. I could really do it.* I stood there for what felt like hours, until my arms ached, until my toes were numb with cold. Then he rolled over and his face moved into the square of moonlight on his pillow and I drew back, ashamed of myself, horrified.

Then it happened. March 22, 1972. I was making coffee and three fried eggs and bacon; Maggie was living in San Francisco by then. Ed was upstairs, shaving. We'd had a bad fight the night before. He'd come home late, drunk. I'd shoved my fingers down my throat to be sick so he wouldn't force himself on me.

I heard a heavy thud, like a sack of new dough dropping. I found him on the bathroom floor with his trousers off and a razor in his hand, and a small bit of toilet paper clinging to his chin, where he'd nicked himself and tried to stop the bleeding. He died even before he reached the hospital.

The doctors told me later it was a heart attack. It happened that way sometimes, they told me. Too much drinking, too much fat in his diet, too much stress. We're all just a collection of wires pulled tight, charged beyond capacity—a tangle of plugs and valves, waiting for a surge to take down the whole system.

He hadn't even finished his shave. When I came into the bathroom, I saw there was still hair stubbling the right side of his face. And after I called the doctor, I don't know what got into me, but I sat there and finished for him. I sat on the ground and pulled his head into my lap and finished so he could have his last good shave. He liked a good shave.

I hadn't expected to miss him. I'd expected only relief. And I was relieved, more than I could say or express—sometimes I'd find myself laughing, and I had to be very careful at the funeral and in front of neighbors to seem sad, when sometimes all I wanted to do was sing. At night I walked the house in the dark and touched all the things that belonged to me: the sofa he would never sit on again, the chairs he would never knock over, all the dishes he would never throw.

But sometimes I woke from the middle of a dream and found myself reaching for him or rolling over toward the place his warmth should have been. The house was so quiet, so still, I listened unconsciously for the sound of his footsteps, the door slamming, the roar of his voice or his laughter from the living room. For months I expected him to call out to me to bring him a beer, hurry up already, where's dinner. For months I threw burned bacon into the trash thinking of Ed, thinking of how foul a mood he would be in, before remembering that he wasn't coming down to breakfast. I had carried the weight of him for so long that without it I felt dizzy. I guess it's the same way trees grow around the very vines that are killing them, so they're strangled and sustained all at once. After a long time, even pain can be a comfort.

I didn't really, deep down, believe he was dead. At least, I didn't believe he was gone forever. I was constantly waiting for him to come back, and dreading it, too, and even the dread was like grief.

Ed liked to smoke his pipe in the bathroom. He'd grown up in rural Virginia and shared an outhouse with five brothers; I think the bathroom might have been his favorite room in the house. Sometimes he'd flush two, three times in a row. He liked the sound of it, he said. And even in deep winter he'd crack open a window and sit there with his pants around his ankles, puffing on his pipe, so over time the wallpaper went yellow with it.

Two months after he died, I woke up in the middle of the night and I knew: he'd come back. I could smell his pipe. The smoke was seeping into the bedroom, clinging to the weave of the sheets. And I knew I had only to push open the bathroom door and I'd see him, his pale thighs and knees like doorknobs, his nightshirt wrinkled and the wispy tufts of his hair sticking straight up, like the feathers of a baby bird. Go back to bed, Alice, he'd say. Can't you leave a man in peace for even five minutes?

But there was nothing: nothing but the toilet, and the bath, and the old yellow wallpaper, and the window, closed. And it was then, in that moment, that I really understood that I was alone and I would be alone.

I sat that night on the toilet seat. I leaned my forehead against the wallpaper. The smell of his pipe was so strong, I could nearly taste it. I stayed there until morning.

T R E N T O N

Trenton was nearly out of time.

Seeing the ghost, and learning about the woman whose brains had gone splat in the den, had made Trenton temporarily reconsider his plan to die. For a few short days he'd felt that he had a purpose; there was a mystery for him, layered underneath the visible world, like a gift nestled inside folds and folds of tissue paper. He'd felt that everything was connected: coming back to Coral River, meeting Katie, and the ghost. Or ghosts. Whoever they were.

Katie had been . . . what? A friend? A kind-of friend? He didn't know.

Now Katie was gone. Vanished. The day after the fire, while Caroline, Minna, and Amy were at the doctor, making sure Amy wouldn't be asthmatic or psychologically scarred for life, or whatever Minna was worried about, Trenton had once again walked the mile and a half to Katie's house, as he had for the party, and found all the doors locked, the house dark, the driveway empty—as if no one had ever lived there at all. He had rung the doorbell anyway and pounded on the door so loudly that a group of birds had startled up from the field and gone cawing together into the sky, like a shadow breaking apart and re-forming.

It occurred to him he hadn't even gotten her number, though

she had gotten his at her party. *Write your number on my arm,* she'd said, uncapping a blue marker with her teeth and pulling up her sleeve. He'd been so happy he nearly got his own number wrong.

But no matter how much he stared at his phone and willed it to ring—or locked it up in a drawer and told himself he didn't care either way—his phone stayed quiet. Maybe, he thought, Katie had never even existed; she could have been a figment of his imagination.

Except that Amy remembered her. He'd had to swear Amy to secrecy, so she wouldn't tell. Katie couldn't get in trouble; she told him so herself.

Minna and his mom were treating him like he was a psych case, like he might go on a shooting rampage if they said the wrong thing. Minna thought there was something wrong with his brain—he'd heard her say so to their mom. She thought he'd started the fire, maybe even deliberately. He wasn't allowed to be alone with Amy anymore. She hadn't said so explicitly, but any time he went to check on Amy or play a game, Minna suddenly materialized, eyes sharp and worried, and whisked Amy away for a meal or a nap or a walk.

Maybe he had started the fire. Maybe it was all his fault. Maybe he was really, truly crazy.

His father's memorial service was tomorrow. The ghosts didn't leave him alone, even for a second, anymore.

"I wish they wouldn't fight so much." She was sitting in the bathtub, or maybe not sitting. It was hard to tell, since she didn't have a clear silhouette. She was just a shadow on the tiles, shifting in the sun. "My mom and my stepdad were always fighting. Then he left. My real dad left, too, before I was born. I never even knew him." Then: "I wish they'd just stop."

She talked to him this way, in sudden bursts, half nonsensical, about people he didn't know and places he had never seen, brief and jumbled outpourings of old memories and whispered complaints.

He still had trouble figuring out how old she was. Sometimes she seemed as old as he was and sometimes just a kid. She had told him she was sixteen; based on what he knew about girls of that age, which admittedly wasn't much, he guessed that she was younger.

She hadn't told him her name, either. Sometimes she claimed to be the missing girl, Vivian. But when he had called her by that name, she had suddenly burst into tears—breaking apart in waves, like a pattern of broken sunlight across a wall—and sobbed that no one knew who she really was, no one would ever know her again, she was dead and she would be forgotten. It made Trenton want to die and strangle her and hold her all at once.

The other voices were still going, too.

"For a newbie, you got a lot of opinions."

"Leave her alone, Sandra. She's a child."

"I wasn't talking to you."

"You can't avoid me forever."

"Hey. Newbie. Tell Alice to buzz off."

"Shut up, all of you!" Trenton didn't realize he'd spoken out loud until there was a sudden silence. He had been trying to count. Now he had to start over.

There was a knocking on the bathroom door. "Trenton?" his mom called out. "Trenton, are you all right?"

"Fine." He shook all the pills back into his palm and began a recount.

"You've been in there a long time," she said.

"I have to dump," he replied.

He heard his mom sigh. "Language," she said, and moved off.

The ghost went on as though nothing had happened. "I'm not a *child*," she continued. "My birthday's in July. My mom said we could go anywhere I wanted. I asked to go to Six Flags." She was quiet for a moment. "Do you think . . . do you think my mom misses me?"

"Please," Trenton said. His head was going to burst; the voices were like insects burrowing through his brain. "Please." He didn't want to care but he couldn't help it; the world was fucked.

Nine. He had nine pills so far.

"That isn't enough to kill you," the ghost said. She was suddenly next to him. He hated that, how quickly she could move. And her touch was like a shiver, like something going wrong in his stomach. "You'll just throw up."

"How do you know that?" He was annoyed because she was right. He'd looked online and realized he needed at least twenty, to be safe. But he couldn't take too many from Minna at a time.

"I saw a story like that on TV." She paused. "It's not fair," she said. She was trembling. They weren't touching anymore, but he could feel it—cold air, the hair on his arms standing up.

"No," he said. He longed, suddenly, to touch her—this fragile, needy, broken child, to kiss the top of her head and pull her down into his lap, as he did with Amy when she was having a bad dream. But she wasn't Amy, and she was only half a child. And, of course, he couldn't touch her. He couldn't even see her face clearly: just shifting patterns of light and shadow, a faint impression of hollow prettiness.

"When you die," she said. "We'll be friends, won't we?" She hesitated, then said shyly, "We can be together all the time."

He felt a sudden wave of panic. He hadn't thought about it like that. He'd thought only of sleep, and of Minna sobbing and blaming herself; and the kids at Andover lighting candles in his name. What if death turned out to be just as awful and depressing as life? What if he was just as powerless?

"Don't count on it," Trenton said. "I'm not planning to stick around." But he had trouble pouring the pills back into an empty bottle of calamine lotion, where he was hiding them, and dropped two. He had to get down on his hands and knees to retrieve them.

"You'll stay," she said. "You'll stay, and then I'll always have someone to talk to."

She grew quiet, and Trenton felt her withdraw, saw her shadow-self shifting across the cold tiles, and the old shower curtain, spotted with mold. Soon, she wouldn't even be a shadow. She would be nothing but a voice, telling stories no one could hear.

"I'm lonely," she said, in a whisper.

He placed the bottle in the back of the medicine cabinet, which smelled like old Band-Aids and nail polish and the bubblegum scent of kids' Tylenol. It comforted him. He thought of Katie leaning forward as she reached behind him to light a candle, her breast bumping his shoulder.

"Me, too," he said.

S A N D R A

Trenton, Minna, and Caroline are locked in separate bathrooms. And not one of them is even taking a piss.

Trenton's shaking out pills into his palm again, like maybe the number magically doubled in the past two hours. Caroline dials and hangs up. Dials and hangs up.

And Minna is in the bathroom with the FedEx man.

It reminds me of an old nursery rhyme I used to like: The king was in his counting house, counting out his money; the queen was in the parlor, eating bread and honey. The maid was in the garden, hanging up the clothes . . .

I always thought it was kind of a fun story. All those people, busy with different work, happy—except for the poor maid, who gets her nose pecked off by a blackbird.

But really, they're all just shut up in different rooms, trying to keep busy so they won't notice they're alone. Just like the Walkers in their big old house, everyone locked up behind closed doors and only speaking to each other through the walls.

Everyone waiting for a blackbird. Or for the roof to collapse.

Yes, Minna says. *Yes. Yes.*

A L I C E

"Close your eyes, Vivian," I say—an automatic command, and a stupid one, since I know she can't. Minna's backside, bare, is cupped in the sink; the FedEx man's fleshy fingers are squeezing her skin. I wish I could give her a sharp poke. But I don't have that kind of control. Not yet.

"My name isn't Vivian," the new ghost says. "And I *know* what sex is."

"Newbie," Sandra says. "Tell Alice to stop being a prude."

"I'm not a prude." I'm tired of Sandra's abuse. Tired of Minna's feet kicking in the air, and the sight of the FedEx man's navy blue pants. Tired of all the Walkers, and the constant buzzing presence of their needs and smells and voices and *aliveness*—a sensation like mosquitoes zapped to death in our light fixtures, ants running over our cabinets, termites chewing us slowly, from the inside out.

I came so close to release. Never, in all the years of my death, have I been closer than I was in those few minutes, with the flames spreading, building warmth through our body, and the smoke like a gentle hand, pushing away memory, pushing away thought.

"Everyone needs a little action sometimes. You know, they

used to treat women for hysteria by setting them up with vibrators. A little orgasm now and again . . . "

"Ew," Vivian says.

If only the fire had spread. "It amazes me," I say, "that your stupidity only seems to increase with time." I say to Vivian, "Tell Sandra that her stupidity—"

"I'm *not Vivian*."

"Did you ever have a vibrator?" Sandra says to me, obviously enjoying herself. Minna slips; the FedEx man grunts and adjusts his grip. Her face is strained, rigid, like someone in the rictus of death. "It might have helped, you know. It might have shaken you loose, given you a little kick. Maybe then you wouldn't be such a sourpuss all the time."

"I had a husband." Minna is moaning now, a low, guttural sound. Her mouth forms a single word, again and again. *Please. Please. Please.* I think of Ed, and of Thomas, and of mornings when the nausea was a fist, punching up my breakfast, doubling me over the toilet.

"Right," Sandra scoffs. "A husband. A lampshade! Don't pretend you loved him."

"I would be more inclined to listen to you," I say, "if you'd had a lasting relationship with anyone—with anything—other than a bottle. How long was it before someone found your body? Was it two days? Or three?"

For a moment, Sandra is silent. In the quiet, Minna gasps, and the FedEx man grunts, and pushes, and says *any second now*.

"It was three days," Sandra says quietly. "And you're right, Alice. You're absolutely right. You had a husband. You had a daughter. You had a lover, too, before Maggie was born. Thomas, wasn't it?" Her voice is very low, very deliberate, and somehow I can sense what's coming, and I want to say don't; please, don't; but these words don't come, either.

And so she says it, still in that same lullaby voice, the question we have sworn, by silent agreement, that she would never ask—in the bathroom the FedEx man begins to howl, and Minna squeezes her eyes shut and digs her nails into his back and says *don't, no, don't.*

"What happened to his child, Alice?"

Rooms. Rooms I have loved in, walked in, remembered, mourned:

The narrow tiles of our bathroom floor in Boston, and steam rising from the bathtub, and my mother's arms, bare to the elbow.

My childhood bedroom, and the dolls clustered on the narrow shelf above my bed, and playing mommy to each of them in turn.

The coat hanger and the pills; the bathroom floor spotted with blood; cottonseed drifting through the open window and settling like snow in the sink.

PART VIII

THE LIVING ROOM

M I N N A

Normally Minna felt calmer after sex, empty, like the world after a blizzard—almost as if she didn't exist at all. But tonight she was full of a deep ache. He had been awful—Gary, Jerry, whatever his name was—but they were all awful, and she knew the ache wasn't physical. It was in her teeth and hair and breathing. It was the ache of something breaking apart, the covering of ice that she depended on, the layers of snow that kept her true self buried deep underground, warm, protected.

Toadie, *Danny,* still hadn't called her back. She must have left him fifteen messages by now, apologizing, then joking, then apologizing again. Nothing. She couldn't have said why it was so important. She was plagued by the continuous sense that she had forgotten something, had failed to do something critical. She triple-checked the arrangements for the memorial service. She imagined she heard Amy shouting, worried she'd forgotten to make her lunch, or give her a bath or her vitamins. Minna signed on to check her bank accounts twice a day, worried that her emergency savings had evaporated—not that she had much of anything to begin with. She set down her sunglasses and instantly forgot where she put them. She turned her phone on and off, and even had her mother send her a text to make sure her messages were working.

But the nagging feeling persisted. Something was wrong. Something was missing.

She'd been taking too much Valium—she was nearly out. She shook one of the remaining pills into her palm and swallowed it down with a sip of red wine. Vintage Bordeaux. The good stuff. The house was stocked: trays of cold cuts, carefully wrapped under thin films of plastic; bottles of gin and whiskey and vodka, arranged in neat rows in the dining room; platters of crescent-shaped cookies and sweaty-looking cubes of cheese; tinfoil trays of lasagna.

And cards—cards addressed in handwriting Minna didn't recognize, sent from people she didn't know, all bearing the same combination of words, *sorry,* and *loss,* and *grieving,* all words that seemed by now to her foreign and meaningless, almost inappropriate. She wanted it over and done. She wanted to get home. She thought she would fire Dr. Upshaw, her therapist, or break up with her, or whatever you did with shrinks.

There had been no healing, no demons laid to rest. There had been two bad fucks, a failed kiss, and a fire.

She felt no closer to her father, and even further from her mom and brother.

It was after eleven P.M. by the time Minna finished organizing the flower arrangements, mopping the floors, counting folding chairs, setting up the guest book, and threading a chain across the stairs to prevent guests from accessing the upper floors. She checked in on Amy for the fifth time—she was asleep, bundled in a sleeping bag on the floor of the now-empty study, her hair, still wet from her bath, scattered over the pillow. She'd been thrilled when Minna had told her they would have to camp downstairs for a bit. The upstairs bedrooms still reeked of smoke, and leaks came through the ceilings, where blackened holes and cracks as thick as a finger had appeared.

Trenton had set up in the basement—Minna didn't know how

he could stand it, and knew he was only proving a point, to get as far from Minna and their mom as possible. So much the better. She didn't trust him. There was something different about him since the accident, a look, a way of speaking, a desperateness she couldn't identify, and it was only getting worse. Her mom wouldn't see it. She never did. But he needed help.

They all needed help.

She went through the house, shutting off lights. Downstairs, she heard the muffled sounds of explosions—Trenton was probably playing that video game he liked, the one where you got points for shooting librarians and policemen. She closed the basement door firmly without bothering to call down to him, and the sounds of gunfire were silenced.

The smell of smoke was still following her. She kept imagining flames behind every closed door, smoke billowing down the staircase.

She wouldn't take another Valium. Not yet, when she had so few left.

In the living room, she switched on a lamp and almost screamed. Her mom was sitting in an armchair in the corner, totally still, in front of a bottle of Jameson.

"Jesus Christ, Mom." Her heart was racing. "What are you doing?" She registered that her mom had been sitting in the dark, apparently for a long time. Her eyes were very red. When Caroline brought a cigarette to her lips, Minna saw she was shaking. "You don't even smoke."

"I smoke sometimes," Caroline said, and she flicked her ashes inexpertly into a heavy crystal tumbler Minna had set out earlier for guests of the memorial, which was posed next to the bottle on a leather ottoman. Caroline had poured her whiskey into one of the tall water glasses, no ice.

"No, you don't," Minna said, crossing the room to haul open

the window. No wonder she had smelled smoke. "And you don't drink whiskey, either." Her mother stuck to vodka—colorless, odorless, like a South American poison in an old murder mystery that kills before anyone realizes it's been administered.

"Tonight calls for whiskey," Caroline said and tipped a little more into her glass. "Do you want some?"

"No," Minna said automatically. The wind smelled like wild heather and rain—a sweet smell that brought back a memory of getting caught in a downpour with her dad outside the supermarket; how they'd run together, laughing, sloshing through puddles that had sprung up in a moment, how the paper bags had gotten soaked through, collapsed, and they'd scattered groceries as they ran. She was tired. And she did want a drink. Badly. She turned away from the window. "Yes. I'll get a glass."

She returned to the dining room and took a tumbler from the sideboard—then, thinking better of it, she grabbed one of the tall glasses and used the tumbler instead for retrieving ice from the freezer. When she got back to the living room, her mom had lit another cigarette.

Minna sat down on the floor next to the ottoman. Her thighs ached, and her breasts from where Gary, or Jerry, had mauled them. But sitting cross-legged, barefoot, in front of her mom made her feel like a kid again and reminded her of childhood Christmases. There had been plenty of Christmases out in California, when they'd gone to church in sandals and T-shirts, opening presents while palm trees hailed them from outside. But nothing compared to the Christmases in Coral River, when the world was blotted out by white, and Trenton toddled through layers of discarded wrapping paper like an explorer fording a river.

The whiskey tasted awful, but left a good feeling in her stomach: a slow spread of warmth, a flushed feeling, like when someone really good-looking leaned in and touched your lower back. It had been a long time since she'd felt that way when a man touched her.

Maybe it had been forever.

They drank in silence for a bit. Minna's head began to feel pleasant and clouded.

"I was thinking about your father," Caroline said, out of nowhere. She was staring out the window. "I was thinking of what I would say tomorrow."

"Tell the truth," Minna says.

"How can I?" she said. "He was a cheater. And a liar. He was selfish." She shook her head. "But there were times . . . I do think he loved us. He did love us, in his way. As much as he could. I'm sure of it." Her voice broke.

Minna said nothing. She wasn't sure of it and had never been. Her throat was tight, and it was difficult to get the whiskey down.

"He was so proud of you." Caroline's words were getting slurry. "You *and* Trenton. When the accident happened . . . I couldn't even tell your father. He was already sick. It would have broken his heart."

"I doubt it," Minna said. She reached back through the cloud, through the fog, trying to resurrect memories of her father; but instead she kept picturing Mr. Hansley, and his wrinkled chino pants, and his soft voice whispering in her ear—"That's it, Minna. Just like that. Beautiful," as he rocked his erection against her back, and she sat stiff and terrified, moving nothing but her hands—playing Chopin's Étude in C Major, Bach's Concerto no. 7, as though she could escape up and out through the music.

Minna poured out more whiskey and was surprised to see they were already halfway through the bottle. She wanted to forget Mr. Hansley. She tried to press him back into the soft darkness of her mind, as she had tried then to ignore what was happening, to deny it—but he stayed, and his hardness stayed, resolute and undeniable, like an accusatory finger pointing at her, marking her.

Her father should have known. He should have protected her.

She had never once, in all her life, allowed herself to think the words—but they were there, suddenly, and she knew she was going to cry.

Caroline was still talking. "He called me every week, just to see how you were doing. You and Trenton. Sometimes he called every day."

"Why didn't he call me, then?" Minna turned to the window, too, fighting the squeeze in her throat, the sharp sudden pain behind her eyes. She took another long sip of whiskey. It didn't taste so bad anymore. It eased the tightness in her throat, too.

"He probably knew you wouldn't pick up," Caroline said. "You're busy. He knew that."

The window showed an indistinct reflection of the lamp and Minna's face, her eyes carved into black hollows. Outside, beyond the screen, she could hear the low song of crickets in the grass. What the hell did they sing for, she wondered? Probably something to do with mating. But it sounded like mourning to her.

"I got fired, Mom," Minna blurted out. She didn't turn to look at her mom's face. She couldn't stand it. She closed her eyes quickly and listened to the cricket song, constant as a tide, in and out, rising up to meet the darkness; bringing darkness down into the song. "I was screwing the accounts manager. My boss found out. Against company policy."

"Minna . . . " Caroline started to say.

But Minna found she couldn't stop, now that she had started to speak. The words, too, were like a tide, long suppressed, suddenly rolling out of her. "Remember when I worked at SKP? There it was the mail guy. And one of the interns."

"Minna, you really don't need to—"

"You want to know why Trenton hates me?" Minna turned, finally, to her mom. Caroline was framed perfectly by the lamplight, stiff-white, horrified, like an actress in a play. "Family weekend. Remember family weekend? I told you I ran into an old friend so you put Amy to bed. But I didn't. I didn't run into anybody. I—I went back to the dorms with one of the seniors. Conrad. He was only eighteen." She looked down at her hands. Her cheeks were burning, but she was surprised when she saw tears appear suddenly on her palms. She didn't know when she had started to cry.

"Trenton doesn't hate you," Caroline said.

Still the words were coming. And the tears, too. Minna couldn't remember the last time she'd cried. It must have been years. But it was like all that frozen stuff had finally cracked open, and now everything was running, pouring, bleeding out, like the ground during the first big thaw of the year. "I slept with Danny's best friend at prom. In the bathroom. I slept with a taxi driver once, in college. He was taking me to a friend's house for Christmas Eve, over break." The crickets were still singing; the note was swelling higher, louder, like a wave about to break. Like the high notes at the end of Bach's Solo for Cello in G Major: one of her favorite pieces of music. "And I hated piano. I hated Mr. Hansley. He used to—*rub* against me when I played. He made me put my hands on him. He made me put my hands all over him."

There. It was done. The cello hit the D note; the crickets stopped singing. Now that she'd said it, Minna felt suddenly empty. There was a long stretch of silence. She was afraid to look at her mom.

"Minna," Caroline said finally, in a voice that sounded very young. But she said nothing else. Minna knew she should be relieved or furious or disappointed—she should be something—but the tears had dried up as suddenly as they'd come, and she couldn't muster up the energy to feel anything.

Caroline picked up the pack of cigarettes, offered one to Minna, and took one for herself. The smoke burned her throat—a good, cleansing burn.

They sat, and they smoked. All around them, the house was silent. Gradually, the crickets began to sing again.

A L I C E

Morning, this morning, tastes like ashes and rosebuds. Minna and Caroline both fell asleep together on the air mattress, a single blanket bundled around them. Caroline snores into her pillow, and a bit of drool is clotting Minna's hair. The room smells like whiskey, and wind from the open window stirs the cigarette ashes scattered across the leather ottoman. Outside smells gray today, like rain.

Today is Richard Walker's memorial, a Saturday. What did Saturdays used to taste like? Like eggs and fried ham and the bitter smell of hair in heavy rollers. Like long quiet hours and making up after a fight. Like ointment and bruising. Like waiting, especially, for something—anything—to happen.

Thomas was going to come for me on a Friday night. He had last-minute things to take care of, and the letter still to write to his fiancée, breaking off their engagement. He told me not to expect him before dinnertime, and I avoided eating, even though I was hungry. I was too nervous, too excited, and I imagined we'd have our first dinner together as a real couple on the road. We'd pull off a no-name highway, miles away from anywhere, when the darkness was pulled tight over the whole world and even the stars seemed remote and unconcerned. We'd find a little restaurant where the food was cheap and awful and we would laugh about it later.

It was nearly ten P.M. by the time I started to worry. I called his house. No answer. Then I was reassured again. He must be on his way to meet me. But another hour passed, and he didn't come. It was a warm night, a perfect spring night, but I thought maybe the roads had been closed—a sudden flash flood, though it hadn't rained more than usual, a portion of the steep hillside by Hayes' farm giving way. Those things happened, back then.

But I would have heard. He would have called. Surely, someone would have called.

Hour after hour, I waited in the sitting room with the suitcase at my feet, while the darkness deepened and spread out around me, like an endless well closing in over my head. For a long time every sound—a coyote crying out, a sudden change in the wind—brought hope again. I imagined the crickets were an engine, drawing closer. I imagined the shush of the wind through the grass was his footstep.

Finally, the darkness began to ebb. The room began to assert itself: the sofa, the suitcase, the lamp, and the telephone all floated out of the deep purple shadows like objects thrown up on a tide, somehow—suddenly—unfamiliar. Deep inside my belly, the baby kicked, restless.

We had names already picked out: Thomas, for a boy; Penelope, for a girl.

That Saturday, too, tasted like ashes.

T R E N T O N

"It doesn't hurt," she said. By now her voice was even quieter than a whisper; it was like the memory of a voice, like a shadow falling across Trenton's mind.

"How do you know? I thought you didn't remember anything." In the living room, the guests were already assembling. Trenton could hear the soft pressure of dozens of feet beyond the bathroom door, and the murmur of quiet conversation. How many of them had really known, or liked, his dad? None of them, probably.

His suit itched.

"The worst part is being scared . . . before," the ghost said. "After that, you just let go."

Thirteen pills and a bottle of vodka. Would that do it? He'd brought in a carton of orange juice, too. He didn't think he could take even a few shots of vodka without puking. And what was the point of that?

He heard Minna say, "Thank you for coming," her voice higher pitched than usual. He had a brief moment of regret, for her and for Amy. He'd loved Minna once, and she'd loved him. He remembered Christmases when she'd heaved him, kicking, into the air, so he could be the one to put the star on the top of the tree.

He wondered whether his memorial service would be full of

assholes pretending to be sad and secretly filling up on free booze and deli sandwiches. He wondered whether his mom would have him cremated, and what kind of urn style she'd pick out for his remains—hair, nails, toes, pimples, singed to fine dust. A plain style, probably, for a plain, nothing-life.

He wasn't sure he wanted to die. But he didn't think he wanted to live, either.

He measured half a glass of vodka, then topped it with orange juice. The first sip almost made him gag. He hated vodka, didn't understand how his mom could drink it plain. He forced himself to take three big swallows, then washed down two Valium. He fought the urge to puke.

In the living room, Minna was saying, "Thank you so much for your flowers, and we're sure that's what he would have chosen." Her voice sounded very faint, as though he were hearing her from the bottom of an ocean.

"I'll be here," the ghost said. "I'll be waiting for you."

Her voice was close. He was hot. His shirt was itchier than ever. He unbuttoned the collar. When he reached for the glass, for a moment his hand was water and broke apart; he saw the sink beyond it, the hard lines of porcelain, the lingering brown silhouette of a cup that had been packed away or discarded—the things that would outlast him, outlast his body and his life. What was the point of trying at all, if in the end you were no better, no longer, no more real than a bathroom sink and a rust stain?

"Where's Trenton?" That was his mother's voice. "Has anyone seen Trenton?"

He shook another pill into his palm. It was very blue. It looked like a breath mint, which struck him as funny. A deadly breath mint.

Was there anything he would miss? Anything at all? Would anyone miss him?

"I'm happy," the new ghost said. At least, he thought she said it. He couldn't tell, anymore. Her voice was an echo, like voices he had heard before but forgotten. "I'm happy you're coming."

He brought the pill to his mouth. He put it on his tongue. There was a faint vibration in his pants, and for a moment he thought he might be having some kind of predeath experience, a just-before-dying erection, a final humiliation; and then he realized that his phone was buzzing, and he had a message. He worked his phone out of his pocket clumsily with one hand, spitting the pill into his other, and placing it carefully on the edge of the kitchen sink.

He was dizzy. He leaned back against the wall, blinked, made the words come into focus.

The text was from an unknown number.

"Don't read it," the ghost said, speaking directly into the darkest corners of his mind, speaking like a footfall that isn't heard, but felt or intuited. He could feel her, still, even though he couldn't see her anymore. Even though every part of her was fading. "It doesn't matter."

It's Katie, the words read. They kept blinking and re-forming, disappearing and reappearing, and he had to hold the phone very steady with both hands. *Where are you? I'm coming. I need to explain.*

"Please don't leave me alone, Trenton," the ghost said; but he was reading the text again and again, feeling the words in his fingers, already imagining the smell of menthol and tobacco and wildflowers, and his head was rising out of the shadows, and he didn't hear her.

I'm at home, he typed back, very carefully, with very clumsy fingers. *I'll wait.*

Then he took another long sip of his drink, and as the guests continued flowing into the living room for his father's memorial, he ran the faucets, bent over the toilet, and let it all come up.

SANDRA

Richard Walker is a lot more popular dead than he was alive.

We haven't hosted this many people in years. It's like standing in an overcrowded elevator on your way to the forty-second floor. Someone's always farting. Too much perfume, too much bad breath, too many murmured conversations and fake smiles, too much lipstick-on-teeth, and too many men trying to scratch their balls in their suits so no one will notice.

Most of the action is in the living room, where Caroline and Minna have set up rows of chairs in front of the fireplace, with an aisle in the middle like they're preparing for a wedding. There's no podium, no priest—just a small standing microphone that Minna rented, a half-dozen flower arrangements, and a huge cardboard poster of Richard Walker's face, a professional shot he must have had taken for his company. He's tan and smiling, leaning forward like he's about to whisper the camera a secret.

"He looked so healthy then," a woman says, shaking her head, as if it's his fault he started aging and stopped looking so good.

"It's terrible," says another woman, sipping her gin and tonic.

"Is he in there?" says a young kid as he points to a small marble urn set up on the fireplace mantel, just behind the photo of Walker smiling.

"Only his body," the kid's mom says, as if that should give him comfort.

The kid keeps staring, fidgeting with his jacket. "How'd they fit him in there?" he asks finally.

The woman with the gin and tonic overhears and turns, smiling, with lipstick-coated teeth. "They burned him, sweetie," she says.

The kid begins to cry.

When I was maybe five or six years old, a woman down the street, Mrs. Gernst, got flattened by a train. When I got older, I realized it probably wasn't an accident—it was a late train, and she was so sick and swollen with age she could barely move, so what the hell was she doing crossing the tracks at midnight on a Tuesday?—but at the time my mom only said that *God works in mysterious ways,* a.k.a. God will make a pancake of a sick old woman who never did harm to anybody, so what do you think he'll do to you if you don't clean your room and brush your teeth and mind your gospel?

Somehow—don't ask me how—they managed to stitch and cinch and stuff her, ice her down, stick her in a big wood coffin, and put her up on display, like one of the glazed carp my dad's friend Billy had hanging on a wooden plaque on the wall of his living room.

That's probably my earliest memory: the funeral of Mrs. Essie Gernst. It was the first time I'd ever seen a dead person. I remember playing rummy in the back of her living room with Billy Iverson and Patty Horn during the speeches and the service, and how the whole house smelled like a combination of my dad's old socks and the kind of powder my mom put down in our drawers and cabinets to keep the ants away.

Billy told me if I kissed Mrs. Gernst on the mouth, she would wake up. I had to do lip-on-lip, he said, and then she'd sit up and throw her arms around me and give me all her fortune—because everyone knew that Mrs. Gernst had a lot of money that she didn't spend.

What the hell did I know? It worked in all the fairy tales.

(Cissy and I once played Prince Charming and Snow White. We were drunk on apple brandy she'd unearthed from her parents' liquor cabinet, lying out by the creek on a big patch of deep purple moss on one of those Georgia summer days like we were living inside of a painted egg: greens and blues and bright splashes of color; everything brighter and better than real life should ever be. I was sleepy from the heat and the brandy and the slow rotation of the minutes, like even the seconds were too hot to move at normal speed. Cissy sat up on an elbow and leaned over me.

"You be Snow White," she said. "I'll be Prince Charming."

Before I could ask her what she meant, she leaned down and kissed me. Her lips were dry and tasted like sugar and her hair was wet from the creek and I could smell her sun cream and deodorant.

"What was that for?" I said when she pulled away, and I remember laughing even though I felt scared for some reason I couldn't name.

"Now you'll never die," she said, and she was smiling, too.)

After the service was over, when the grown-ups had drifted into the kitchen to talk about nothing and drink coffee and watch the clock sideways, wondering how quickly they could leave without looking impolite, Billy gave me a boost so I could reach the casket. I remember Mrs. Gernst collected porcelain figurines and there were two cats nestled next to her, perched on tissue paper, eyes up, watching me. Her skin smelled like the inside of a garage, like spilled chemicals and someone's wooden workbench; her lips were thin as paper and just as dry.

And I remember the sudden scream, and falling backward on top of Billy, who was laughing like a maniac. My mother came charging out of the crowd like the devil was at her heels, yanked my skirt up where I was, and gave me a solid spanking right there in front of Mrs. Gernst's body, until my father intervened and dragged us both into the street.

Funny enough, I thought at first my mom was mad because I'd done it wrong. Mrs. Gernst hadn't woken up. She was still dead as dead.

That was always my favorite part of the story, anyway. Not the happily-ever-after part—even as a kid I could see that that was a load of honky—but the kiss, the reversal, the waking up, like the past had never happened at all. It was better than confession and getting Jesus to absolve you after a few Hail Marys.

Maybe that was my problem all along, and Alice's, too. We were waiting for Prince Charming and that magic kiss.

We were waiting—*are* waiting—for forgiveness.

MINNA

Minna saw Danny slip into the living room just after her mom started speaking her dad's eulogy. At first she thought he'd come to show support, to listen to her apologize; but then she saw he was in uniform and was accompanied by another cop in uniform. She tried to gesture to him several times—which was hard, because she was sitting in the front row and was supposed to be paying attention—but he kept his eyes glued to her mother.

Where the hell was Trenton? She didn't see him anywhere.

"You can never really know anyone else," her mother was saying, and Minna turned around, guilty, feeling as though her mom was speaking a private message to her. And Caroline *was* looking at her. This wasn't part of the speech, Minna knew, at least it wasn't part of the speech her mom had rehearsed with her earlier, while they were stashing the roll-away beds, carefully avoiding discussing what they had said to each other last night, how they had slept side by side, as if Minna was still a little kid.

"I was married to Richard for almost twenty-two years, and in some ways he was still a stranger to me," Caroline said. It was very quiet in the room. Someone coughed. Minna was embarrassed by her mom's eye contact, and the pleading look of her expression. She wanted to look away but couldn't. "But I know certain things for a fact. Richard enjoyed life, truly enjoyed it, in a way very few people do. Sometimes he enjoyed it a little too much." Several people laughed. "One time, he decided we should all go camping as a family. He spent weeks researching the best tents, the best fishing poles, the best places to pick berries in the summertime. He wanted to *do* it. He didn't want to bring even a can of beans. Well, that lasted about half an hour. We spent the night in a Regency near Lake George, after I got eaten alive by mosquitoes, Minna picked a handful of poison ivy, and everyone got hungry."

Now everyone laughed. Minna felt a sudden gripping terror: she had forgotten about the camping trip, but now she remembered her father suited up in a broad hat decorated with feathers and ornaments, wading into a flat river the color of sky, calling for her to come swim. She remembered, too, how he had taken her arm, bloated with poison ivy, onto his lap, squinting with concentration as he applied calamine lotion.

What else had she forgotten about her dad? How many other moments had she let slip? She knew he had loved life, almost to the point of poor taste. That was the problem, in some ways. The rest of them had been like passing shadows on the brilliant high-noon photograph of his life; she had *felt* like a shadow next to him.

For the first time it occurred to her that maybe, maybe, it wasn't entirely his fault.

"Death makes it easy to forgive," Caroline was saying. She looked down and shuffled the notes in her hand, even though Minna knew she wasn't reading from them. When Caroline looked up again, she had the same pleading expression in her eyes. "We all do our best," she said, speaking very deliberately. Then she broke eye contact, finally, and looked out over the rest of the crowd. Minna wondered whether her mom was sober. It was hard to tell. She didn't usually speak so truthfully, even—or especially—when she was drunk. "I loved Richard very much, even after all this time.

We stayed very close." Her voice broke slightly and Minna gripped the sides of her chair, to keep from feeling like she might be bucked off. "I forgive him for everything. I forgive him for dying, too, although I'll miss him very much. There were things I still wanted to say. But there always are."

It took the audience several moments to work out that Caroline's speech was over; it was a strange, abrupt ending, and it wasn't until Caroline had sat down heavily in the seat next to Minna's that the tension, the silence of waiting, broke. If this had been a play, the audience would have applauded. But it wasn't a play, and instead there was just the sound of shuffling and chairs creaking and mints being unwrapped, as Minna's cousin, Greg, came silently up the aisle and took his place behind the microphone.

"How was I?" Caroline leaned in to whisper to Minna. She reeked of vodka. Not sober, then, not that it mattered. Minna reached out and squeezed her hand. She was worried if she tried to talk, she would cry again.

It was over soon, thank God. Greg spoke, and so did his father, Richard's sister's husband, since Richard's sister had spent half of her adult life feuding with Richard and had even refused to come to the memorial service. Richard's longtime business partner spoke, and Minna focused on the fact that he looked pretty good, better than she remembered, but before she could wonder whether he was still married and whether it would matter, he was finished talking and the service, at least the formal portion of it, was over. Then she was crowded from all sides. People slipped hands over hers—smooth hands, rough hands, hands as old and thin as parchment, and whispered, "I'm so sorry," and exhaled the smell of breath mints and alcohol.

She spotted Danny moving toward her, politely but forcefully, pushing through the crowd. He still wasn't looking at her, though. Before she could call his name—before she could say anything—he had moved past her without even a glance and had stopped in front of her mother.

"Mrs. Walker, is there somewhere we could go and have a talk?" he said, in a voice very different from his usual one. At the same time, Minna realized that the second cop was standing just behind Danny, thumbs hooked into his belt, shifting his weight. He had acne scars and a fat cold sore on his lower lip and looked like a bad actor doing a tough cop routine.

"I told you," Caroline said. "I go by my maiden name."

"What's this about?" Minna stepped next to her mother, forcing Danny to look at her. He did, but only for an instant.

"I'm sorry we have to do this now," he said. And he did sound sorry. "If there's somewhere more private . . . ?"

"What's this *about*?" Minna repeated, so loudly that several people looked. She lowered her voice. "Danny?"

Danny sucked in a deep breath. "This really isn't the place."

"This really isn't the time," Minna said, getting angry. "We're having a memorial service, in case you hadn't noticed."

At least the room was emptier now. The crowd was flowing out toward the dining room, to refill on drinks and make inane comments about the circle of life.

"And like I said, I'm very sorry," Danny said. "But we received a complaint—"

"A complaint?" Minna repeated.

"I didn't do anything," Caroline said simultaneously. But she swayed slightly, and Minna had to steady her.

Danny looked at his partner—Minna assumed the guy with the acne scars was his partner—for help. When he didn't say anything, Danny went on, "A woman named Adrienne Cadiou got in contact with the station. Apparently she's been having trouble with harassing phone calls. Sometimes *thirty* in a day. You know anything about that?"

"She's a liar," Caroline said quickly. Then, to Minna, "Get me a drink, Minna."

Minna didn't move. The name was familiar to her, but it took her a second to place it. Then she did, and she realized. "Mom," she said and brought her hands to her forehead. There were explosions of pain behind her eyeballs. She thought of the Fourth of July when she and Danny had snuck out of Lauren Lampert's party to make out on the wooden raft in the middle of Gedney Pond. What had happened? She opened her eyes again and the colors dissipated.

"She's lying, Minna, I've never even spoken to the woman, I—"

"All the calls originated from this number," Danny said, interrupting her. Caroline went quiet.

Christ. Her mom probably had no idea that people had caller ID. That phone calls could be tracked.

Minna felt like laughing or crying or both. "All right," she said to Danny. "What now?"

"Well . . ." Danny turned to his partner again, but then something began beeping and Acne Scars yanked a phone out from his waistband. "It's Rogers," he said, and then he turned his back to Minna and Caroline, speaking words too quietly and rapidly for Minna to make out. People were still watching them, whispering, doing a bad job of pretending not to stare. Minna wanted to scream at them to get out, to go get sauced in the dining room like normal guests.

"I'm sorry for all the trouble," Danny said for the third time, and Minna nearly slapped him. "It looks like she wants to press charges."

"Charges?" Caroline repeated, as though she'd never heard the word. She clawed at Minna's arm. "The drink, Minna," she said urgently.

"You can't arrest her." Minna was speaking as forcefully as she could while still whispering. "Are you crazy?"

"I'm not going to cuff her," Danny said with a short sigh, as if

Minna were the one being unreasonable. "After the service is over, maybe you or your brother can drive her into town. We can talk about what's what when we get there."

"We haven't seen Trenton in hours," Minna said, seizing on Danny's suggestion that Trenton drive as if she could prove the absurdity of the whole complaint. "And he's not allowed behind the wheel of a car, anyway."

Caroline teetered again, and Minna steadied her. "Where's Trenton?" Caroline said. It was like she had somehow delayed the effect of the alcohol she must have consumed; now it was hitting her all at once. "Did he see my speech?"

"She can't come down to the station," Minna said. "Look at her. And don't say you're sorry again."

"Trenton! Trenton!" Caroline's eyes were wide with panic. She was gripping Minna's arm so tightly, Minna was sure she was leaving marks. "Minna, where did Trenton go? We're burying Dad this afternoon. We have to bury the ashes . . . "

Danny's partner finished his conversation. He pivoted and flipped shut his phone. "Rogers is on his way," he said. His voice was surprisingly high pitched and did not at all match his face.

"He's on his way over *here*?" Danny said.

Caroline seized her opportunity. She lurched forward, nearly upsetting a chair; before Danny could stop her, she had barreled around him and passed into the hall.

"There's been a development." Acne Scars barely registered Caroline's departure. "Vivian Wright's cell phone went on an hour ago."

Danny went still, like a deer listening for danger. "Someone found it?" he said.

Acne Scars shook his head. "She sent a text," he said, "to a 516 number." He turned to Minna. His eyes were very shiny, and his lips wet. "Registered to one Trenton Walker."

T R E N T O N

Trenton still felt woozy, even after puking twice. He splashed cold water on his face, getting his shirt collar all wet in the process. He didn't care. In the medicine cabinets he found a few miscellaneous toiletry items that Minna had skipped over or missed, among them a half-used tube of toothpaste and a travel-size bottle of mouthwash. He scrubbed his teeth and tongue with his finger, nearly puking again. Then he rinsed four times with mouthwash. The whole time, he was expecting the ghost to start badgering him—*hurry up, please Trenton, you promised me*—but she was, uncharacteristically, quiet.

By then, Katie had texted again. *You didn't tell me you were having a party.*

Before he could write back and correct her—not a party, a memorial service—she had texted again. *Where are you?*

The room was still revolving a bit. Trenton eased the bathroom door open and peeked into the hall, which was crowded with people—all of them were shuffling slowly out of the living room in unison, like zombies gearing up for attack. Minna had booted up the speakers, and soft music intermingled with the sound of murmured voices and repressed laughter. Someone had farted.

Trenton had missed the whole service.

Mrs. Anderson, his first-grade English teacher, spotted him and waved. Trenton ducked quickly back into the bathroom and closed the door.

Go toward the music, Trenton texted. *I'll watch 4 u.*

This is the worst party I've ever been 2, she texted back.

The song was an acoustic version of "Born to Run," by Bruce Springsteen. Trenton had to admit: Minna was a genius for picking it. Trenton's dad was a Bruce fanatic, partly, Minna said, because Richard Walker identified with his story: the everyday, working-class guy who makes it big on his own steam. Trenton remembered being five or six years old and sitting in the passenger seat of his dad's new Mercedes, summertime, windows down, sunlight streaming so brightly through the windshield it was practically blinding, the bass reverberating so hard through the dashboard Trenton could feel it in his teeth. And Richard was singing along, and drumming with one hand on the wheel, and Trenton had felt very old, then: like his father's best friend.

Trenton checked the hall again and saw her: red hoodie cinched tight, sunglasses on, a bright spot of color in a sea of blacks and grays, startling, like a spot of blood on a clean floor. He started to move out into the hall to greet her, but she put a hand on his chest and piloted him backward into the bathroom again and closed the door behind her.

"Look," she said, taking off her sunglasses and wrenching off her hood. "I don't have much time."

She had changed her hair color again. It was dark brown now, like his.

He was filled with sudden joy. The world shrank down to the size of a single room: Katie was here, with him. "I thought you ran away," he said.

"That's funny," she said.

"Or your parents shipped you off."

"My parents don't know where I am," she said. A brief look of pain, or maybe worry, passed across her face. "Listen, Trenton. I need you to listen to me. I have to explain a few things to you, okay?"

"I've been up shit's creek since the fire," he said. He was still dizzy, but now he thought it might be because they were standing so close. He could see individual freckles under her makeup, like tiny stars. "But I made sure Amy didn't tell."

"*Listen.*" She grabbed both of his arms. Surprised, he sat backward, onto the toilet. Thankfully, the lid was closed. "Just shut up for two seconds, okay? I have four things to tell you." She released him and straightened up. He said nothing. She began pacing. The bathroom was so small she could only take two steps in either direction before having to pivot and return. "One. I have to go away soon." She was ticking off items on her fingers.

"Where are you going?"

"Just *listen,* for Christ's sake. Two. I'm a liar. I've lied to you about a lot of things. But I'm not a bad person."

"Okay." Trenton wondered if he should stand up again. He didn't like how she was pacing. It was making him nervous. But he didn't want her to yell at him, either.

"Three." She stopped in front of him. Her eyes were like an animal's—big and pleading. "I like you. You're kind of an idiot, but I do."

Trenton was going to protest, but then the weight of her words hit him—*I like you*—and he felt like something had just knocked into his chest. He couldn't even breathe. He was afraid that if he so much as moved, he would send the words scattering back into nonexistence, into untruth, like cockroaches startled by a sudden light.

But Katie was watching him, expectant, clearly anticipating a reply.

"What's the fourth thing?" Trenton asked, in a voice that barely sounded like his.

For the first time, Katie smiled. "This," she said, and dropped onto her knees on the rug in front of the toilet, and put her hands on his shoulders, and kissed him.

For a half second, he was seized with terror; then, just as quickly, his anxiety passed, and when she slipped her tongue into his mouth, he found he wasn't worried about what to do, or whether he was using too much pressure or too little. He just let go. It was like falling into a warm bed after an exhausting day. It was dark and sweet and soft. Now even the room disappeared. Now there was only her mouth and her breathing, her warm hands on his shoulders.

The kiss lasted for minutes, hours. He was dimly aware of a growing crescendo, as if applause were swelling from an unseen audience. At a certain moment, the crescendo crested, and a sudden flood of awareness passed over him, and he realized he was hearing not applause but footsteps and shouting.

The bathroom door swung open, smacking hard against the tub.

Katie accidentally bit his lip.

Trenton drew back, wincing.

Minna was standing in the doorway, gripping Amy's hand. Crowded next to her were two cops. Trenton recognized one of them as the guy Minna used to date.

Danny was breathing hard, as if they'd come from a long distance. "Vivian Wright?" he said.

Katie looked at Trenton and sighed. "Busted," she said.

Amy touched a finger to her lips and said, "Shhh."

A L I C E

"I knew she was a liar." The new ghost is bitterly disappointed: Trenton is still alive. She begins to cry, and Sandra hushes her sharply.

"Stop it," she says. "There's no use blubbering. It won't do you any good."

"Nobody *asked* you," she says. Then: "I told you I wasn't Vivian."

"You told us different things," I say gently. I feel a momentary ache of sadness for her: the ache of an empty room after a party has dispersed. Every minute, she forgets how to be alive. She loses her lines and separateness; she is drawn into the air, blown apart on the wind coming through the open windows. "Who are you, really?"

She sniffles, a sound like the faint stirring of mice in the walls. "My name's Eva," she says at last. "It *was* Eva. I don't know what I am now. I—I don't even know why I'm here."

"Join the club, sister," Sandra says, but without conviction. I can tell that she, like me, is tired of pretending.

Trenton, Minna, Amy, the two policemen, and Katie—or Vivian, rather—have returned to the living room, which is now empty of other mourners. The cops have placed six chairs in a semicircle and everyone is seated.

"Detective Rogers will be here any minute," the cop with the bad complexion says. "Everyone just sit tight."

"What I want to know," Danny says to Vivian, "is why you picked the Davison house. How'd you know they'd be away?"

"Can I see your badge?" Amy asks him.

"Shhh, Amy," Minna says. But Danny passes the badge over.

"Internet," Vivian says. She almost—*almost*—sounds embarrassed. "Their house was listed on vacation rentals."

"Why did you do it?" Trenton asks her in a low voice.

She looks down, picking at the hem of her jacket. "I don't know. Just to get away for a while. Be somebody else. It felt kind of nice to have everybody looking for me, though." She looks up at him. "Will you?"

"Will I what?" Trenton says.

A smile flickers over Vivian's face, moving so quickly it doesn't touch her eyes. "Will you look for me?"

"Yes." Trenton's voice cracks. He clears his throat and tries again. "Yes."

"Are we done here?" Minna directs the question to Danny. "In case you've forgotten, we were in the middle of a memorial service. We're burying my dad today."

Danny looks embarrassed. "We're still going to have to take your mom down to the station." Then he looks around, as if for the first time noticing her absence. "Where is your mom, anyway?"

That's when the gun goes off.

PART IX

THE HALL

S A N D R A

Here's Caroline:

Gripping Richard Walker's pistol tightly in one hand, while a man tries to wrestle it away from her; ignoring the crowd of people shouting instructions, pushing past her, calling for the police. There is a small hole in the ceiling, and a fine sift of plaster raining down onto the assembled guests. The front door hangs open like a mouth; standing on the front porch is a woman.

The man with the black hair has Caroline in a bear hug. "No, Caroline. Caroline, *stop*."

"What the hell is she doing here?" Caroline's voice is shrill. "Get her out. I want her *out*."

"*Mom*." Then Minna comes tearing around the corner, and Trenton, and Amy, until Trenton seizes her around the waist and forces her to stay back. The cops follow, eyes bulging and chests puffed out like they're about to cream in their pants with importance. Vivian hangs back.

"Move aside," Danny says, squeezing through the knot of people. "Everyone clear out. Move aside."

The other guests hang back, conversing in whispers, trying hard not to show their excitement. They look like scavengers tailing a dump truck.

"Mom, come on. Come with me." Minna puts an arm around her mother. Caroline is trembling like a wire about to snap.

"*Get her out.*" Her voice crests to a high shriek, like steam out of a kettle. Everyone is frozen and horrified. One woman has a smile plastered on her face, as wide and ugly as a Halloween jack-o'-lantern.

Minna puts an arm around Caroline's shoulders. "Shhh, Mom. Come on." Caroline doesn't budge.

"She shouldn't be here," Caroline says. "She has no right, do you hear me? *No right.*"

"It's okay, Mom." Minna glares at the woman on the porch. "Who the hell are you?"

She's dressed in black, and for a moment, backlit by the sun, her features are all in shadow. Then she takes a step into the hall. She looks like a dog that's been kenneled and only half groomed: she has a bewildered, panicked look, like she has no idea where she is, and even though she's dressed for a funeral, the hem of her slip is showing beneath her skirt and her black top is stained. She has dark red hair, frizzy, graying at the temples, hanging in a long braid down her back.

Her jaw is moving soundlessly—up and down, up and down. It takes me a second to realize she's saying *I'm sorry,* barely breathing it, so quietly I'm sure no one else can hear.

Danny unhooks a pair of handcuffs from his belt and takes two steps toward Caroline. Trenton steps quickly in front of his mother.

"You must be fucking kidding me," Minna says.

"I'm sorry, Minna," he says quietly. "I really don't have a choice."

"No way." Now Trenton steps up.

Amy starts to cry.

"Look." Danny leans in close to Minna. "I don't like this any more than you do. But your mother just fired a gun at someone. And we have a complaint about her on file already. I don't want to have to cuff her. If she'll just come with me quietly—"

"Screw you, Danny."

"Don't make this worse." Danny moves Minna forcibly out of the way. "Caroline Walker, you're under arrest for aggravated assault—"

"My fault."

The two words, spoken quietly from the doorway, make even Danny go silent.

The woman clears her throat and tries again: "It's my fault. I'm sorry."

"Who *are* you?" Trenton says.

Her big eyes keep traveling over everyone, like insects refusing to settle. "My name is Adrienne," she says. "Adrienne Cadiou."

PART X

THE DINING ROOM

C A R O L I N E

"Drink," Minna said, refilling Caroline's coffee.

"I don't want any." Caroline took her coffee with sugar, cream, and preferably a nip of something stronger. This coffee was black and very strong; Caroline had already forced down a cup, while Danny and Minna watched her with identical expressions of concern, as if she were a child and they were the overattentive parents. Between them was a vast array of used cups and plates smeared with mustard, platters still piled with sandwiches arranged on wilted lettuce leaves.

"Just drink it," Minna said. Caroline was too tired to argue. She was still drunk, but not drunk enough. The gun in her hand, the sudden, blinding fury that had gripped her, the sound of screaming—it was achieving reality, floating out from the dream-fog in which it had been comfortably encased.

Minna had gotten rid of all the other guests, thank God, and they'd convinced Danny to delay Caroline's arrest, at least until after they had buried Richard's ashes. Caroline couldn't have faced a crowd. She couldn't bear to see her former neighbors and so-called friends staring at her, whispering, the hiss of their insinuations about Richard and the woman.

The Woman.

Adrienne was sitting on the far side of the dining room. She hadn't moved or spoken since she had announced her name, except to ask for some water. Caroline should have ordered her out of the house. She should have commanded it. Instead, she was forced to sit and watch Minna try to appease her, offering her cookies or a glass of wine, speaking in the voice she reserved for when Amy was sad or injured: a voice meant to say *Please, please, don't be angry at my mother. She's harmless, she's drunk, she didn't mean to.*

But Caroline had meant to.

"So you're telling me"—Danny and Minna were conversing in low voices, but not so low Caroline couldn't hear them; they probably thought she was too drunk to understand—"that this is a *different* Adrienne Cadiou? That she's not the one your mom's been calling?"

"She's not the one," Caroline said. It was the first time she'd spoken to Danny since he'd attempted to place her in handcuffs, and he turned to her in surprise. She deliberately avoided looking at him.

This was, in fact, the last and final insult: Adrienne was not the Adrienne Caroline had expected. Caroline wished she'd read more about *this* Adrienne. She remembered only an article she'd barely skimmed—a hit-and-run, a drunk driver. Now she fought vainly to recall details. She had the sense that it would make her feel more secure, less like she was drowning in open air, as if by knowing a person you could avoid being hurt by them. You might at least anticipate which way the blow would fall.

Suddenly, Adrienne turned to Danny and Minna, who were still standing by the windows, silhouetted in light. "Can we have some privacy, please?"

Neither Danny nor Minna moved. But it was as though Adrienne believed they had. Now she turned and spoke directly to

Caroline, pleading with her almost. What had she come for—forgiveness? Understanding? Caroline wouldn't give her any.

"I didn't ask for any money," Adrienne said abruptly. "I haven't spoken to Richard in ten years. He never answered any of my e-mails. I'd stopped calling a long time ago." Now that she had started speaking, it was as if she couldn't stop. She was trembling like someone in the grips of a bad fever. "It's blood money. I don't want it."

"I don't understand," Caroline said coldly. She was playing the part of the queen. Adrienne was the penitent. Except that the part felt wrong. Caroline was the one who felt like begging—for Adrienne to go away, for Danny and Trenton to go away, too, for everyone to leave her in peace. She wanted to curl up in her bedroom—the bedroom that had been hers and Richard's—and drink until the world started to soften and forgive.

"My daughter, Eva." Adrienne's voice broke on the name. "She was . . . his."

For a moment there was silence. Minna turned away, rubbing her forehead. Caroline heard the seconds ticking forward, and then remembered that the big grandfather clock in the hall had been wrapped up and shipped off to the auction house, along with everything else of value.

She was seized by a sense of the absurdity of the scene: the big dining room table and the litter of food and plates and glasses; the narrow wedge of sunlight shining between the curtains; and Danny stuffed into his ridiculous uniform, like a sausage in a too-small casing.

The kitchen door slammed, and Trenton came into the dining room, stamping dirt from his sneakers. "We're burying Dad under the weeping willow," he said. Then, seeing Adrienne, he froze in the doorway. "Sorry. I thought she was . . . " He trailed off before he could say *gone*.

When Adrienne turned to Trenton, her expression was full of such open hunger that Caroline's stomach rolled. "How old are you?" she asked.

His eyes ticked temporarily to Caroline, as though requesting her permission to answer. "Sixteen," he said.

"Eva would have been thirteen in July," Adrienne said. A smile flickered over her face, but her eyes remained empty, huge, like open wounds. "She wanted—she wanted to go to Six Flags for her birthday."

Trenton stiffened, as if a current had gone through him.

Caroline said. "Is she . . . ?" She couldn't bring herself to say dead.

"I called Richard from the hospital. I don't know why. We only met once. It was a mistake. We both knew it." Adrienne's voice cracked again. Caroline felt like spitting at her. She, Caroline, was the one who should have been crying. All this time, this other person, this phantom-child, had been running parallel to Caroline's life, waiting to destroy it. "Still, I sent him pictures. Letters. A cutting of hair." She didn't stop herself from crying this time; she picked up a napkin Caroline was sure was dirty and wiped away the tears when they came. "My poor Eva. The doctors told me she would never make it. I—I thought Richard could make it untrue." Adrienne's face was white, like the center of a very hot flame. "But Richard was dead. Someone answered. 'Don't call back,' she said. 'He's dead. He's dead and he left you nothing.' "

Minna inhaled sharply. Trenton pulled a chair out from the table, letting it scrape on the floor, and sat down heavily.

"They were going to bury her," Adrienne said, her expression wild, begging. "They were speaking her favorite psalm. *The Lord is my Shepherd. I shall not want. He maketh me to lie down in green pastures . . .* I couldn't watch. I couldn't bear it. I was in Buffalo before I knew where I was going—before I knew I was coming here."

She was shaking so hard that the ice cubes rattled in her glass. "It was my fault. All my fault. I was driving—I should have seen the other car. I should have known . . . I should have saved her."

"Holy shit," Trenton whispered. "My sister."

"Minna," Caroline said sharply. "Get Adrienne something to drink."

They sat rigidly, in silence, until Minna returned with whiskey. She had to physically remove Adrienne's empty water glass from her hand, as though Adrienne had forgotten how to move her fingers. Caroline watched her drink. She remembered, now, that she had seen pictures of Adrienne's daughter: a girl with a wide, frank face, freckled and grinning, like a child you would see on a commercial for pancake mix. She'd had bright blue eyes, like Richard's. Like Trenton's.

She remembered, too, the phone call from the police the night of Trenton's accident; the blind drive through the dark, when the sky had seemed like a lid that might suffocate her.

People, Caroline thought, were like houses. They could open their doors. You could walk through their rooms and touch the objects hidden in their corners. But something—the structure, the wiring, the invisible mechanism that kept the whole thing standing—remained invisible, suggested only by the fact of its existing at all.

Caroline stood up. Adrienne froze, as if she expected Caroline to lean across the table and strike her. But Caroline wasn't angry anymore—not at Richard, not at Adrienne. All at once, in one second, the past and its ruin of promises and disappointments had released its hold on her. She was filled with a golden warmth that made her limbs feel loose and light; it made her forget her swollen ankles and the fact that she was not drunk enough to ward off the beginnings of a hangover.

She didn't have to forgive him—the idea came suddenly, like a deep breath of air after a long submerging. It was all over now. She didn't have to forgive him, and she could love him and hate him at the same time, and it was all right.

She closed her eyes and felt, for a split second, a hand pass across her neck; and in that moment she had a vision of rooms like atoms, holding a universe of secrets; and she, Caroline, gripped in the small bounded nucleus of the past.

Now she was free.

She reached across the table to take Adrienne's hand. "It's not your fault," she said.

"My sister," Trenton whispered again. This time he spoke quietly and addressed the word to the walls.

S A N D R A

"I always wanted a brother," Eva says quietly. She pauses. "Mom would never tell me anything about my dad. She said I was born from a tube. But she was lying."

"Now you know," Alice says softly.

"I think . . . I think that's all I wanted," Eva says. "To know." In the quiet, her mother continues sniffling into Caroline's shoulder. "I wish she wouldn't cry. It wasn't her fault. I know it wasn't." Then: "I think I'm ready now."

"Ready for what?" I say. But she doesn't answer. For a second, I feel her trembling like a violin string, vibrating out a high note of fear and loss. "Ready for what?" I say, a little louder.

A sharp pain goes through me, a feeling like being socked in the stomach. Alice cries out. For a second, everything goes dark. When everything comes into focus again—the dining room, the bones of our staircases and the doors like jaws that open and close—I feel lighter, and emptier, too. Like I've just taken the world's most epic dump.

"Eva?" Alice whispers. No answer.

She's gone.

"Well." I don't know why I feel sad about it. But I do. I'm sad and sorry and jealous, all at once. "There you have it. Vivian and Eva. That's two out of three missing children accounted for."

"Stop, Sandra." Alice's voice is shaky, like *she's* the victim, like I'm the bad guy.

"It's too late, Alice," I say. "There's no use in pretending anymore."

She sucks in a deep breath: a whistle through a teakettle. "What about you?" she asks.

"Not even for me."

There's a moment of silence. In that minute, I can practically feel our walls coming down, slowly down, pulled earthward by the pressures of gravity and decay.

Alice says, "Why did you tell me Martin shot you? For all these years, all our years together, you lied about it. Or did you really forget?"

"Does it matter?" I haven't felt so tired since I was alive—too tired to keep the truth back, to stuff it into dark corners and keep it shored up behind heavy walls. It comes creeping out into the open, like a mouse sniffing around a darkened house. "You knew the truth all along. You were there."

"I was there," Alice agrees. "I was waiting for you to remember."

"I remembered," I say. It hurts to speak, to think, to remember. As if we've been planed and sawed down into splinters—as if everything is about to fall. "I just didn't want it to be true."

We're quiet for a bit. Adrienne is still staring dull-eyed as an idiot. Trenton has torn her napkin to strips. All of them so clear and sharp, like individual cardboard cutouts. In that moment I'd trade places with any of them, just to have a beginning and an end.

"Why did you do it?" Alice asks quietly.

"I don't know," I say, although that's not exactly true, either. I did it for a hundred reasons and for no reason at all. Because Martin told me I needed help and I knew it was his way of saying he was getting tired of me. Because I couldn't stand to keep drinking and I couldn't stand to stop. Because I was so tired that even sleeping didn't help me at all.

But mostly because I was lonely. It was like living at the bottom of a pit. There was only one way out. "They're digging," Alice says. She's gotten her voice under control. "Under the willow tree."

"I told you," I say. No point in lying anymore. I blamed Martin for not loving me, until the blame and what happened became the same story.

Everything comes up in the end.

T R E N T O N

A sister. Trenton had—or used to have—a sister. He wished he'd known earlier.

He was alone in the dining room. The woman, Adrienne, had gone to wash her face in the bathroom. The ugly cop, who had skin just as bad as Trenton's, was waiting outside in Adrienne's car. Everyone agreed she was in no state to drive; there was talk of getting her a place to stay the night, until a relative could come and get her. Caroline had gone to change her clothes, and Danny was waiting outside her bedroom door, like Caroline might shimmy down the drainpipe and make a break for it. Trenton thought Danny was enjoying himself, even if he was pretending to be sad and apologetic. He probably didn't get to arrest people very often.

Poor, lonely Eva. Trenton had always wanted a younger sister—had dreamed of it, especially after Minna moved out and went off to college and left Trenton alone with his mother. He would not have tortured her, as some older brothers did, or locked her in the bathroom after he'd used it or put her in headlocks until she screamed for mercy.

He would have showed her how to catch toads by making a cup of his hands, as Minna had done with him when he was very small. He would have taken her to the creek behind Mulaney's so they could root out newts together, shrieking over a sudden flash of orange belly; he would have told her stories at night, saving the scary ones for when she was older.

Adrienne emerged from the bathroom. Her shirt clung to her shoulders where it was damp. Trenton got quickly and clumsily to his feet. He hadn't expected to see her; he had assumed she would go out the way she came in, through the hall. But of course she didn't know the house.

He felt embarrassed in her presence—embarrassed that he got to live, when he had wanted to die; that her daughter had died, when she had wanted to live. He wanted to say he was sorry, but the words felt insufficient. What would that mean, coming from him? From anyone?

Instead, they stood there in silence. Trenton was aware of the slow drag of time, the air in the house stifling, thick with funeral smells.

Adrienne spoke first. "You have her eyes," she said. "Beautiful eyes."

Trenton didn't know how to respond. "Are you going to be okay?" he asked her.

She smiled, but it was the saddest smile he'd ever seen. Trenton remembered the first time he had seen Eva's ghost in the greenhouse—the dry rustle of her voice, like autumn leaves tumbling over a barren riverbed. He was as sad now as he had been then—sadder, even, than he had ever been for his father.

"I don't know," she said. "Am I?"

"You will," he said, although he didn't really know. He felt a subtle shift, as if the air had suddenly begun rotating in the other direction. This was why people lied: sometimes, it was only the stories that mattered.

After Adrienne had gone, Trenton stood for a while in the quiet, listening hard to the familiar sounds of the floors creaking and the house settling minutely on its foundations—listening, too, for a voice, a whisper, a word of forgiveness, maybe. But there was nothing.

He cleared his throat. He knew his mother and sister couldn't hear him, but he still felt embarrassed speaking out loud. "Eva?" he said, and then, a little louder, "Eva?"

There was only silence. He wondered whether she was upset at him, because he hadn't gone through with killing himself. But no. The silence was dull and complete—not even the faintest rustle or whisper or creak. The ghosts were gone, or he had stopped hearing them. He wondered if it had been like a virus, and he had gotten it out of his system when he puked.

Was it because he had refused them? Because at the last moment, he had refused to cross over?

"I'm sorry, Eva," he said. "I let you down." He hated to think of the ghosts trapped in the walls, with no one to listen or hear.

But the problem with death was that you could never get tired of it and go home. No one would ever come and put a jacket around your shoulders, as Detective Rogers had done with Vivian, and put you in the backseat of a warm car and send you back to being alive. If only bodies were like rooms, and people could pass in and out of them at will.

He wondered whether Minna was almost finished digging. The hole didn't have to be very deep to bury an urn. He moved to the window to check, but his view was obstructed. There was a white work van parked in the driveway. Connelly Roofing was stenciled in black on its side. Connelly. The name seemed familiar somehow.

"Hello?" a man called out. Before Trenton could go to the door, he heard it open; heavy footsteps came down the hall.

"Can I help you?" Trenton said, when the man passed into view. He was old—at least sixty—and dressed in gray work pants and a T-shirt saggy as a loose skin. But his shoulders were wide and his arms still roped with muscle.

"Who're you?" the man said.

"Who're you?" Trenton fired back.

"Joe Connelly," he said. "I got my guys working the job upstairs." His skin was webbed with burst capillaries, and Trenton smelled beer on him. But he must have been okay-looking, back in the day. Joe seemed to register the food on the dining room table for the first time. "Sorry. I didn't know you were having a party."

"It isn't a party," Trenton said. He didn't feel like explaining what it was. "Anyway, it's over."

"You Caroline's kid?" Joe asked, and Trenton nodded. "One of my guys left a ladder up there. We need it for another job. You mind if I go up?"

"I guess not," Trenton said. Why, he wondered, were they even bothering to fix the roof? Would they ever come back? He couldn't imagine it. It wasn't their house anymore—it wasn't his house—no matter what the will said. They should leave the roof open and give the birds a place to nest.

Joe didn't move right away. He stood there, sucking on his lower lip, like he was debating whether to say something else. Trenton thought he might not know where the stairs were. "Straight down the hall," he said.

Joe nodded. "Yeah," he said, but still didn't move. "Yeah. I remember this place. Did some work here years ago. It was a lot different then. Smaller." He shook his head. "Time flies."

Then Trenton remembered: Joe Connelly. Joe Connelly was the name of the man who'd found the dead woman, the one with her brains blown out—Sandra.

"Wait!" Trenton took two quick steps forward, nearly tripping over the rug. Joe stopped, turned to face him. "Wait. You—you were the one who found her. The woman who died here."

Instantly, Joe turned guarded. "How'd you know about that?" he said, wetting his lips with his tongue.

"My sister dates a cop," Trenton said. He could never explain what had really happened: the voices, the visions, the sense of touch whenever Eva came near—like a cool blade running through his very center. It was all true. There was an invisible world; there was meaning gathered like clouds on the other side of a mountain.

"Oh." Connelly was clenching his fists and unclenching them, like he was squeezing an invisible rope. "Yeah. Wrong place, wrong time. That was a bad winter. Lots of snow. Poor lady's roof caved in."

"Sandra," Trenton said, watching Joe carefully.

"Something like that," he said. "Screwy the things you forget. She didn't have a face by the time I got to her. That I remember."

"What happened to her?" Trenton asked. "The police—I mean, they never found out who did it, right?"

"No," Joe said hoarsely. He turned away. "No, they never did find out."

Trenton grasped for another question, something that would keep Joe in the room and talking to him. His pulse was going wild. He didn't know why it was important for him to know about some stranger who'd died here decades ago, only that Joseph Connelly's arrival seemed like a sign. There was something he was missing, something he'd forgotten. Eva had told him that the ghost Sandra had been shot; there had been an important letter, too, which was stolen.

"What about the letter?" he blurted out, and Joe stiffened like Trenton had just reached out and electrocuted him.

"How—how'd you know about the letter?" Joe asked. When he

turned around, his face was awful: white and frightened, older than it had looked just a minute earlier. "Who told you?"

Trenton didn't answer. He couldn't. Joe stood there, still trembling like a wire, his eyes like two dark gashes in his face. Then he pulled out a chair, abruptly, and sat down.

"Are you all right?" Trenton said cautiously.

But when Joe spoke, it was in a normal voice. "Blood pressure," he said. "I'm an old shit. You got any water?"

Trenton went to the sideboard, where Minna had lined up pitchers of ice water for their guests. He poured a big glass of water and passed it to Joe at the table. Then he sat down.

"Thanks," Joe said. But he didn't drink. He just spun the glass between his hands. After a minute, he said: "I got rid of it. I thought it was the right thing to do. Seeing her like that . . . There was blood everywhere." He shook his head. "It doesn't help to know the reason. People say it helps. But it doesn't."

"Know the reason for what?"

Joe looked up, frowning. "For why they do it in the first place."

Trenton suddenly understood. He'd been chasing this story of an old murder, feeding on it like carrion birds did, but it was a sadder story than that: digging up the old, dry bones of someone's misery.

"So it was suicide," Trenton said.

Joe put two hands on the table and pushed himself to his feet. "My dad roped himself when I was a kid. My mom told everyone he bust an artery in his brain. Aneurysm. She was embarrassed. Even changed our name back a few years later, from Houston to Connelly. Connelly was her maiden name." He shook his head again. "It doesn't help to know. It doesn't make it easier. Still, I shouldn't have burned the letter. It wasn't my business."

Trenton sat there for a long time, thinking of his father's many conferences and Adrienne's letters, unanswered; thinking of a man hanging from the ceiling and his wife lying about it because she was embarrassed. He thought about faceless women. He thought about time coming down slowly around their ears, like a roof under the pressure of snow.

It was time, he thought, to bury his father. It was time to put the ghosts to rest.

A L I C E

"Don't go." I've been trying to ignore Sandra for the length of her death, trying to expel her; and now I'm begging her to stay, like a child. "Please don't go."

"The jig's up, isn't it?" Already Sandra sounds fainter, as if I'm hearing her from a distance. "It's about damn time, too."

"Don't leave me." I hate myself for saying it, but I can't help it: she's my other, my boundary. Now there will be no one to hear me. It's almost the same thing as not-existing, but worse. Lonelier. The Walkers will go home, and I will remain here, alone, openmouthed and silent in the doorways; frozen in the ice box; full of the darkness of empty closets and rooms that no one enters.

"You need to let go, Alice. That's the whole trick. Let go of everything."

"Tell me how," I say. "I'm ready to learn." Silence. "Sandra? Are you there?"

The only answer is a hole, a deep bottoming out, as if I still had a body and all the bones had suddenly vanished. Then—a sudden sickness, a reverse nausea, the sickness of something good and necessary going out.

Everything comes up in the end.

Sandra was right: old crimes expiated, truths revealed, curiosities satisfied.

How could I have been so blind? Sitting, watching, waiting, like a fat cat in a patch of sunlight, for years before she came along—but seeing nothing, really, feeling nothing but the slow crawl of time and minutes hardening like plaster in my veins. I remember Sandra's death, vaguely. I saw the last fight she ever had with Martin, and the twenty-four hours that followed: the glass refilled and refilled, the stumbling and vomiting, the crust of blood on her lips.

I saw her load the gun, of course. How could I not? We can't choose what we see.

But afterward . . . was I happy that she came to join me? Was I secretly pleased when she elbowed her way through the soft folds of my new nonbody, like a splinter beneath a surface of skin? Probably. And so I barely noticed the cleanup, the police, the sad small group of strangers who came to haggle over her pots and lamps and sofas when they were put up for sale.

I didn't notice little Joey Houston, all grown up to become Joe Connelly, whom I had last seen sitting next to his mother at his father's funeral service. I didn't see the resemblance in the proud, hooked nose and determined chin, in the ears that stick out just a little more than usual.

Joseph Houston. Thomas's son.

I've been so wrong—so wrong about everything.

I want to tell Sandra. *You were right.*

And Thomas: *I forgive you.*

And our little baby girl, the small promise that grew inside me like a flower under glass: *I'm sorry. I'm so sorry.*

But those are just words, and words are just stories, and eventually, always, stories come to an end.

* * *

Caroline has changed into old jeans and a nubby sweater, and she returns to the dining room with her makeup scrubbed off and her hair tied in a ponytail. She must have snuck a few drinks. She is brighter eyed than she was just twenty minutes ago.

"Trenton, are you ready? Do you have the ashes?"

"Minna has them," Trenton says. "I was just going to check—" Trenton is cut off. The kitchen door bangs open, and a second later Minna appears in the dining room, breathless, her hands covered with dirt.

A shadow moves across the sun; the house, my rooms, my mind goes dark. The end is very near.

"Come quickly," Minna says, speaking not to her mom or brother but to Danny. "I—I found something. Holy shit."

"What kind of something?" Trenton says.

Minna's hands tighten on the door frame. I feel as if every single door in the house had been slammed shut at once—tight with expectation and terror. "It's a kid."

"A *what*?" Danny says.

"A baby." Minna swallows and pushes her hair back, leaving a smudge of dirt on her cheek, like a single tear. "In a box."

PART XI

THE KITCHEN

A L I C E

The kitchen has been emptied of its furniture. Even the Spider has been packed up and carted away, and the old fireplace stands cold, clean-swept, dark, like a mouth open in a scream. Bits of cottonseed have found their way in through the window.

There is nowhere to place her but on the countertop.

Bits of the blanket remain, shreds and tatters, most of it eaten away by insects. The box is mostly intact: dark wood, laminated, it has stood up well to time. My initials are still faintly visible, although much of the rest of the paint has flaked away. It was yellow, I remember, and decorated with painted lilacs. It had been a gift from my mother on my seventeenth birthday, for holding my Sunday hat, fitted with lace as fine as a spider's web and smelling of the lavender salts she placed next to it.

I wrapped her up in a blanket. I thought she would be safe, there, in the small yellow box that smelled like flowers.

Her bones are thin as a baby bird's, her skull no larger than a palm.

She was blue when she came out—blue, and so cold.

I thought she would be warm—in the blanket, in the ground, under the willow tree.

TRENTON

The bones were small, far too small. Trenton felt a swinging sense of unreality, as he did sometimes in dreams, just before waking. It must be some kind of a sick joke.

But then Danny said, "Shit. Shit," and Trenton knew it was not a dream.

"Who—who could have done this?" Caroline said. And then, without waiting for an answer, "Trenton, I need a drink. Please."

But Trenton couldn't move. The baby's head was as small as an apple. It looked like it would blow apart to dust if he tried to touch it.

"Whoever buried her, it was a long time ago," Danny said quietly.

"Her?" Minna said. "You think it's a girl?"

Danny lifted an edge of the blanket, now hanging in tatters, that had once enfolded the child. Pink.

"Oh my God," Caroline said, and turned away, cupping a hand over her mouth. Trenton felt a flicker of irritation—she was making this about her—and he hung on to it, tried to coax it into anger or some other familiar emotion.

"Amy made me dig under the willow tree," Minna said, looking around the room as though she expected to be accused of unearthing the body deliberately. "She insisted. You know how Amy gets." She turned pleading eyes to Trenton.

"What do we do with it—with her?" Trenton corrected himself quickly. Immediately, he wished he hadn't asked. The words sounded so awful—like she was trash that needed to be dealt with.

Danny shook his head slowly. "I don't know," he said. "I don't know." Then he straightened up. "We'll take her downtown. There might be something in the archives, but I doubt it." He reached out and lowered the lid of the box gently, and Trenton was glad.

"Jesus," Caroline muttered.

Amy appeared at the door, her face mashed up against the screen. What is it, Mom?" She opened the door before anyone could stop her. "Why won't you let me *see*?"

"Trenton, get her out of here," Minna said sharply. To Danny she said, "We'll follow you. In our car."

"Come on, Amybear." Trenton lifted Amy, grateful for the excuse to leave the room. She wrapped her legs around his waist. Her breath smelled like ginger ale, and he could feel her heart beating through her ribs. He imagined all the fine, fragile bones holding her together, the caverns of her lungs, the thin tissue fabric of her organs, so easily disintegrated, and felt suddenly like crying. "Want to help me pack up the cars?"

"We're leaving?" Amy said.

"We're leaving." Trenton almost added, *And never coming back*. He knew it was true instinctively. They would never return to Coral River.

"What about Penelope?" Amy asked.

Trenton jogged her a little higher in his arms. Minna and Danny were speaking together in low voices, planning, figuring out who would drive Caroline to the station. "Who's Penelope?" he asked.

"Penelope is the girl in the box," Amy said, swinging her feet.

Minna went silent. Trenton froze. Caroline and Danny stared.

"What do you mean, Amy?" Minna whispered.

"The book!" Amy said, as if it was obvious. "In *The Raven Heliotrope* they put Penelope in the ground so she'll come back to life."

Minna was very white. "Oh my God." She flinched. "Oh my God. She's right."

"They bury her under the willow tree," Amy said happily, wiggling in Trenton's arms. "It's magic. And the tree learns to cry, and then Penelope can come back to life. Remember, Mommy?"

"I remember, sweetie." Minna tried to smile and couldn't. Her eyes met Trenton's again. She looked old—older than she should have. He felt a message pass between them, strong and wordless. *I love you, too.* The words were there, suddenly, in his mind.

Amy was still babbling. "And then the army of Nihilis comes to raid the palace and drive out the Innocents."

"All right, Amy," Trenton said. He tried to sound cheerful. "You can tell me about *The Raven Heliotrope* while we get everything ready to go. Sound good?"

"But the Innocents escape through the tunnels and they burn the palace down so that the Nihilis die. It's sad because they love the palace, but they have to burn it or else. The fire is so big it goes all the way to the sky." Amy stretched her hands toward the ceiling, gesturing.

"Wow." Something stirred in Trenton—a memory, an idea. Fire. "That's pretty big." Trenton pushed open the screen door with the toe of his sneaker. Outside, the sun was blazing, and the sky was white as ash.

A L I C E

I didn't mean for her to die. Believe this, if you believe anything.

I thought I could erase her. I thought I could will her back into nonexistence.

Ashes to ashes, dust to dust.

That year, too, there was cottonseed. I remember how it trembled in the screens, like small alien creatures, sent to bear witness; how I wished that it were real snow and would bury me when I slept. Maybe I should have died. Maybe that's what I deserved.

But I didn't.

Ed was on his way home from the war.

I couldn't return to my family. I had no close friends besides Thomas.

And Thomas, too, I meant to erase.

I'd heard rumors in Boston, when I still lived at home, about girls who'd gotten into trouble. There were doctors who'd do operations, I knew, but operations cost money; there were other ways. Pills and poison. A coat hanger, even.

I thought she would just vanish. One day I would be pregnant. And the next day: a chance to start over. I would be a better wife to Ed. I would learn to love him again. I would pray to God every day for forgiveness.

At least that part of the bargain, I kept.

But she held on. Little Penelope, my poor little Penelope, who didn't know how to do anything but live. I swallowed bleach and took pills to make myself throw up. I prayed for her to wither, like a flower on a stalk. I even tried to fall down the stairs. But at the last second I couldn't let go of the banister.

She came at last, Queen Penelope, riding a carpet of blood: blue and cold, like someone left too long in the ice. Wise Penelope. She refused to take even one breath of this new world, where mothers were monsters; and men were at war; and nothing and no one could be believed.

T R E N T O N

They were done in Coral River. Minna had arranged for Holly, a local woman who'd cleaned for her dad, to come later and deal with the dishes and trash from the memorial service. The luggage was loaded. Adrienne had gone, escorted to a motel in town by Danny's partner. Richard Walker was buried, as he had requested, on the land he had loved.

Trenton wanted to walk through the house one last time.

He went through every room, touching walls and curtains and the remaining pieces of furniture, hoping to feel some further connection to his father, to his past, to Eva, even. But they were just rooms, many of them empty and thus unfamiliar, like the rooms of a stranger's house. It didn't much matter. The past would come along with you, whether you asked for it or not.

In the kitchen, he paused at the window. The squad car was idling in the driveway. Trenton's mom was just visible in the passenger seat. Minna was chasing Amy around the BMW, trying to distract her—or maybe trying to distract herself, to forget what they had just seen. Trenton could see birds wheeling in the sky, and the soft waterfall silhouette of the weeping willow. Even now, Trenton thought, his dad's ashes were there: intermingling with the earth, someday to be swept up by the wind, spiraling up to the afternoon sky and the clouds like new milk. He thought of the girl, the tiny little child in the box, and felt an ache in his chest. So much better to be released into air and sky.

That's what everyone wanted, in the end: to be a part of something bigger.

Then, in the bare silence, Trenton heard a voice so soft that afterward it seemed like a memory of a memory: *Release,* it seemed to say. *Release.*

He stood very still. He held his breath.

Fire. The voice was a flickering impression in his mind, a sense of shadow and heat. *Please. Fire.*

Trenton felt a finger of cold go down his back, as though someone had reached out and stroked him. He thought of the lightbulb that had exploded above his head, and the sudden push, the force of wind, that had tipped all the candles in the attic.

He thought of how terrible it would be to be trapped forever in a body like a box; to have only the long hours for company, only rooms and walls and divisions, keeping you from the open air.

And he knew what he would do—what he had to do.

Trenton leaned over the sink and closed the window, making sure it was latched tight. He felt surprisingly calm. He felt almost as if there were a force moving through him, controlling his body, as if he were experiencing a kind of possession. It couldn't look deliberate; he had to be careful.

A burner leaking gas. A spark from a faulty wire, an exploding bulb, an overturned candle. An accident.

He moved to the stove. The burner let out a hiss of escaping gas, like a satisfied sigh.

"Trenton." He jumped when he heard his name. Minna was leaning into the kitchen, one hand on the doorknob. "Are you ready? We really have to get going."

"I'm ready." He was filled with the sudden, desperate urge to stop, to turn off the gas, to go through the house again, memorizing every corner, every curtain, every patch of sunlight. But he forced himself to cross the room toward her.

Minna stopped him before he could get out the door.

"Hey." Minna frowned. "Do you smell gas?"

Trenton didn't blink. "Nope," he said.

They stood there for a second. And it came to him; they could still, after everything, speak without words.

"Let's go home," she said, putting an arm around his shoulder.

Trenton made sure the door was closed tightly. At the last second, fitting the key in the lock, he thought he heard a voice—fainter than a whisper, barely louder than a thought. *Thank you.* But it might have been the wind singing through the grass, the leaves rubbing palm to palm, the far-off hum of the crickets.

He couldn't bring himself to look back at the house. And what was the point, really, of looking back?

He wanted to be far away by the time the fire trucks came.

The fire begins in the basement.

Does it hurt?

Yes and no. This is, after all, what I wanted.

And I'm beyond hurting now.

The fire grows quickly. Trenton, good Trenton, gave me the chance I needed. A single spark was all it took: a memory of a high yellow sun, of a first kiss, of spinning around in a circle with my sisters, believing that we would always be happy.

The smoke is thick as a dream. In the smoke, they return to me: Maggie and Thomas; Ed; little Penelope and her small, cold hands. Out of the darkness, they come: chanting silently, eyes like holes.

They've returned to take me.

And I return now to the great open jaw of the sky.

From the kitchen, to the pantry, to the dining room and the hall; up the stairs, a choking smoke, darkness, soot, and stifling heat.

From the attic to the roof, from the roof to the basement.

Smoke becomes wind becomes sky. Somewhere, the crickets sing of joy.

Read an excerpt from Lauren Oliver's next young adult novel,

Vanishing Girls

BEFORE

MARCH 27

Nick

"Want to play?"

These are the three words I've heard most often in my life. *Want to play?* As four-year-old Dara bursts through the screen door, arms extended, flying into the green of our front yard without waiting for me to answer. *Want to play?* As six-year-old Dara slips into my bed in the middle of the night, her eyes wide and touched with moonlight, her damp hair smelling like strawberry shampoo. *Want to play?* Eight-year-old Dara chiming the bell on her bike; ten-year-old Dara fanning cards across the damp pool deck; twelve-year-old Dara spinning an empty soda bottle by the neck.

Sixteen-year-old Dara doesn't wait for me to answer, either. "Scoot over," she says, bumping her best friend Ariana's thigh with her knee. "My sister wants to play."

"There's no room," Ariana says, squealing when Dara leans into her. "Sorry, Nick." They're crammed with a half-dozen other people into an unused stall in Ariana's parents' barn, which smells like sawdust and, faintly, manure. There's a bottle of vodka, half-empty, on the hard-packed ground, as well as a few six-packs of beer and a small pile of miscellaneous items of clothing: a scarf, two mismatched mittens, a puffy jacket, and Dara's tight pink sweatshirt with *Queen B*tch* emblazoned across the back in rhinestones. It all looks like some bizarre ritual sacrifice laid out to the gods of strip poker.

"Don't worry," I say quickly. "I don't need to play. I just came to say hi, anyway."

Dara makes a face. "You just got here."

Ariana smacks her cards facedown on the ground. "Three of a kind, kings." She cracks a beer open, and foam bubbles up around her knuckles. "Matt, take off your shirt."

Matt is a skinny kid with a slightly-too-big nose and the filmy expression of someone who is already on his way to being very drunk. Since he's already in his T-shirt—black, with a mysterious graphic of a one-eyed beaver on the front—I can only assume the puffy jacket belongs to him. "I'm cold," he whines.

"It's either your shirt or your pants. You choose."

Matt sighs and begins wriggling out of his T-shirt, showing off a thin back, constellated with acne.

"Where's Parker?" I ask, trying to sound casual, then hating myself for having to try. But ever since Dara started . . . *whatever* she's doing with him, it has become impossible to talk about my former best friend without feeling like a Christmas tree ornament has landed in the back of my throat.

Dara freezes in the act of redistributing the cards. But only for a second. She tosses a final card in Ariana's direction and sweeps up a hand. "No idea."

"I texted him," I say. "He told me he was coming."

"Yeah, well, maybe he *left*." Dara's dark eyes flick to mine, and the message is clear. *Let it go.* So. They must be fighting again.

Or maybe they're not fighting, and that's the problem. Maybe he refuses to play along.

"Dara's got a *new* boyfriend," Ariana says in a singsong, and Dara elbows her. "Well, you do, don't you? A *secret* boyfriend."

"Shut up," Dara says sharply. I can't tell whether she's really mad or only pretending to be.

Ari fake-pouts. "Do I know him? Just tell me if I *know* him."

"No way," Dara says. "No hints." She tosses down her cards and stands up, dusting off the back of her jeans. She's wearing fur-trimmed wedge boots and a metallic shirt I've never seen before, which looks like it has been poured over her body and then left to harden. Her hair—recently dyed black, and blown out perfectly straight—looks like oil poured over her shoulders. As usual, I feel like the Scarecrow next to Dorothy. I'm wearing a bulky jacket Mom bought me four years ago for a ski trip to Vermont, and my hair, the unremarkable brown of mouse poop, is pulled back in its trademark ponytail.

"I'm getting a drink," Dara says, even though she's been having beer. "Anyone want?"

"Bring back some mixers," Ariana says.

Dara gives no indication that she's heard. She grabs me by the wrist and pulls me out of the horse stall and into the barn, where Ariana—or her mom?—has set up a few folding tables covered with bowls of chips and pretzels, guacamole, packaged cookies. There's a cigarette butt stubbed out in a container of guacamole, and cans of beer floating around in an enormous punch bowl full of half-melted ice, like ships trying to navigate the Arctic.

It seems as if most of Dara's grade has come out tonight, and about half of mine—even if seniors don't usually deign to crash a junior party, *second semester* seniors never miss any opportunity to celebrate. Christmas lights are strung between the horse stalls, only three of which contain actual horses: Misty, Luciana, and Mr. Ed. I wonder if any of the horses are bothered by the thudding bass from the music, or by the fact that every five seconds a drunk junior is shoving his hand across the gate, trying to get the horse to nibble Cheetos from his hand.

The other stalls, the ones that aren't piled with old saddles and muck rakes and rusted farm equipment that has somehow landed and then expired here—even though the only thing Ariana's mom farms is money from her three ex-husbands—are filled with kids playing drinking games or grinding on each other, or, in the case of Jake Harris and Aubrey O'Brien, full-on making out. The tack room, I've been informed, has been unofficially claimed by the stoners.

The big sliding barn doors are open to the night, and frigid air blows in from outside. Down the hill, someone is trying to get a bonfire started in the riding rink, but there's a light rain tonight, and the wood won't catch.

At least Aaron isn't here. I'm not sure I could have handled seeing him tonight—not after what happened last weekend. It would have been better if he'd been mad—if he'd freaked out and yelled, or started rumors around school that I have chlamydia or something. Then I could hate him. Then it would make *sense*.

But since the breakup he's been unfailingly, epically polite, like he's the greeter at a Gap. Like he's *really* hoping I'll buy something but doesn't want to seem pushy.

"I still think we're good together," he'd said out of the blue, even as he was giving me back my sweatshirt (cleaned, of course, and folded) and a variety of miscellaneous crap I'd left in his car: pens and a phone charger and a weird snow globe I'd seen for sale at CVS. School had served pasta marinara for lunch, and there was a tiny bit of Day-Glo sauce at the corner of his mouth. "Maybe you'll change your mind."

"Maybe," I'd said. And I really hoped, more than anything in the world, that I would.

Dara grabs a bottle of Southern Comfort and splashes three

inches into a plastic cup, topping it off with Coca-Cola. I bite the inside of my lip, as if I can chew back the words I really want to say: This must be at *least* her third drink; she's already in the doghouse with Mom and Dad; she's supposed to be staying out of trouble. She landed us both in *therapy*, for God's sake.

Instead I say, "So. A new boyfriend, huh?" I try to keep my voice light.

One corner of Dara's mouth crooks into a smile. "You know Ariana. She exaggerates." She mixes another drink and presses it into my hand, jamming our plastic cups together. "Cheers," she says, and takes a big swig, emptying half her drink.

The drink smells suspiciously like cough syrup. I set it down next to a platter of cold pigs in blankets, which look like shriveled thumbs wrapped up in gauze. "So there's no mystery man?"

Dara lifts a shoulder. "What can I say?" She's wearing gold eye shadow tonight, and a dusting of it coats her cheeks; she looks like someone who has accidentally trespassed through fairyland. "I'm irresistible."

"What about Parker?" I say. "More trouble in paradise?"

Instantly, I regret the question. Dara's smile vanishes. "Why?" she says, her eyes dull now, hard. "Want to say 'I told you so' again?"

"Forget it." I turn away, feeling suddenly exhausted. "Good night, Dara."

"Wait." She grabs my wrist. Just like that, the moment of tension is gone, and she smiles again. "Stay, okay? *Stay*, Ninpin," she repeats, when I hesitate.

When Dara gets like this, turns sweet and pleading, like her old self, like the sister who used to climb onto my chest and beg me, wide-eyed, to wake up, wake up, she's almost impossible to resist. Almost. "I have to get up at seven," I say, even as she's leading me outside, into the fizz and pop of the rain. "I promised Mom I'd help straighten up before Aunt Jackie gets here."

For the first month or so after Dad announced he was leaving, Mom acted like absolutely nothing was different. But recently, she's been *forgetting*: to turn on the dishwasher, to set her alarm, to iron her work blouses, to vacuum. It's like every time he removes another item from the house—his favorite chair, the chess set he inherited from his father, the golf clubs he never uses—it takes a portion of her brain with it.

"Why?" Dara rolls her eyes. "She'll just bring cleansing crystals with her to do the work. Please," she adds. She has to raise her voice to be heard over the music; someone has just turned up the volume. "You *never* come out."

"That's not true," I say. "It's just that you're *always* out." The words sound harsher than I'd intended. But Dara only laughs.

"Let's not fight tonight, okay?" she says, and leans in to give me a kiss on the cheek. Her lips are candy-sticky. "Let's be happy."

A group of guys—sophomores, I'm guessing—huddled together in the half-dark of the barn start hooting and clapping. "All right!" one of them shouts, raising a beer. "Lesbian action!"

"Shut up, dick!" Dara says. But she's laughing. "She's my *sister*."

"That's definitely my cue," I say.

But Dara isn't listening. Her face is flushed, her eyes bright with alcohol. "She's my sister," she announces again, to no one and also to everyone, since Dara is the kind of person other people watch, want, follow. "*And* my best friend."

More hooting; a scattering of applause. Another guy yells, "Get it on!"

Dara throws an arm around my shoulder, leans up to whisper in my ear, her breath sweet-smelling, sharp with booze. "Best friends for life," she says, and I'm no longer sure whether she's hugging me or hanging on me. "Right, Nick? Nothing—*nothing*—can change that."